THE REFORM ARTISTS
A Legal Thriller

By

JON REISFELD

HOT GATES PRESS
COLUMBIA, MD

AUTHOR'S NOTE:
This book is a work of fiction. Names, characters, places, or incidents either are a product of the author's imagination or are used fictitiously, and any resemblance to actual persons, living or dead, business establishments, events or locales is entirely coincidental.
ISBN-13: 978-0-9965878-0-8
ISBN-10: 09965878-0-2

To Zach, a young man with a big heart and an even bigger gift for writing and storytelling.

Prologue

Heather Barnes pounded impatiently on the steering wheel as her red Mini Cooper raced through the residential neighborhood at twenty-five miles per hour above the posted speed limit.

When the green light suddenly turned red, she slammed on the brakes. The car came to a screeching halt, hurling her against the seatbelt and scarring the pavement with broad, incriminating tire marks.

Heather's eyes darted everywhere looking for police cruisers. Finding none, she glanced at her wristwatch. *Six-thirteen. I should have reported in to Tim eighteen minutes ago,* she thought, as a wave of panic overtook her. *God only knows where that twisted mind of his has gone!*

Sweat poured down Heather's forehead and into her eyes stinging them and making her mascara run. She couldn't believe she had allowed her boss to buttonhole her on the way out the door with more questions about that new ad account. *I should have told him I'd call him from the road!* But, Heather realized, her demanding boss was now the least of her problems.

She glanced again at the red light, then at the lifeless cell phone lying beside her on the passenger seat. "Come on!" she screamed, grabbing the phone and staring at it. "What the hell's wrong with you?" She shook the phone fiercely and whined, "Pleeease, please charge!"

Then, Heather saw it for the first time. The left side of the phone's charging jack was slightly ajar. "Oh, my God!" she screamed, cramming it back in place. She wanted to cry, but there was no time.

Heart racing, Heather nudged the car forward, looked left, then right, and gunned it. Tires screeched, houses flew by and neighbors looked up in alarm, as she tried to make quick work of the remaining three blocks to her home.

When Heather finally pulled into a parking spot in front of her house, the cell phone suddenly sprang to life. She glared at it, threw open the car door and leapt out.

Tim, tall, thin, and muscular, stood motionless in the front doorway, intently watching her.

At the sight of him, Heather instinctively slipped her right hand back onto the car door handle. Then, she thought about her two young children. She frowned, bracing herself against the coming onslaught, and ran toward her husband as if her life depended on it.

*　　　　*　　　　*

The triple murder-suicide dominated the evening news in Maryland and across the nation. At McCredie's Sports Pub, in downtown Silver Spring, every flat screen TV offered a different channel's take on the tragedy, which had become breaking news shortly before 7:00 p.m.

The screen facing the rear corner booth, where two middle-aged men sat nursing drinks and talking, showed James Holt, star reporter for WQDP News, standing just outside the victims' family residence, in Rockville—site of the tragedy. Crime scene tape and flashing police cruisers littered the background.

"In the latest case of domestic violence taken to extremes," Holt said, "Tim Barnes, a 35-year-old unemployed construction worker slit the throats of his two school-aged children, Donald, 10, and Amy, 7. Then, he raped and murdered his wife, Heather, shortly after she returned home from work. His brief reign of terror ended moments later, when Barnes shot himself in the head."

As Holt talked, pictures of the victims, taken in happier times, flashed across the screen. Elementary school yearbook photos of little Donald and Amy were followed by a business promotional shot of Heather, a strikingly beautiful 32-year-old graphic designer with a sleek figure and dirty-blonde hair; and finally, by a family photo of Tim, a six-foot-three, tautly built man with a thick moustache and a wild mane of dark, curly hair. Tim was holding up a metal spatula as he posed, in his chef's apron, beside the family grill.

"At 6:33 p.m. a neighbor called 911 and reported hearing a single gunshot coming from the Barnes home. Police arrived minutes later and discovered the gruesome murder scene.

"I am standing with Penelope Trask, a neighbor and friend of Heather's. Penelope, did you know or suspect that Heather and her children were in any danger?"

"Heather, yes," Trask said. The plump redhead, who looked to be in her late twenties, repeatedly rubbed tears from her eyes. "But she denied it. Several times, I saw big bruises on her arms, and once, she even had a black eye.

"'Is Tim doing this to you?' I asked her the last time. Heather nodded and began to sob. She said Tim had become insanely jealous. 'You've got to get out of there,' I told her. 'It's not safe!'"

The two men in the booth watched the report and grimaced.

"Cassie," the older one said, signaling his waitress, a skinny, energetic, fortyish brunette with her hair pinned up in a hot mess. When she looked his way, he continued. "Another scotch on the rocks for me and a Tom Collins for my friend, here." Then, he quickly lowered his right hand, which had begun to shake, and slipped it below the table.

"Sure thing, hon!"

The older man turned to the Tom Collins drinker. "What a mess, huh?"

"It doesn't get much sicker than this."

"No."

They both shook their heads.

Then, the Tom Collins fan continued. "So, are you cancelling the Face Off?"

"Why would I do that?" The older man's voice grew clipped.

"I don't know."

"We go forward. You be there, tomorrow, when he gets on the train. This guy needs us now more than ever. And, like most, he's probably clueless. His picture's in here," he added, tapping a manila envelope lying before him. He slid it toward his companion with his left hand.

"This makes our work so much more difficult," the Tom Collins drinker said.

The older man stared at him. "So, what's your point? Is this suddenly about how tough *we* have it?"

His companion thought for a moment. "No. I guess I don't have a point. Forget it."

"Already did." Then, he looked up and smiled. "Here come our drinks!"

Cassie put their new drinks down and collected their empties. "Will you be wanting another round, Mr. Hannah?" she asked.

"No, this should do it," the older man said.

At that, Cassie smiled and turned away. The two men raised glasses and clinked.

"To the Face Off," Hannah said.

"To the Face Off...and all that follows."

Chapter 1

The `incident occurred at the D.C. Metro's Farragut North stop, as Martin Silkwood boarded the northbound train for his return commute to Maryland. It ended as quickly as it began, and no one—save the participants—seemed to notice or care. But it would forever change Martin's life.

Martin had entered the subway car at the head of a surging crowd that heaved and pressed against him with the dumb force of an enormous beast. He was pushing back and maneuvering toward an empty seat, when a casually dressed man, with the look and bearing of a drill sergeant, suddenly sprang up, lurched forward, and rammed into him.

"Watch it!" the man barked, his steel-gray eyes underscoring the challenge.

Martin recovered his balance, if not his senses, and pushed back hard. "No, you watch it!"

For an instant, the two squared off. Then, as a faint smile appeared on the stranger's face, his right arm shot forward, palm out, catching Martin square in the diaphragm. Martin doubled over in pain, gasping for air, as the stranger grabbed his arm and drew near.

"I already have watched it, Martin," he said under his breath. "Now, it's your turn." Then, he turned up the collar on his beige windbreaker and slipped out the door, disappearing into the crowd.

Martin struggled to breathe as he dragged himself toward an empty seat. He swung his left arm wildly to clear a path and steadied himself by grabbing onto a nearby handrail with his right. When he finally reached the seat, he turned around and gingerly dropped into place.

As he did, Martin felt something in his left pants pocket. Hand shaking, he dug in and retrieved a tiny video disk in a slim vinyl case. The disk was silver, unmarked, and small— only half the diameter of the videos Martin normally played on his home entertainment system.

"Huh," he grunted to himself between steadily decreasing, but uneven, chest heaves. He flipped the disk over in his hand several times. He had no idea what it was, why the stranger had given it to him, or how he had known his name.

After a few moments, Martin put the disk away. He decided he would deal with it later, when he got home, but try as he might, he couldn't get this latest incident out of his mind. Martin kept wondering if it somehow fit into the disturbing chain of events that had begun to unfold the previous Friday night, when he had returned home to an empty house—without Katie, the kids, or the dog. All he had found was a brief note, in Katie's handwriting, lying on the kitchen table.

"I tried, Marty. Really, I did," it read. "I'll contact you when we get settled." That was the last time he had heard from any of them.

Martin spent all night Friday calling around to Katie's friends. (He used to consider them his friends, too, but now he knew better.) Had they seen her and the kids? Did they know anything about where she had gone or what was up?

Some of them, the nice ones, apologetically said they couldn't discuss it. They had promised Katie to keep her whereabouts a secret, but they said everyone was safe, not to worry. Others, her "true sisters," uttered startled, indignant gasps at the mere sound of his voice and then hung up the phone.

The nastiest, most self-righteous ones said things like: "Really, Marty! Haven't you caused enough trouble already? Leave her alone!"—or—"If you call here again, I'm going to report you to the police! Do you understand?" both of which were followed by a sudden resumption of the dial tone.

Martin couldn't believe these were the same women who had welcomed him and Katie into their homes for years on end, the same women who had joked with him, occasionally flirted with him, and who, once or twice, seemed to forget themselves and sent him signals he wisely chose to ignore. And, he wondered, where were their husbands—his supposed friends? Only one of them ever picked up the phone to say anything to him at all, and it went something like this: "Hey, Marty, I was sorry to hear about you and Katie. Let's grab a beer sometime soon." And then, when his wife realized he was speaking to Martin, "Oops, got to go now," and again the damned dial tone.

Martin wondered what Katie had been telling these people and how they could possibly believe her without first hearing his side of the story. But these thoughts quickly evaporated as Martin grasped, for the first time, the full impact of Katie's decision. Disillusion turned to anger, fear and finally desperation as Martin realized that, in leaving him, Katie had stolen nearly everything that gave his life meaning: his children, his marriage, and his home life. Of the three roles Martin dutifully performed each day, those of husband, father, and breadwinner, only the later remained.

Katie had left the one thing she couldn't take: Martin's senior partner position at the accounting firm of Findley, Feldman, and Santori. Martin had earned senior partner status through years of hard work, self-discipline, and self-sacrifice. While he drew some personal satisfaction from this, he found accounting work, in general, to be rather dull and unfulfilling.

Martin had long ago realized that he did his job, day-in and day-out, primarily to pay the bills. His partner's salary made possible the life and future he had been building for himself, Katie, and the kids. Now that his marriage appeared to be unraveling, Martin felt the wind go out of his sails. He wondered where he would find the motivation to continue to put in the long hours and to suffer the painful deprivations that life on the road, as an auditing team leader, demanded.

Deep down, Martin sensed he only had one option. Somehow, someway, he would have to get his children back in his life. He could not accept the harsh new reality Katie was forcing upon him.

Despite this realization—or perhaps because of it—Martin had a hard time accepting the fact that his marriage to Katie was over. In the first place, her timing made no sense to him. Yes, they hadn't been getting along that well lately, but only a few months earlier, when the trouble started, Katie had agreed to see a marriage counselor with him. They hadn't even attended their first session yet!

Why would she 'throw in the towel' now? Could she really walk away from our marriage—especially after starting a family and bringing two new lives into the world? Good parents—and Katie and I clearly are that—good parents don't just 'bag it' when the going gets rough, do they?

The next day, Martin gained further insight into the depths of his problems, when an ATM machine rejected his debit card. The joint household account that previously held $9,600 now claimed to have insufficient funds to cover his one-hundred-dollar cash withdraw.

As these thoughts once more flashed through his mind, Martin's stomach began tying itself up in knots. He hated feeling this way, and since all he could do for now was spin mental wheels, he redoubled his efforts to put his troubles out of his mind. He decided to focus exclusively on his accounting work. That usually helped.

Martin began by taking stock of preparations for the upcoming Great Plains Company audit and by mentally reviewing the members of his newly formed auditing team. Martin always handpicked his auditing crews. The following Thursday they would all fly out of Dulles airport to Chicago for an extensive review and compilation of the food processing giant's books.

There was so much to do. Gradually, ever so slowly, Martin slipped back into the endless sea of accounting management minutiae, and soon he found himself back in that numb, safe place his work often provided. Before he knew it, the train had reached his suburban Maryland stop, and he was crossing the parking lot to his car.

Chapter 2

It was nearly seven o'clock when Martin finally turned his Acura off the rural road that ran past his gated community in Olney, Maryland

He drove by the guardhouse and turned into his asphalt driveway, following it to the oversized brick colonial that occupied a hilltop at the center of his five-acre lot. As expected, Katie's car was not in the driveway. The house looked dark, empty, and abandoned, even under the intense glare of the floodlights Martin had installed the previous summer. He got them so Katie would feel less isolated and vulnerable when he was away. She only had complained a few times, in passing, about how empty the house felt when he was away on audits. She didn't make a big deal of it when he had them put in, but he was sure she appreciated that he really had "heard" her. At least, he thought so at the time.

Martin entered the house through the garage—which, as always, smelled faintly of sawdust, cardboard, turpentine, and a blend of the various solvents that comprised his arsenal of touch-up paints and building-repair products. He put his briefcase down on the breakfast table, took off his jacket and prepared to make dinner.

The house, which usually greeted him with the sounds of kids, pets, and people—and with the inviting smell of Katie's home cooking—was now lifeless, odorless, and silent. Somehow, it seemed as if it had grown several sizes larger and more than a few degrees colder. He was surprised to discover just how much he already hated coming back to this empty reminder of his suddenly former life.

Had his family been there, Martin's six-year-old son, Justin, would have paused his game console and come running across the living room floor the moment he heard the front door open. He would have been wearing a big smile on his face and shouting, "Daddy! Daddy! Daddy!"— Martin's favorite greeting. Justin always managed to intercept his dad while he was still in the foyer, wrapping his arms around him in a knee-high embrace that would have made any NFL special teams coach proud. Monica—only three—would have been in her gated play area in the kitchen, playing with her toys, grabbing at Maxie's tail as the dog walked by, and watching her mom prepare dinner. When Martin would have turned the corner, Monica would have looked up, smiled, opened her arms wide and jumped up and down in anticipation, waiting for him to scoop her up, rub noses with her, twirl her around a few times and then gently return her to her play area. And Katie? She would have leaned away from the kitchen sink as he approached her from behind, given him a peck on the cheek and handed him a glass of their favorite California Cabernet or Riesling to take the edge off his day.

Instead, this evening Martin received a cold blast of air from the freezer as he inspected the assorted frozen dinners he had picked up at the supermarket over the weekend. He took one out and started to pry open the lid while he listened to messages on the flickering answering machine. There was nothing from Katie, just a concerned call from his mother checking to see if he had heard anything yet.

Martin put the video disk on the kitchen table and fixed himself a frozen Salisbury steak dinner. He ate it alone, in silence, staring at the disk. After a quick clean up, he headed for the den.

Martin placed the disk in the entertainment center and pushed "play." He grabbed the remote and sank into the leather couch, not knowing what to expect. The screen went dark for several moments. Then the phrase, "Decoding Image Overlay," appeared in red at the center. He watched as the words gradually faded to black and the screen dissolved into the image of a middle-aged man in a dark-gray business suit.

The man sat alone in a leather armchair, his face partially obscured by shadow. He appeared to be speaking from a private, residential study. He looked to be in his late fifties or early sixties, had short-cropped gray hair and the proud bearing and rugged build of a professional athlete or soldier. As he started to speak, a small register of white numbers appeared at the bottom right-hand corner of the screen and steadily began counting down from 300.

"Hello," the man said. "Please excuse me for not introducing myself, but, for security reasons, I must remain anonymous. We even have altered my voice, slightly, to prevent identification. I don't know who you are or the year in which you are viewing this. I may not even be alive anymore. But the underground organization my associates and I started, an organization uniquely equipped to help you right now, lives on.

"Since you're viewing this video, we can assume that my associates have determined that you are currently facing some imminent form of personal threat. My guess is that sometime within the next twenty-four hours, you will learn the details. Don't be surprised to discover that at least one branch of our government may be involved and that it will attempt to deprive you of certain protections guaranteed by the Bill of Rights.

"You may think you are immune to government assaults on your liberties, but I assure you, you are not. Every member of our organization previously has had his or her hand bitten by government institutions we supported and, in many cases, bled to defend.

"We formed our volunteer network to stop these kinds of civil-liberties abuses. We love this country and we would never harm it. But we will not allow its sacred institutions and principles to be turned against the very citizens our founding fathers intended for them to serve.

"That's why we've contacted you. Very soon, you will need our expert help, and we're prepared to give it, provided you are willing to meet certain conditions.

"One of our operatives will contact you within the next forty-eight hours. This is important: We will only give you one opportunity to meet with us and accept our assistance. Should you refuse our help, we will withdraw our offer immediately—and forever."

"Good luck."

With that, the image turned to snow. Martin got up and pressed "play" again several times but nothing happened. He even restarted the entertainment center and reinserted the disk: still nothing. Martin sat there on the couch staring at the snow-filled screen for some time, before finally switching it off.

The silence that followed should have filled the room with a comforting, reassuring peacefulness. But that night Martin sensed something altogether different. A hungry, uneasy dread had somehow slithered inside the house, and Martin could feel it weaving its way toward him among the shadows.

At first, Martin thought it was the man's warning that had set him on edge. But gradually, he realized he was worried about this self-proclaimed patriot and the mysterious, underground group he represented. For reasons, still unknown to him, these people—an organized and determined outlaw element—had him in their sights and, quite possibly, under surveillance.

Martin suddenly stood up, strode to the front door, and switched the floodlights back on. Then, he returned to the den where he poured himself a tall glass of Scotch. As he put the cap back on the bottle, Martin caught his reflection in the bar's mirror and stopped dead in his tracks. His face was drenched in sweat.

He fumbled in his pocket for a handkerchief and used it to wipe his face and forehead. Then, he killed the lights and slowly sank back down into the couch. There, in the comfort and anonymity of total darkness, Martin polished off his drink in one long, hot, desperate gulp.

Chapter 3

Martin had heard that sound before, he was sure of it, but where? Then, he remembered. It was the sound of the back-porch door smacking against the wood frame of his grandparents' summer beach house in Cape Cod. It always did that before a squall, if he or his brother, Jeb, forgot to secure the latch when they went out. Where was Jeb, anyway? Maybe he had gone looking for shells again. Martin knew he was going to have to get up, eventually, and fix the latch, but he was too comfortable to do so at that moment. "Jeb did it," he muttered to no one. "Ask him."

"Mr. Silkwood! Mr. Silkwood!" voices shouted as the banging continued.

Martin shot up, alert, awake and terrified. This wasn't the beach house after all, and it was far too dark for late afternoon. He heard the men's voices and the pounding again, and he realized he was back in his suburban Maryland home. He was a grown man of forty-one, not a thirteen-year-old, and the pounding sounds and strange voices were coming from his front door. Could they have found him already?

"Sir, we know you're in there!" a voice shouted. "We need to speak with you. Police business."

Now, Martin's head was reeling. *Police business? What do the police want with me? Have those subversives done something to Katie and the kids?* He rose and felt his way through the dark, along the edges of furnishings and walls, until he had reached the door.

"Hold on. I'm coming!" he shouted. He put his eye up to the peephole and saw the tan, festooned hat that he was sure only Maryland State Troopers wore. He opened the door and found himself confronted by two sheriff's deputies.

"What's the matter?" he asked.

"Are you Martin Silkwood?" the younger, taller deputy asked as he held up his Sheriff's Department I.D. and pointed a flashlight in Martin's face.

"Yeah, that's me," Martin said. Out of the corner of his eye, he could have sworn he saw the older deputy unfasten his gun holster.

"Mr. Silkwood, we have a court order demanding that you vacate this house. You have fifteen minutes to gather your belongings and go, sir."

"What, are you crazy?" Martin protested. "This is my home. I'm not going anywhere!"

"Sir," the younger deputy said, handing him a stack of papers. "Your wife has sworn out a petition for a protective order against you. Take your time and read it, if you like, but you have to leave."

Martin took the stack of hand-filled forms and official-looking papers from the deputy and began flipping through them. The first page was a Temporary Restraining Order, signed by a district court judge. It required him, the "respondent," to vacate his house and refrain from contacting his children, visiting their schools—including their Sunday school—and from going anywhere near his wife or her place of work for the next seven days. The reason given was his "repeated acts of violence, threats, and abusive behavior" against his wife and children.

The judge, the documents said, had awarded his wife temporary custody of the children and exclusive use of their home, pending a hearing on the charges. The judge had not required him to surrender his car—since his wife had one of her own, and he had not yet specified any child support amount. But the issue of enforcement was quite clear. If Martin violated the Temporary Restraining Order to any extent, the document said, he would be held in contempt of court and subject to arrest, fines, and imprisonment.

"I can't believe this," Martin said, as he turned the page. "Not one word of this is true!" He looked intently at the deputies. "How can something like this happen?"

The deputies stared back at him awkwardly. Martin's hands already had started shaking from the panic-induced adrenalin rush, when he flipped to the page in the petition that his wife had filled out against him and had signed under oath. As he read it, shock turned to panic and panic to nausea. He thought he was going to vomit.

Martin could not believe what he was reading. His wife, the woman he had been married to for eight years, the person he had trusted more than anyone else in his life, had accused him, under oath, of committing repeated "escalating acts of physical and verbal abuse" against her and the kids. What's more, she wrote, "the police have been called to the house on numerous occasions."

"What's this about the police being called here on 'numerous occasions'?" Martin asked the deputies. "As far as I know, the police have never come to our house, at least, not when I was here."

The younger deputy directed him to the next page, where his wife had elaborated on her charges. There, he found a chronology of fictitious, or at best, grossly distorted accounts of past arguments they had had. But far worse, he found four occasions on which his wife claimed he had been so abusive and threatening that she had called 911 and had the police come to the house. Then, he noticed something strangely familiar about those dates.

"My God!" he said, looking at the deputies. "Every time she says she called the police, I've been out of town on audits. I'm a senior partner in an accounting firm, and we routinely take audit teams to our clients' businesses to review their books!

"Didn't anyone check out the facts about these 'alleged' incidents before issuing her a restraining order? And, shouldn't I have, at least, been present in court? Don't I have the right to tell the judge my side of the story?"

Now, the deputies were looking a bit uncomfortable. "It was an *ex-parte* proceeding," the older deputy said. "See there, where it says that?"

"*Ex-parte*? What's that?" Martin asked.

"In cases of alleged domestic abuse," the deputy said, "the courts routinely hold emergency hearings with just the party seeking protection. This ruling's only temporary. You have a right to a hearing within seven days. It's all there in the papers.

"See," he said, taking the report from Martin and flipping to the appropriate page. "You're scheduled for a hearing before the judge at 9:00 a.m. next Monday, a week from today."

"This is unbelievable," Martin said. "What am I supposed to do until then? And what about seeing my kids?"

"You've got to vacate, sir," the younger deputy repeated. "I'd suggest checking into one of those low-cost, extended stay motels until the hearing. Or, if you have family in town, you could arrange to stay with them. But you cannot see your kids."

"Wait a minute," Martin said. "She signed this under oath, right?"

"That's right, sir," the older deputy said.

"So, she's committed perjury! She's going to have to answer for that, isn't she?"

By now, the deputies seemed to have lost all enthusiasm for their work. "Well," said the older one, "I suggest you contact an attorney as soon as possible, sir. He or she can advise you about what to do. But, we've got to get going. We have a whole stack of these to serve tonight."

"But this is nothing but a pack of lies!" Martin protested.

"It's not that uncommon," the older deputy said.

"What do you mean?"

"I'd say, on average, about half of the Temporary Restraining Orders we serve are based on bogus charges." The deputy smiled sheepishly as he wiped the back of his neck with a handkerchief.

"Half?" Martin repeated, in amazement. "Then, why do you bother serving them at all?"

"We have to, sir," the younger deputy explained. "It's our job."

"I don't know how you guys can stand doing this kind of thing to people day-in and day-out," Martin said. "Doesn't it bother you?"

"The judges make the rulings, Mr. Silkwood," the younger deputy said. "Nothing's going to change until they do. Please sir, we've got to get going. Can you get your belongings together now?"

"I guess I have to," Martin said as he gestured for the deputies to come inside. He went upstairs, quickly packed a suitcase and returned.

"We're sorry about all this, Mr. Silkwood," the older deputy said.

"That's OK. I know it's not your fault."

As Martin began leading them out the door, he suddenly stopped in his tracks and turned around. He had a look of panic on his face. "Hey guys, I just realized I forgot something really important. Can you give me just one more minute to go and get it?"

The two deputies looked at each other. Already this stop had taken longer than they had expected. Then, the younger one sighed and turned to Martin. "Sure," he said, nodding. "But please make it quick, OK?"

Martin forced a smile. "Thanks!" He rushed up the stairs and went to the master bedroom. There, on the dresser, he found what he was looking for: two framed photos: one, of Justin, and the other, of Monica. He snatched them up, tucked them under his arm like a football and bounded back down the stairs.

"OK, guys. I'm all set. Thanks, again!"

Martin picked up his bulging suitcase and led them out the door. Then, when they were all on the front stoop, the older deputy paused for a moment and cleared his throat. "Uh, sir, we're going to need your copy of the house key."

"Oh, of course," Martin said. He nervously worked his key chain until he had removed his copy of the key and handed it to the deputy. Then, he waited while the deputies tried the key in the door and locked up the house.

Chapter 4

Celia Gardner frowned when the doorbell rang at 8:45 p.m. *Who could that be at this hour?* she wondered, as she hurried down the main staircase of her sprawling Tudor home. Celia had just finished tucking her two-year-old daughter, Jessica, into bed.

"Ted, are you expecting someone? Ted?" she shouted in the general direction of the great room, where her husband was preoccupied, watching an NBA basketball game. No reply.

"Predictable," she chuckled to herself as she looked through the peephole and saw Martin Silkwood standing on the doorstep.

"Marty, what a nice surprise!" she said, opening the door. Celia flashed him a big smile as she shouted, over her shoulder, "Ted, it's Marty! Did you hear me?" She adjusted the storm door's sticky latch to get it open.

"Come on in, stranger!" she said, grabbing Martin by the arm.

A petite woman, with soft, delicate features, fashionably coiffed, shoulder-length brown hair and stunning, turquoise eyes, Celia looked considerably younger than her thirty-eight years. She stood on tiptoes to plant a kiss on Martin's cheek as Buddy, the Gardner's Labrador retriever, bounded toward them with eight-year-old Timmy close behind.

Buddy barked excitedly, wagging his tail as he tried, unsuccessfully, to break his momentum by back-peddling his paws against the foyer's highly polished marble finish. No such luck. He slammed into Celia, who quickly grabbed him by the collar to keep him at bay.

"I'm sorry to barge in on you guys," Martin said over the fray.

"Don't be silly," Celia said, glancing up at him as she struggled with the dog. Then, turning to Buddy, who was drooling and still trying his best to get past her to Martin, she scolded, "Knock it off, you big galoot!"

Little Timmy stepped forward. "Hi, uncle Marty."

"Hey, kiddo." Martin said, rubbing Timmy's mop of dirty-blond hair.

Celia gestured in the direction of the great room. "Ted's sitting in there, like a zombie."

Martin raised an eyebrow and stared at her blankly.

"Wizards basketball. Remember? Your buddy's their biggest fan?"

"Right!"

"What's with you tonight?"

Martin shrugged. "Would you join us, Celia?"

"Is everything OK?" she asked, following.

"Not really."

Ted was seated on the couch at the far end of the great room, watching the game on a large, flat-screen TV that hung like a painting above the fireplace. The Wizards were closing in on the Nets with just two minutes left in the first quarter. The score: twenty-eight to twenty-two. He glanced briefly in their direction as Buddy wedged himself between him and the coffee table, licking his hand and angling for attention.

"Hey, Marty," Ted said. "Grab a seat!"

"I'm going to join you too, honey," Celia said, after Timmy had raced ahead and sat down on his dad's left. "Marty's got something on his mind."

"Can it wait till half-time?"

"Sure," Martin said.

"Ted!" Celia chided. "Your best friend has come by to talk. Don't you think that's a little more important than—?"

"It's all right, Celia, really," Martin interrupted. "Frankly, I could use the distraction."

Ted glanced up at his friend. "Guess who's got a C-note riding on this—with an eight-point spread?"

"Someone with more money than sense, I guess."

"Marty," Celia broke in, "can I get you a beer in the meantime?"

"Sure."

"Would you get me another one, too, Hon?" Ted asked, dangling his now empty bottle before her at arm's length, without taking his eyes off the game.

"Sure, Arrchie," she said in her best Brooklyn accent. Then, to no one in particular, "How about some nachos?"

"Yeah, Mom!" Timmy said. "And can I stay up till halftime, please?"

"If I let you, mister, you better jump out of bed in the morning."

"I will. Promise!"

By halftime, the score was fifty-one to fifty. Timmy kissed his parents "goodnight," gave Martin a hug, and reluctantly stomped off to his room alone. Then, Ted put the TV on mute and turned to his friend. "So, what's up?"

"Well," Martin said, "I've got bad news and *really* bad news."

"Let's start with the bad news," Ted said.

Martin sat up. "I'm homeless."

"You're *what?*" they both said in unison.

"Homeless. Out on the street."

Ted smiled. "So, the repo man finally caught up with you?"

"Ha-ha," Martin said. "I still own the house; I'm just not living in it. And that brings me to the really bad news. Katie and I have separated."

Celia gasped. "Oh my, Marty!"

"As of when?" Ted asked.

"Friday night. I found out when I came home to an empty house, with a note from Katie waiting for me on the kitchen table."

"I'm so sorry, Marty," Celia said.

Ted frowned at his friend. "So, why are we only hearing about this now?"

"Well, I spent Friday night calling Katie's close friends, trying to figure out where she was. I was in shock, and I guess I was hoping the whole thing would blow over. Telling you guys only would have made it seem more real."

"So, you spent the weekend alone?" Celia asked, a concerned look on her face.

"No. My brother and mother came by taking turns keeping the 'wounded soldier' company."

They all sat for a moment in silence.

"I'm confused," Celia said, at last. "If Katie moved out on Friday, why are you suddenly without a house now?"

"I had one until about an hour ago," Martin said. "Then, two sheriff's deputies came and kicked me out."

Ted looked appalled. "They did *what*?"

"They knocked on my door at about eight-fifteen and served me with a Temporary Restraining Order that Katie had gotten. Then, they told me I had fifteen minutes to gather up my belongings and leave."

"Just like that?" Celia asked. "No warning?"

"Uh huh."

"They must have had some kind of grounds to do it, didn't they?" Ted asked.

"Yeah," Martin said, blushing. "Katie had accused me of repeated acts of verbal and physical abuse against her and *the kids*, for Christ's sake! Can you believe that?" Martin shook his head, grunted, and threw his upturned hands into the air, as if to say, 'What's the world coming to?'

"Well...Marty," Celia began hesitantly, clearing her throat. "Have you ever threatened her...or the kids?"

"What?" Martin asked, taken aback. "Are you kidding me, Celia?"

"No need to attack me, Marty," Celia said. "I'm just asking."

"I wasn't. But do you actually think I'd be capable of doing something like that?"

"Well, a restraining order, that's pretty serious stuff, Marty," Celia continued. "Doesn't a judge have to sign it?"

"Let's be clear," Ted interjected, "there was a hearing, right?"

Martin nodded as his blush deepened. "It's a *Temporary* Restraining Order, guys. It expires in seven days."

"Unless the judge makes it permanent," Ted interjected.

"I-I can't believe you," Martin said, shaking his head.

"Marty, do you understand how serious these charges are?" Celia asked.

"I'm the one who just got kicked out of his home, Celia. I think I have *an inkling*."

"You could go to jail for this."

"Now, Celia," Ted said, trying to diffuse the situation a little. He waved his finger at her mischievously. "Remember the O.J. Simpson trial, honey? Let's not 'rush to judgment.'"

"Interesting choice, dear. O.J. was a celebrity, and no one had any idea of what he was capable of, either—no more than they could have predicted what that horrible Barnes man would do."

"What?" Martin said, leaping up, shaking his head, and waving his hands in the air. "Tell me the two of you are not comparing me with those psychos!"

"Whoa, whoa," Ted said. "No one's suggesting anything of the kind."

He turned to his wife. "And, for the record, Honey, the jury found O.J. not guilty, remember? 'If the gloves don't fit, you must acquit!'"

Celia shook her head and waved a finger at Ted. "O.J. was guilty as hell, dear. The prosecution never should have allowed his defense team to put so much weight on those gloves. Instead, they should have been telling the jury, "If the shoes fit, you must nail this shit!"

Martin broke in as he resumed his seat, "Hey guys, remember, I haven't been tried, or convicted, of anything."

"You haven't, Marty?' Celia said with surprise. "How can that be? There was a hearing. You said so yourself."

"It was an *ex-parte* hearing," Martin repeated.

"What kind of hearing?" Ted asked.

"*Ex-parte*. Only Katie and her attorney were present."

Celia looked puzzled. "I thought both sides always had to be there."

"Me, too, but the deputies assured me that *ex-parte* hearings are 'standard operating procedure' in domestic violence cases. I get a hearing...eventually, but it won't be till next Monday. And Katie and her attorney will be there as well.

"Meanwhile, the judge has thrown me out on the street. He's ordered me not to speak with Katie or the kids—or to have any contact with them at all. I have to put myself up in a motel. And, believe it or not, I'm lucky. He could have confiscated my car and given it to Katie, if she didn't already have one."

"Wow," Ted said, shaking his head in disbelief. "It's like they've tried and convicted you in advance. And this is America?"

"Apparently."

"That's really something," he continued. "And none of this has anything to do with your separation?"

"Oh, I think it has everything to do with it," Martin said. "Katie made the whole thing up. It's all lies!"

"Well, didn't Katie have to make those charges under oath?" Celia asked.

"Yeah."

"Do you really think she would be reckless enough to lie then?"

"What's your point?"

"All I'm saying is I've known Katie a long time. She's smarter than that. I'm wondering...is it possible, Marty, that you might actually have done something wrong?"

Martin shook his head. "I haven't."

"Marty, did you ever hit her?" Ted asked, abruptly.

"No!"

"What about the kids? Did you ever lose it with your boy? I mean, kids can get extremely frustrating at times."

"No, no. What, are you both out of your minds? I love my kids! I would never strike them. This is sick!"

Ted stared intently at Marty for a moment. Then, his expression gradually relaxed. "Are you sure you haven't stashed a riding crop in your nightstand, Marty, just in case the wife might need a little 'disciplining'?"

Martin wasn't sure what to make of this last remark, until he saw the edge of his friend's lips curl upward.

"You, jackass!" he said, shaking his head, and starting to laugh. Martin looked away for a moment and took a deep breath, but as he did, his smile suddenly disappeared.

"Wait a second," he said. He raised his index finger near his forehead, as if catching himself in mid-thought. Then he turned back in Ted's direction. "You really don't believe me, do you?"

"I want to. I'm trying to. My instincts tell me I should."

"But, you have your doubts?"

"I don't know."

"What about you?" he said, now facing Celia.

She just sat there shrugging her shoulders.

"Listen, you two," Martin said, determined to make them understand. "Katie's lying. What she claims happened never took place—and I can prove it."

"How are you going to do that?" Celia challenged.

"Katie says she called the police to our house four different times. Now, maybe she did call them. That's possible. But I was never there when she did. I wasn't even in town on the days she claims all this stuff happened. I was away doing audits."

"Oh—?" Celia said, surprised. She hesitated for a moment before continuing. "But that still doesn't explain why she would be foolish enough to lie under oath."

"Beats me, Celia, but from what I hear, she's got plenty of company. No offense, but women apparently lie about this stuff all the time."

"Really, Marty? Celia said, folding her arms, and raising an eyebrow. "Where did you dig up that plum?"

"The deputies told me. They said half the Temporary Restraining Orders they enforce are based on, and I quote, 'bogus charges.' I'll know more when I speak to an attorney, which I need to do as soon as possible."

"You don't have one yet?" Ted asked.

"No. I could ask our firm's counsel, or a few of my D.C. lawyer friends, for referrals, but I don't have that kind of time. And I'd prefer to fly under my firm's radar on this, if I can help it. So, I was wondering, do you know anyone locally who is good and who handles divorces?"

"Yeah," Ted said. "Jeff Bishop, one of my construction supers, went through a nasty divorce two years ago, and he was represented by a guy with an office right here, in Olney. He said the guy saved his ass. Do you want me to call him and see if I can get a name and number?"

"Yeah, that would be great."

Ted excused himself and went to his study to make the call.

"I'm sorry, Marty," Celia said, after a moment. "God knows we have no reason to doubt you, but Katie has accused you of something truly awful. You claim she's lying...which would make her actions wholly unforgivable...and yet I don't get it. Why would she turn on you like this? What could possibly make her hate you that much...unless—?"

"Unless I did something to warrant it? I get it, Celia."

"I know, I know. I feel terrible about it. But *domestic violence*, Marty? It's such an ugly, scary thing. Just look at that awful Barnes case! I've never known anyone accused of it."

"So, that's another first for me? Nice!"

"God, I'm sorry!" Celia said. "Listen, you've always been a gentleman to Katie around us. You've always seemed extremely attentive and considerate. You're a great dad, too, from what I've seen. And, for what it's worth, I really don't think you could hurt a fly."

"Thanks, I *think*."

"The problem is...no one really knows what goes on in other people's homes, you know? I mean, who could ever have predicted that a young father would slit his own kids' throats, murder his wife, and then take himself out. It's inconceivable to me! But I'm really worried for you, Marty. I'm also a bit shocked. We had no idea you two were having any problems. You always seemed like such a solid couple."

"We were," Martin said. "For years. Rock solid. Did I ever tell you how we met?"

"No."

"It was a blind date, when we were both in our early thirties. A 'fix up.' We hit it off. I think we were both looking to settle down.

"I've never told this to anyone, but the night of that first date, after leaving our friends' house, we slipped away to a little hole-in-the-wall bar and sort of 'interviewed' each other."

"No kidding, like Larry King?"

"Yeah. I had never done anything like that before. We compared notes about what we wanted in life, and we discovered we pretty much wanted the same things. So, we began dating exclusively, and not long after that, we decided to get married.

"We were always, to borrow your term, 'solid.' We were extremely comfortable with each other. But I'll tell you what we weren't, Celia," he said, looking at his friend. "We were never madly in love, like you and Ted. At best, we were mildly in love.

"Our marriage may not have been perfect, but it was still pretty good most of the time. And once we had the kids, which happened pretty soon in our case, it was over for me. I believe adults have special responsibilities to their kids. Once they're here, we need to do everything we can to give them our best."

Martin felt a sudden chill as he heard himself saying those all-too-familiar words. *Could Katie's actions wind up rendering them meaningless?* Even before he was old enough to articulate them, those principles had become his life's mission and private mantra—the salve, and promised cure, for his own secret pain.

As a child, Martin repeatedly had promised himself that, when he grew up, he would give his children the positive, stable, and secure home life his parents had never provided. He would do everything in his power to insulate them from the senseless cruelties and hardships of the adult world.

Martin and Jeb had not been so fortunate. As kids, they had watched, helplessly, as their father's unrestrained gambling addiction wrecked his life and theirs. Charles Silkwood made a good living as a construction project super, but his need to stay constantly in the action, and to offset steadily mounting losses, led him to bet on everything and anything: baseball, football, and basketball games; the ponies; even the stock market.

While Charles Silkwood occasionally enjoyed big, even spectacular, wins, the family saw little of it. He might have taken the boys and their mother out for a celebratory dinner, but then he would plow every remaining cent of his winnings right back into making his next big score.

The family's collective fortunes rose one week, on hollow hopes and empty promises, only to crash the next. But their overall trajectory soon became apparent: The Silkwoods were steadily slipping toward financial ruin and into ever-deepening desperation and despair.

Martin remembered late-night yelling matches between his parents, when his father would stumble in from high-stakes poker games, reeking of liquor and, more often than not, smarting from fresh new losses. As his gambling debts mounted, Martin's father blew through his salary, the family savings and even much of his aging parents' retirement nest egg in ever more desperate attempts to reverse his fortunes. Yet it seemed, each new attempt only left him deeper in the hole.

Finally, with nowhere else to turn, he approached the loan sharks. This proved to be his undoing. To pay their exorbitant interest rates, Charles Silkwood began taking bribes at work. He would 'look the other way' when vendors substituted inferior goods for the first-rate materials his company had ordered. When he finally got caught, Charles lost his job and went to jail.

No one in the Silkwood extended family had ever sunk so low. The trauma and shame were palpable. Martin's immediate family never spoke of it to anyone; but the shame, though not his own, left an indelible stain on Martin that had dogged him ever since.

For a moment, Martin considered telling Celia what those words meant to him. He wanted her to know why he would do anything in his power to preserve the peace, stability, and innocence his children had enjoyed. He wanted to share why he would have taken his own life before he ever would have allowed himself to harm them or shatter their world.

Celia and Ted were among his closest friends. It would have been so easy to let them in, if he could just say the words. But he realized he couldn't. Martin had allowed Katie in, only to have her betray him. He simply could not risk another betrayal, no matter how unlikely. The invisible wall of separation that had served him so well, for so long, would remain in place—at least, for the time being.

Celia had listened intently, nodding her head, as Martin had discussed his marriage and his child-rearing philosophy. She liked what she heard, but that only made her more confused.

"Marty," she asked when he finished, "why do you think your marriage fell apart now? Was there a triggering incident of some sort?"

"I wish I knew, Celia," he said. "I know that sounds like a cop out, but I lay awake nights now, struggling with just that question.

"All I can tell you is, a couple months back, something in our marriage changed. I'm not sure what. Katie started picking fights with me all the time. Our shared beliefs seemed to go out the window.

"I pushed for us to see a marriage counselor, and she agreed, in principle," he continued, "but it never amounted to more than lip service."

Martin's eyes began to water as the realization gradually hit home. He shook his head. "My God, it's really over, isn't it? The marriage and the life Katie and I were building together for the kids? It's like I'm witnessing some horrible train wreck and I can't do anything to stop it."

"Worst of all," he said, "this restraining order has cut me off completely from Justin and Monica. I can't see them or even talk with them on the phone until after the hearing next Monday. I can't even send them a note or send Justin a card for his birthday this Saturday. If I do, I could go to jail! And what if I lose, Celia? The judge already has given Katie sole custody of the kids. It's as if I suddenly don't even exist."

Celia stood up, walked over, and sat next to him. She placed her hand on his shoulder. "It's awful, Marty. I don't know what to say."

Ted returned with the attorney's name and number. They called him at his home and scheduled a meeting for the first thing in the morning. Then, Ted and Celia tried to convince Martin to spend his first homeless night as a guest in their home, but he declined.

"Under the circumstances, it just doesn't feel right," he said. "Besides, I've got a motel room."

Martin said goodnight to his friends and let himself out. He walked slowly to his car, bent over, and mumbling to himself. He looked like a death row inmate, who had just learned that his desperate, eleventh-hour appeal had been denied.

Chapter 5

Early Tuesday morning, Martin met with Chester Swindell in the restored Victorian home that served as his law firm's Olney office. The meeting did not go well.

Swindell, one of the area's most noted divorce attorneys, sat behind his large mahogany desk in a cluttered office that smelled of equal parts freshly brewed coffee and stale cigar smoke. He shook his head from side to side as he reviewed Martin's copy of the Temporary Restraining Order and petition.

As he read, Swindell repeatedly made the same "zzt, zzt, zzt" sound doctors often make when reviewing particularly disturbing test results. He wore a pained look on his face that Martin found appalling but that Swindell had discovered, over the years, to be particularly useful in preparing his clients for the gargantuan legal bills divorce matters he tried typically generated. At his $300-an-hour rate, litigation clearly wasn't going to be a bargain.

Swindell, at sixty-eight, was a tall, aristocratic-looking man, whom nature had blessed with the constitution of a rhino and the face of a terminal lung-cancer patient. The combination gave him the good fortune of looking much older than his years—and far more sympathetic than his conduct usually warranted.

Swindell's sole hint of vitality was the shock of gray hair he combed straight back from his forehead. Everything else about him suggested weariness and infirmity. His naturally loose olive skin, painstakingly weathered to a rawhide-like appearance under an endless succession of sun lamps, had the look, and feel, of a well-broken-in baseball mitt. His considerable jowls, darkened eye sockets, and droopy eyelids—all suggestive of long nights spent "burning the midnight oil" for his clients—were a convenient accident of birth. He was, in fact, the spitting image of his father, who had spent most of his adult life as an underemployed "gentleman" farmer.

Swindell came from an old Maryland family of tobacco farmers and horse breeders. His ancestors were distant relatives of the Lees, a family of pre-revolutionary war origins noted for two things: its extensive real estate holdings and its claim of direct lineage to General Robert E. Lee. This historic connection was a source of great pride for Swindell—so much so, in fact, that he affected a slight southern lilt whenever he spoke.

Swindell fancied himself to be a true "southern lawyer," and he played the part to the hilt. His southern affectations made him seem like an anachronism in the progressive, increasingly cosmopolitan Maryland suburbs of Washington, DC.

"Your wife," Swindell finally said, looking up from the papers and over the rims of his reading glasses, "appears determined to skin you alive and then keep your hide around as some sort of souvenir."

"None of the charges are true," Martin insisted.

"Of course, of course" Swindell replied, with what appeared to be a pained effort at a smile. "Unfortunately, Mahr-tin," he said, "she has the court, if not the law, on her side."

"How's that?"

"You saw how easy it was for her to get a temporary restrainin' order against you?" Swindell asked.

"Yes."

"Well, that's because, in today's 'politically correct' environment, no judge in his or her right mind ever wants to be accused of bein' 'insensitive' to the plight of women who fear for their safety or for the safety of their children. They'd rather blindly issue a thousand of these TROs, as we call them—*carte blanche*—than risk denyin' protection to even one woman in real physical peril."

"But what about the truth?" Martin blurted out. "Doesn't that matter anymore? And what about my civil rights? Don't I have a right to 'due process?' Aren't I supposed to be protected against unreasonable 'searches and seizures'? And, more importantly, don't I have a right to see my kids and to stay actively involved in their lives?"

Swindell cocked his head to one side and squinted. "Yes, sir, Mahr-tin, those are all fine principles—the bedrock of American society."

"But—?"

"But, they don't amount to crap in these judges' minds, at least compared to the thought of them bein' ridiculed by the press for makin' a mistake that leaves just one abused wife lyin' face down in a ditch, beaten to death.

"They don't want to be caught sippin' coffee one mornin' while the TV news reports that a woman they denied protection to a day earlier—someone like that poor Barnes woman—had been summarily executed, along with her two children, upon her return home from court.

"You see, Mahr-tin, it's not really about justice or the law anymore. It's all about protectin' reputations: theirs, not yours. They want to position themselves for advancement, not embarrassment."

"But my wife's apparently been spreading lies about me to everyone we know, and now she can start using this TRO as some form of proof."

"That's unfortunate," Swindell said, "unfortunate, but largely unavoidable."

"Well, what about this hearing I've got in seven days. Can we expose her lies then? And where will that leave me?"

"Of course," Swindell said, smiling to himself. "You should, and you shall, have your day in court. But please understand the position you're in."

"What position is that?" Martin asked, growing increasingly exasperated.

"Well," Swindell continued, "it's hardly like you are goin' in front of an impartial judge, now, is it?"

"You mean the judge already has made his mind up against me?"

"Well, what do you think? Hasn't he put himself on record as believin' you're capable of violent, abusive acts?"

"Yes, but—"

"And won't we be askin' that same judge to now reverse that earlier decision?" Swindell continued.

"Well sure, but—"

"And, Mahr-tin, do you know anyone who likes to admit he's wrong—and to do it publicly?"

"No, of course not. But the judge hasn't even met me yet. If he's received bad information from my wife and her attorney, if she has misled him, then certainly, she's responsible, not him, right?"

"Well," Swindell said, "he's still the fool who believed her, isn't he? I mean, isn't that the essence of the point you want me to make?"

"OK, OK. I get it."

"You see," Swindell added, "all of this nonsense—and excuse me, I don't mean to trivialize your situation, Mahr-tin—but all of this could have been avoided, if the judge had simply asked your wife or her attorney some probin' questions at the *ex-parte* hearin'. Then, they would have gotten much nearer the truth. But judges in these cases don't want to ask probin' questions. They want to grant the petitions, so the less conflictin' information they turn up, the better.

"I mean, why go out of your way to question the propriety of a course of action you prefer to take? Wouldn't that be counter-productive?"

By now, Martin looked dumbstruck. He shrugged his shoulders, shook his head, and let out a mild snort.

"These judges don't care if they fail to establish future grounds for perjury charges, either," Swindell continued, "because they don't consider what they're askin' you to sacrifice to be such a big deal, after all."

"Are you crazy?" Martin said, with sudden fury. "I've been summarily thrown out of my house. My wife is dragging my name in the mud. My best friends doubt me. I've been denied access to my children, and now it looks like my entire case has been prejudiced, to boot."

"Yes, but that is not the way *they* see it."

"Well then, how do they see it?" Martin asked bitingly, throwing his hands up in the air.

"Since this is a civil procedure, rather than a criminal one, they see themselves as temporarily inconveniencin' you, but not doin' you any real, long-term harm. No matter what happens at the hearin', you won't have a criminal record doggin' you in the future. It will all soon be forgotten."

"Not by me, it won't."

"Of course, not," Swindell said. "But they will be able to put this matter behind them. They will forget about your inconvenience a lot sooner than they'd forget their own embarrassment and guilt, if anythin' unfortunate happened to your wife or children."

"So, what you're saying is the whole system is rigged against me, because I'm a man—and all in the name of 'political correctness?' You're saying that I'm being judged on stereotypes about men being more violent—and that most judges care more about their personal reputations and careers than they do about making sure justice is served?"

"Yes," Swindell nodded, "that's it—precisely. But don't you dare go around quotin' me on that. I'll deny it, because I have to work with these judges. My livin' largely depends on my ability to influence them. And remember, Mahr-tin, filin' false petitions still is a drastic, risky, nasty, despicable act. Yes, women do it all the time, more and more. But it remains slightly more the exception than the rule. Unfortunately, your wife and her attorney appear more than willin' to make this a very dirty fight." (Swindell tried hard to let his smile shine only on the inside.)

"So, what are my odds of getting this TRO, as you call it, reversed next Monday?" Martin asked.

"Dependin' on the evidence we can produce, probably somewhere in the range of fifty-fifty, but if you're lookin' for justice, or to give your wife her comeuppance for subjectin' you to this, I think that's a real stretch.

"Right now, your wife has everythin' she wants," Swindell explained. "She's got your kids; she's got your attention; and she's got the court's sympathy. I would expect an offer to be tendered soon."

"You mean, like a *settlement* offer?" Martin gasped, looking dumbstruck.

"Somethin' like that."

"Well, she can forget it!" he said, slamming his fist down on Swindell's desk. "I'd rather lose everything I have in a court fight than let her take what she wants from me in this manner."

"I understand, Mr. Silkwood," Swindell replied, growing all warm and mushy on the inside. "You want your day in court, and I'm goin' to see that you get it."

"Damned straight," Martin said.

Swindell shook his new client's hand, promising to be in touch.

Chapter 6

It was almost eleven o'clock when Martin stepped off the elevator and into Findley, Feldman, and Santori's stately reception area on the fourteenth floor of the Washington Square building, in downtown D.C. He glanced past the Chippendale sofas and chairs and waved 'hello' to Monique, who was sorting mail behind the reception desk.

Young, slim, attractive, and impeccably dressed and coiffed, Monique—the temporary agency's 'flavor of the month'—exuded a *Vogue*-like, left-bank sophistication that Martin initially found somewhat intimidating. She was of a type: an aesthetic, actually. All the full-time receptionist candidates that the agency had been auditioning for hire of late—whether male, female, African, Asian, or European—

looked like they had just stepped out of a fashion spread for *Elle* or *GQ.*

They all also came well-schooled in high-end client greeting and phone-answering etiquette. They never asked a guest to choose between generic "bottled water" and "coffee," for instance. Instead, they inquired as to whether the visitor would prefer 'an Evian' or 'a Keurig?' They excelled as office furniture, complementing the reception area's bespoke décor of parquet floors and fine antiques. But their luster faded rapidly whenever they had to navigate even the most mundane, unscripted conversation.

"Any messages?" Martin asked.

"Oh, yes!" Monique beamed.

Martin stepped forward and extended his upturned hand, as Monique's face suddenly blushed crimson.

"Oh, I'm sorry, Mr. Silkwood. They weren't for you."

"Of course," Martin smiled and sighed. Then, without missing a beat, he turned right and began the long walk down the corridor toward Joe Santori's office at the southern end of the building.

"Is Mr. Santori in?" he asked her over his shoulder.

"Yes, sir."

"Would you let him know I'll be stopping by?"

"Certainly."

"Thanks."

Such minor, daily annoyances were a byproduct of David Feldman's endless cost-cutting efforts. Feldman, the firm's managing partner and fiscal hawk, kept this revolving door of 'fetching incompetents' turning, to avoid hiring a permanent receptionist and causing the firm to incur the one-time placement fee that would equal twenty-five percent of the new hire's annual starting salary.

Feldman further greased the wheels of ineptitude by refusing to provide the temporary placement firm with any meaningful feedback on why he chose to reject its candidates.

Feldman's penny-pinching behavior had intensified in the past year, as the now sixty-four-year-old partner rapidly approached the firm's mandatory retirement age of sixty-five. (His buyout would depend on the strength of the current year's P & L statement.) He was becoming more tight-fisted and risk averse with each passing month.

In his prime, Feldman had focused on creating value, rather than on squeezing it out of niggling operational decisions. His farsighted, strategic thinking had allowed the firm gradually to take over the top three floors of this landmark office building, at the corner of Connecticut Avenue and K Street, without ever paying a rental premium. Feldman accomplished this feat by negotiating a 'right of first refusal' clause into the firm's original lease. That clause allowed FF&S to exchange office space it let elsewhere in the building, at par value, for comparable space on the top three floors the moment it became available.

Martin preferred to meet privately with Santori when he had anything 'delicate' to discuss. The less pleasant and more personally painful the topic, the more he felt compelled to seek out Santori and to dodge Feldman altogether—if possible. These two men not only occupied identical, glass-enclosed octagonal office suites at opposite ends of the fourteenth floor, they also represented polar extremes in temperament.

Feldman was a true "inside man:" obsessive, detail oriented and brash, if not downright blunt. A slight, thin man, with a black comb over and bushy eyebrows, he looked significantly older, and frailer, than his sixty-four years would suggest. Feldman had a temper, too, and when agitated, he would hurl invectives at the targets of his displeasure. At such times, it seemed that Feldman's shrill voice could cut through thick safety glass, insulated sheet rock and steel support beams with the ease of a high-powered laser.

Santori, on the other hand, was the firm's "outside guy" and its primary rainmaker. Big, tan, affable, athletic, extroverted, and upbeat, he exuded an off-the-charts self-confidence and likability. At six-foot-two and 205 pounds, with a thick head of curly gray hair, Santori looked like a former college linebacker. He had developed a slight gut in recent years, but that seemed more related to a naturally slowing metabolism than to any reduction in physical activity. In fact, the fifty-nine-year-old kept on the go seven days a week. He played tennis Mondays, Wednesdays, and Fridays, completed eighteen holes of golf every weekend and had recently started attending a spinning class with thirty-eight-year-old wife number three.

What Martin admired most about Santori was that he knew his strengths and his passions—and he led with them.

In fact, Santori successfully arranged his business and personal life to accommodate his interests.

He blocked out his competitive sporting activities on his calendar each week as "networking time," which they were. He split the rest of his time between providing financial advice to the firm's top clients and serving on the boards of at least a dozen non-profit trade groups, whose membership just happened to represent key FF&S target markets. At those board meetings, Santori used his no-nonsense, creative approach to business problem solving to impress his peers and elicit referrals. He was a consummate politician, plying his trade in the most politically vital city on earth. Each day, he brought new business contacts together for their mutual benefit...and frequently, for the firm's eventual profit.

Santori's door stood slightly ajar, so Martin rapped on it gently and then poked his head inside. He found Santori standing in the middle of the room, sans business jacket, in his custom-tailored, pinstriped shirt, silk tie, silk suspenders and slacks, practicing his putting swing on the office's forest-green carpet. Santori had just tapped a ball in the direction of an aluminum putting cup, which stood about eight feet away from him, and Martin watched the ball rapidly close in on, and find, its target.

"Nice shot," he said.

"All in a day's work, my boy," Santori said. He smiled and waved Martin in, while he began queuing up another ball. His eyes never left the carpet.

"Wanna make this interesting, Dave?" he asked Feldman, whom Martin now saw was seated on a couch at his far left. "Say, a Hamilton or two?"

"Not while you're in your kill zone, Joe—unless, you want to play left-handed?"

Santori ignored him, lined up the putter and hit the ball firmly. This time, it looked like a repeat of the previous shot, until the very end, when the ball suddenly trailed off to the right.

"Damn!" Feldman whelped.

Santori shook his head. "Woulda, coulda, shoulda." He winked at Martin and smiled wryly at the older man as he parked the putter against his desk and came over to join them.

"You did that on purpose—to spite me," Feldman complained.

"I'm not that good."

"Oh, yes, you are!"

Santori stepped forward, gave Martin a firm handshake and guided him to a seat by Feldman, who was studying his wristwatch.

Feldman frowned. "I hear you just got in. Don't we have enough work to keep you busy?"

Santori bowed flamboyantly and deferentially before the older man. "Nice twofer, Dave." Then, to Martin: "He's busting both our balls with that one.

"I'm impressed," he added, turning back to Feldman. "It appears you've still got your mojo."

"Damned right, I do."

"Actually," Santori said, "I told Marty to sleep in, today. I'm worried that if he doesn't slow down a little, he might wind up looking like you in a few years."

"Those would have to be some mighty rough years," Feldman said, and they all laughed.

Santori took a seat facing the couch and turned in Martin's direction. "What's up? I hear you wanted to see me. Everything going OK with the Great Plains audit?"

"Oh, yeah. That's shaping up well."

"Good."

"Nice billable hours on that job!" Feldman chirped.

"Yep. We should make out pretty well," Martin said.

"Like bandits," Feldman cooed.

An awkward silence followed before Martin finally blurted out his news. "Listen guys, Katie and I have separated. I'm living in a motel, and I spent the morning meeting with an attorney up in Olney. I just thought you two should know."

Santori and Feldman exchanged quick, relieved glances.

"I'm sorry to hear that, Marty," Santori began.

"A real shame," Feldman added.

"Any chance the two of you might patch things up?" Santori asked.

"Not likely," Martin said, privately feeling the sting of his words.

Santori leaned forward in his chair. "She wants custody of the kids, I presume?"

"Yeah. And fighting that is probably going to be an uphill battle, what with all the traveling I do. You know, the worst part of this is the effect the divorce will have on the kids. They don't deserve it."

"So, what happened?" Feldman asked, unable to leave Martin's sudden vulnerability alone. "Did she catch you making out with the babysitter or something?"

Martin looked Feldman coldly in the eye and held his gaze until he finally saw the man's Adam's apple twitch. "I'm really not sure what's behind it. We hit a bit of a rough patch, lately. But we were planning to see a marriage counselor and work things out."

"At least, you were planning to—" Feldman sniped.

Santori glared at Feldman. "Knock it off, Dave! Can't you see the guy's in pain?" Then, turning back to Martin, he continued. "Do you think things might get ugly?"

Martin hesitated. "I really don't know."

"Well, let's hope not. These matters can become pretty distracting and draining, if they get out of hand. That would not be good for you...or the firm."

"I agree."

"So, what can we do to help? Do you need to take some time off? Could you use extra staff on the Great Plains gig?"

"No, I'm all right. Really."

Santori's face lit up. "Say, what if I ask my nephew, Tony, to bone up on the Great Plains account. That way, he could work Chicago as your backup—just in case you need it."

"No!" Martin snapped. "I'm fine. I don't need any 'back up.' And if I did, I would decide whom to pick."

"OK, OK. I was just trying to help."

"Are you sure that's all you were doing?"

Santori blinked. "What the hell is that supposed to mean?"

"I don't know," Martin said, "but you suddenly seem unusually free with the resources, especially considering the way our partner, Mr. Scrooge, over there, has been pinching pennies of late. This is also the first time you have ever suggested that I might need an understudy."

Feldman cleared his throat. "For the record, I 'pinch pennies,' as you so crudely put it, to reduce costs and improve margins. And I would never 'pinch' to the point where it put our profits at risk."

"I should hope not," Martin said.

Santori raised a hand. "Let's take things down a notch, shall we? First off, Marty, let me say that Dave and I have the utmost confidence in you and your abilities. You should know that by now. But for many reasons—Dave's retirement being one—it's critical that we proceed cautiously.

"I offered some extra manpower and suggested Tony as a possible backup, because the firm could face considerable exposure if, and only if, your divorce took a particularly ugly turn and it began to affect your work. As you know, we currently have an unusually large number of audits in the pipeline.

"I want to be supportive, that's all—and to look after our common interests. Remember, I've been in your shoes before. I know what a shit storm divorce can be."

"And yet, you voluntarily keep slipping those shoes back on," Feldman jabbed, "which suggests you've learned nothing." He flashed a deep, satisfied smile.

Santori waved him off and continued. "Would you take some advice, Marty, from a twice-divorced guy?"

"Sure."

"Whatever happens, keep it amicable. And by that, I mean, first-and-foremost, keep it out of court. The only ones who make out in a contested divorce these days are the attorneys."

"Actually, if memory serves," Feldman interjected, "your first wife did quite well by ignoring that advice."

"Oh, I don't know," Santori said, looking vaguely annoyed. "She probably would have gotten the house, half the savings and half my retirement anyway, but we could have avoided all those costly attorneys' fees—"

"Fees the judge made you pay."

"Yeah. But it was a wash, really," Santori explained, primarily for his younger colleague's benefit. "Paying those court costs probably saved me from having to foot the bill for years of anger-management therapy for my ex."

Feldman cupped his hands now, as if he was going to whisper a secret to Martin. Then, he shouted, "That's because wife number one caught Joe getting a blow job from wife number two—just a few feet from where we are sitting now. Walked right in on them."

"Is that so?" Martin said, trying to suppress a smile.

"She was my personal secretary," Santori shrugged. "Back then, everyone had one. Now, we all have PCs and laptops."

"Actually," Feldman said, "it could be argued that *she* was your laptop."

"That's funny, Dave. Who are you paying for all this new material?"

"No need for professional help, Joe, not the way you keep setting me up."

Martin decided this was a good time to leave. He stood up. "Well, I guess I should be getting back to work."

Santori walked over to Martin and draped his arm around the younger, and shorter, man's shoulders. "Despite Dave's irreverent, hell, annoying demeanor this morning—"

"Thanks for that!" Feldman interjected.

"I want you to know that we appreciate you sharing this information with us. I'm sure it wasn't easy. But it helps to know about any potential bumps in the road—particularly now, with everything that's going on. The partner agreement may shield us financially, but, as you know, an ounce of prevention—"

"No problem," Martin said.

They were now standing at the door. Santori gripped Martin's arm above the elbow and searched his face. "I know some of what I said didn't sit well with you, but please consider my offer of help to be genuine and open-ended. Whatever you need, we'll provide it."

"OK," Martin said, somewhat dismissively.

"Marty, before you go, is there anything else we should know about? Anything regarding the divorce that you think could cause us trouble?"

"No," Martin said, with a gulp. "As you said, I think this is my personal problem, not the firm's."

"I hope you'll consider talking with Rick Wainwright at some point, if for no other reason than to get a second legal opinion. That's why we pay him that fat retainer of his— and, of course, it would be free advice for you."

"Let me sleep on that, Joe, OK?"

"Sure. Now, one last piece of advice, boychik: Make sure you tell your team about the divorce—preferably, today. Don't make a big deal about it; but they have a right to know, and they should hear it from you. You've earned their trust; now, keep it. OK?

"Sure, Joe."

"Good. Hang in there, pal."

"I will."

As the door shut behind Martin, Santori turned toward Feldman. "The poor bastard has no idea what he's in for."

"Yeah. Well, he's real close to his kids."

"Do me a favor, Dave."

"What?"

"Call Wainwright. Marty's so damn tight-lipped, I doubt he will. Ask Rick to find out what he can about the wife's case: who is representing her and how they typically play. I don't want our boy getting blindsided—especially now, with so many audits in the pipeline."

"Now that you mention it," Feldman said, suddenly straightening up in his seat, "neither do I."

Chapter 7

The rest of the day passed slowly for Martin. He worked through lunch, finalizing the Great Plains Company audit strategy, and then met briefly with his staff at two o'clock to tell them about his separation. Everyone seemed to take the news rather well, he thought. But, as the day wore on, he kept mulling over his meeting with Santori and Feldman. Each time he did, Martin grew more concerned. He now realized how wise he had been to keep most of the details about the divorce to himself.

Martin shuddered to think how Santori might have reacted had he known about the Temporary Restraining Order and the domestic violence charges. Instead of "suggesting" that his nephew, Tony Battaglia, serve as a backup audit team leader, Santori probably would have insisted on it—and not just for the Great Plains audit, either. He might have demanded that Martin start preparing understudies for all his big accounts. Feldman would have been all over him, too, if only for sport.

Both men clearly were worried about the firm's bottom line, but for completely different reasons. Feldman wants the firm to achieve record-breaking profits—to assure him the highest-possible buyout. That's obvious. But what has gotten Santori all stirred up?

He doubted that Santori had only just now realized that the firm's most profitable work—its audits—was under the control of a single person. Then again, there was no mistaking the look of relief he saw the two men exchange when they realized he had come to discuss his pending divorce—and nothing more.

What had they expected? Did they think I was going to 'hold them up?' Were they afraid another firm had made me a better offer?

Santori had seemed uncharacteristically anxious. What was that about? Was he worried that Feldman's departure would leave too big of a management void?

While it was true that Feldman had single-handedly run the firm's day-to-day operations for years, he had been carefully grooming Nancy Spellman and Ed Rosenzweig to share his responsibilities. For the past six months, the two junior partners had been doing most of Feldman's work, without so much as a hiccup. (Eventually, the senior partners figured, the stronger candidate would emerge to become the firm's next managing partner.)

So, if Feldman's departure isn't making Santori anxious, what is?

Then, it hit him. Perhaps, in dealing with Feldman's retirement, Santori, who was next in line to step down, had become aware of the financial risks associated with the firm's most glaring management shortcoming: its lack of effective succession planning and leadership training.

That could explain a lot.

Unfortunately, none of this made Martin feel any better about his current situation. Instead, it made him keenly aware of just how potentially damaging Katie's actions might be. If he wasn't careful, she might not only destroy their marriage; she could end up derailing his career as well.

Whatever hesitancy Martin initially had felt toward the underground group was now completely gone. It began to disappear the moment the Sheriff's deputies had served him with that Temporary Restraining Order and kicked him out of his home. Everything that had happened since then had only served to confirm just how precarious his life had become.

Martin longed to take the offensive. He desperately wanted to turn the tables on Katie, and he wanted to do it as soon as possible. But if that were to happen, he was going to need far more help than he could expect from Chester Swindell. The underground group was beginning to look like his only real option, but he hadn't heard a peep out of it since the run-in with the man on the subway, almost twenty-four hours earlier.

With his mind made up to accept their help, Martin entered into a constant state of readiness. He saw underground operatives everywhere. When the phone rang, he jumped. He studied every new face he encountered and looked for hidden meaning behind every harmless gesture or casual remark.

His overreaching efforts caused him to give every new person he encountered the third degree. Even the deli delivery boy appeared rattled when he left Martin's corner office at lunchtime. "What's with that guy?" he had asked a member of Martin's support team. "He asked me all kinds of questions, and he seemed overly interested in everything about me. It was creepy. I thought he might have been coming on to me or something."

"No, I assure you," she said. "He just hasn't been himself lately."

"Well," the delivery boy said, "until he is himself again, I'm going to leave his lunch orders with you, OK?"

For Martin, the day proved to be an excruciating awakening of sorts. As word of his pending divorce spread through the firm, sympathetic associates began coming out of the woodwork. More than half a dozen colleagues approached him and shared their own intense, deeply personal divorce stories. Previously, the most information he had exchanged with many of them had been mutual grunts of recognition on the elevator, at the water cooler or in the hallways. But now, they were suddenly bound together by tragedy.

At 5:00 p.m., when he folded his coat over his arm and headed for the elevator, Martin knew that he had been living in a bubble most of his married life. Divorce and divorce-related horror stories appeared to be everywhere, and yet he hadn't had a clue. Martin wondered whether he had been unusually oblivious or if divorce was just one of those deeply personal disasters that victims prefer to talk about strictly among themselves. He finally decided that, in his case, at least, it was a little of both.

Chapter 8

"You're an hour late," Esther Finch announced as her daughter stepped through the front door of the family home. "You promised me you'd be here by four at the latest."

Katie Silkwood put down her pocketbook and shopping bag, hung her coat on the front hall banister and sighed. "I'm sorry, Mom. After my shift at the hospital, I had a few quick errands to run. Everything took longer than I imagined."

"I don't like being taken advantage of, dear."

"I know. You're right. But cut me a break, will you? I'm new to this 'single mom' business."

"Whose fault is that?"

Katie frowned. "Do you really want to go there, Mom? Besides, you got to spend an extra hour with your grand kids. How terrible was that?"

"That's not the point."

"OK, OK: *Mea culpa.*"

"Precisely, dear. Call ahead next time—and ask."

"All right, I will." Katie picked up her shopping bag, stepped forward and kissed her mother on the cheek. Then, she looked around the pristine living room.

"I don't know how you do it," she said with genuine admiration. "The place is spotless…and so quiet. Where are the kids?"

Esther smiled. "Monica's taking a nap, and Justin is playing one of his video games in the den."

Katie walked toward the kitchen. "How were they for you?"

"Monica's just like a little baby doll, so sweet and pleasant."

"And Justin?"

"That boy never stops talking! He gave me an earful. Told me all about some game he and the other kids invented at lunchtime. He started talking about it the moment he got off the bus, and he didn't stop until about a half-hour ago."

As Katie emptied the shopping bag, Esther began putting the various items away. "I think they're happy to be home, dear."

"Of course, they are, Mom. This is what they know."

"Justin really misses his dad. He kept asking me when Marty was coming home. I think he's hoping his dad will be here for his birthday party, Saturday."

Katie froze. "He won't be, Mother."

"Not even for Justin's party, dear? The boy only turns seven once."

"No, Mother. I've already explained this to you. The restraining order says 'no contact' until after the hearing next Monday. And 'no' means 'no.'"

"Justin doesn't know from restraining orders, sweetie. And you don't need to tell the judge everything, do you? Let the boy have his daddy at his party!"

Katie stopped emptying the grocery bag. She closed her eyes and frowned as she took a deep breath. "Why don't you just MIND YOUR OWN BUSINESS Mother?!" she finally blurted out. "Justin will get over this a lot sooner than you think. Kids, these days, are very resilient. At least, that's what all the studies say."

"So, that's it, dear: marriage over?"

"Yesss!" she hissed, attempting, once more, to reapply the dampers. "Please respect my wishes on this."

"I can't. I'm not sure you've thought this through. You're willing to destroy your marriage and to turn your kids' lives upside down...for what? I think you are making a huge mistake."

"After everything I've told you about Marty's behavior, I would think you'd understand."

"Just what did he do that was so bad? Call you a few names? Raise his voice now and then?"

"Yes! And whether you know it or not, that's abusive behavior."

"Says who?"

"My lawyer, for one."

"Of course, *she* says so, dear. That's how she makes a living, by getting clients like you all riled up. Did you tell her how you get when you're angry?"

Katie put her hands on her hips and glared. "Just what is that supposed to mean?"

"Oh, come on, dear! You forget; I raised you. I've lived with that mouth of yours—and your temper. I've heard you yell at Marty during your 'special times.' I've heard the vases and dishes break, too. And Marty wasn't the one throwing them. So, by your own definition, you're as much at fault as he is—maybe more."

"That's not true, Mother."

"Of course, it is!"

"No," Katie said, lowering her head, and turning away. "Marty assaulted me."

"What?!" Esther grabbed her daughter by the shoulders, spun her around and searched her face. "Marty hit you, honey? I had no idea. That changes everything. Where? When?"

Katie tried to dodge her mother's piercing gaze. "He didn't actually *hit* me, Mom."

Esther threw up her hands. "Then I don't get it," she said, pulling out a kitchen chair and collapsing into it. "How could he have assaulted you without hitting you?"

Katie looked down at her mother with disdain. "You're not a lawyer, Mother. You wouldn't understand."

"Try me, dear."

"Beverly, my lawyer, said the true test for assault is if Marty's actions ever made me feel scared or threatened, in any way; and they have. 'Assault' means any kind of threatening, abusive behavior. You're confusing 'assault' with 'battery.'"

Esther looked at her daughter as if for the first time. Then she burst out laughing. "What kind of nonsense are you and that lawyer of yours peddling, Katie? Do you really expect me to believe that you're afraid of Marty?"

"I am, sometimes."

"Good luck with that, dear."

"You don't know what happens in this house when you're not around, Mother."

"Katie, the man treats you like a queen!"

"Oh, really?"

"He lets you sleep in on weekends, doesn't he?"

"Sometimes."

"He still opens doors for you and carries your bags?"

"Yes."

"He didn't object when you took over all the master bedroom closets, did he?"

"What does that prove?"

"Just answer the question, dear."

"Who *are* you, Denny Crane?"

Esther stared at her daughter and waited.

"OK, yes. He didn't object."

"—even though he had to store all of his clothes in the spare bedroom closet down the hall?"

"Yes."

"He shares the household chores with you?"

"More or less," she sighed, rolling her eyes.

"He lets you manage the joint checking accounts, too?"

"Uh huh."

"He never asks you to return anything you buy for yourself—no matter how expensive, frivolous or extravagant?"

"That's right."

"He adores the children and dotes on them?"

"Yes."

"Well, no wonder you want a divorce. The man's a freak, a total monster! And just like all the abusive husbands that I've ever read about, his personality profile sounds so controlling and demanding, too."

"I guess we won't be calling you to testify on my behalf at the trial."

"Not if the truth would hurt your case, dear, as it appears it would."

"Mother, you don't know what the truth is in this matter. You think you do, but you are only here a fraction of the time."

"Well, since we're discussing 'the truth' dear, how much of this has to do with 'Uncle Eddie?'"

Katie went to the sink and poured herself a glass of water. "Who?" she asked over her shoulder.

"Uncle Eddie, dear. Your friend. The one your children have told me about."

Katie remained at the sink but now turned around to face Esther. "Oh, Eddie. He's just a friend. A concerned friend. That's all."

"A concerned friend who takes you and the kids out to dinner and to the movies and spends his evenings here with you?"

"Where are you getting all this information?"

"From the children, dear. They see what's going on, even if they don't fully understand it. Have you lost your mind, Katie? This is madness!"

"Mother, please stay out of my personal affairs. And if you can't be on my side, please keep your opinions to yourself. I know what I'm doing."

"Do you?"

"Yes. My marriage to Martin is over. Over. We've been in a rut for some time now, and yes, if you must know, I finally have a chance to be happy...with Eddie. I've hired a great attorney, who comes highly recommended. She says she can help me end the marriage, come out on top, and begin a new life. So far, she's helped me get a restraining order, sole custody of the kids, and exclusive use of the house; and that is just the beginning.

"Beverly says Martin has an enormous amount to lose, professionally, if he were to fight me on this, far more than I do. We worked up a reasonable settlement offer for him— one Beverly says he would have to be crazy to refuse. She expects to have everything wrapped up in just a few days' time. OK?"

"No, it's not OK. Are you now comfortable lying to get your way? I raised you better than that. You're perjuring yourself, dear, and that has consequences."

"Oh, *my God*, Mother," Katie said, laughing, and shaking her head. "Do you really think anyone's going to send me 'up the river' for this? I'm the battered spouse, here, the injured party. Marty is the abuser. Besides, Beverly says perjury is extremely hard to prove. The courts rarely, if ever, even pursue perjury convictions in these kinds of cases. Did you know that?"

Esther shook her head, "No, I didn't."

"Of course, not! Well, those are the facts, Mom. Beverly West has represented hundreds of women like me, in similar cases, for more than twenty years, and do you know how many of her clients have ever been charged with perjury?"

"No."

"Zero. And do you know why?" Katie asked, without waiting for a reply. "Because, Beverly says, in these cases, the victims actually determine whether or not they have been assaulted.

"As long as the victim can honestly say that she felt scared or threatened by her husband's actions, then he has committed assault. It's that simple. The charge stems directly from how the behavior makes the victim feel. And how can you dispute someone else's feelings? You can't."

"But, Katie," Esther said, "Marty is a reasonable man. Why not do this nicely? Why do you have to make everything so ugly and mean spirited?"

Katie sat down at the table now and took her mother's hand. "If I could do this nicely, Mother, don't you think I would? Marty's far too attached to the kids. He loves them and will not allow me to end this marriage, or give me full custody, without a fight. He makes a lot of money, Mom, and the children deserve to get as much financial support from their father as the law allows.

"If he were to get angry enough over this, he might try to hurt me by refusing to provide full support for the kids. I have a parental responsibility to protect them from that."

"Why would Marty do such a thing?" Esther asked. "He loves the children. I can't imagine him denying them anything."

At that, Katie forcefully withdrew her hand from her mother's—as if the older woman had suddenly contracted Leprosy. "Whose side are you on, Mom?"

"Well," Esther began, a bit startled and fumbling for the right words, "I-I'm on the kids' side, of course...and yours, too, dear. After all, you are...my blood."

"Glad to hear it, Mom!" Katie said with more than a hint of sarcasm. She closed her eyes and sighed deeply. Then, she leaned forward, opened her eyes again and, once more, took her mother's hands in hers.

"I'm glad you feel that way," she said, a smile slowly returning to her face, "because the last thing those kids need now would be to lose their grandmother, too."

Chapter 9

Late Wednesday morning, Swindell called Martin at work with the details of the settlement offer he had received the previous afternoon.

"These are the main points," he began. "Your wife wants to make the temporary custody arrangement you now have permanent. She wants substantial child support payments from you, free use of the family home for three years, your promise never to come inside the house again—under *any* circumstances—and an agreement acknowledgin' your mutual consent to begin seein' other people immediately.

"In return," Swindell continued, "her attorney, Beverly West, said your wife would agree to drop the domestic violence charges now before the court and grant you the standard 'weekend warrior's' allotment of time with your kids: dinner one night a week and visitation every other weekend.

"What do you think?" Swindell asked, with carefully suppressed anticipation.

"I think she's out of her effing mind! I want you to have a detective tail her for a couple of days. I'm pretty sure, based on her offer, that she's been having an affair."

"Of course," Swindell said, positively glowing inside.

"I also want you to reject her offer out of hand."

"Are you sure?" Swindell asked, in a last ditch, half-hearted attempt to appear impartial.

"Have you been smoking something other than those Honduran cigars I saw on your desk the other day?"

"OK," Swindell said, with a chuckle, "but there's somethin' else you need to know."

"What's that?"

"Even if the detective can prove your wife has been committin' adultery, Mahr-tin, Maryland law still does not consider that to be sufficient grounds for awardin' custody to the father."

"Naturally," Martin said. "Why should I be surprised? What if she had been convicted of prostitution?"

"Then, *maybe*, you'd have the beginnin' of a case."

"The news just keeps getting better and better," Martin said, in disgust.

"Yes, it does," Swindell chimed in, with barely hidden enthusiasm. "Yes, it does."

Swindell hung up the phone and immediately logged the call and the details of his conversation with Martin into his desktop computer's case-management program. He used his own, makeshift brand of shorthand: "M.S. rejects settlement. Believes wife cheating. Hire PI. No counter offer. Trial."

Then, he keyed in the next call he would make that day—the one to Beverly West, in which he would tell opposing counsel that there would be no deal in the case, at this time.

That should put a smile on her face. Now, she can make an even bigger down payment on that beach-front property of hers.

Swindell hit the Enter key with a flourish, restarting the program's live timer, the proverbial 'meter' that accumulated billable hours for him whenever it ran. It had been idle for all of two minutes. He smiled. Everything was on track. The case of Silkwood v. Silkwood was proceeding nicely.

Then suddenly, despite years of careful conditioning, Swindell felt a slight tinge of guilt. He wondered if he should have pressed Martin harder for a counter offer. After all, he knew this was the best time to negotiate a more favorable custody and visitation arrangement for his client. He was convinced Martin would not have cut off negotiations if he truly had understood the implications of that Temporary Restraining Order.

Even though the court had granted the order solely on Katie Silkwood's say so; even though it was temporary in nature and, therefore, should have no permanent bearing on the case; even though a one-sided *ex-parte* hearing decision deserved minimal legal standing, at best; Swindell knew better. The order, by its mere existence, already had changed the custodial *status quo* in the case. It could, and probably would, do his client grave harm.

When the two parties were to appear in court the following Monday, Katie Silkwood would command the legal 'high ground,' as the children's new, court-appointed sole custodian. Meanwhile, Martin would begin the proceedings as a non-custodial parent—with no presumptive right to custody at all! What Martin could not know, because Swindell had never told him, was that, in deciding matters of custody, Family Court judges almost always prefer to maintain the custodial *status quo*, no matter how new, tenuous, or questionable its award might have been.

Swindell winced over the discovery of his newly resurrected conscience. He picked up the phone and briefly considered calling Martin back. Then, he returned it to its holder and, instead, retrieved the small key to his desk's top-right drawer, where he kept his private stash of hand-rolled, contraband Cuban cigars. A moment later, he finished rummaging through the drawer and withdrew the prize he sought: one of his cherished, six-inch long, H. Upmann Magnum Fifties.

Swindell clipped the end and gently rolled the cigar between his thumb and forefinger several times, taking its measure. He closed his eyes and brought it to his nose to savor its rich, pungent aroma. *What is it about this Silkwood fellah,* he asked himself, as he struck a match and lovingly puffed the cigar to life, *that has allowed him to get under my skin?*

Swindell took a deep, long puff, held it a second and then slowly released a fresh, new blast of smoke. As the roiling cloud fanned out and dissipated in the air above his desk, he shook his head and chuckled. He thought he was long past caring about these poor schlubs who couldn't keep their wives in line. Like most of the men Swindell represented, this new one clearly loved his kids. *A sign of the times,* he thought. *After all, he's part of a new breed of husband— our second generation of fully 'liberated,' co-parentin' males.*

But there was something decidedly different about Martin. When Swindell had asked him the perfunctory background questions about his family life, he was surprised, almost touched, by the spontaneity and sincerity his client had exhibited.

Martin's entire demeanor had changed, brightening considerably, when he spoke about a recent afternoon he had spent at the park near his home, teaching his six-year-old boy, Justin, how to field ground balls and how to perfect his Tee Ball swing. Martin also went on and on, bragging about his three-year-old daughter, Monica's, prowess in toddler tumbling class. Martin took her there every Saturday morning, he said, so his wife could 'sleep in.'

Initially, Swindell had found all this paternal gushing on Martin's part to be a bit excessive, almost bordering on the effeminate. At the same time, though, it made him painfully aware of the lack of closeness in his relationship with his own thirty-three-year-old son, a marine biologist now living in southern California. He and Randall rarely spoke, and Swindell normally had to board a plane just to affect a face-to-face meeting with him. But that was to be expected, he thought, when he considered his own emotionally starved childhood, growing up in a household dominated by his distant, demanding, and aristocratic father, Chester, Sr.

Swindell may have envied his client for the closeness of his relationship with his children, but he found little else appealing about Martin's present life or circumstances. Late the previous afternoon, for instance, he had received a disturbing phone call from Gloria Cheswick, a fellow divorce attorney, who served with Swindell on the county bar association's Civil Procedures committee. Swindell secretly disliked Gloria, whom he considered to be a women's rights zealot and a bit of a nut case.

"Chester," Gloria had begun somewhat sternly, once she had dispensed with the usual pleasantries, "*please* tell me the rumors I'm hearing aren't true."

"What rumors, Gloria?"

"Tell me you are not representing that *awful* man."

"Who?"

"Martin Silkwood. Tell me, it's not true."

"I'm not tellin' you anythin', Gloria—one way or the other. What's your interest in this case, anyway? You representin' the wife?"

"My interest is strictly personal, Chester. Katie Silkwood is a good and dear friend."

"Then, you might not want to stick your nose where it doesn't belong, Gloria. If your intent is to interfere with my representation of a client by slanderin' that individual, you could end up gettin' yourself sanctioned by the court."

"You would report me to the judge, Chester—over this?"

"I'd do it before I'd allow your actions to compromise me, yes."

"He's a monster, Chester. An absolute monster!"

"Where's all this fervor comin' from, Gloria? You got any first-hand knowledge you want to share?"

Gloria thought a moment before replying. "No, I don't. But I know what this man is capable of. Katie has told me everything."

"That's all hearsay, Gloria: inadmissible in court and inappropriate here.... Did the Silkwood woman put you up to this?"

"Of course, not!"

"Then, I guess she's got more sense than you!"

"You *are* representing him, aren't you, Chester?" Gloria said with a gasp. "And all along, I thought you were one of the good guys!"

Swindell laughed. "I've been called a lot of thin's, in my time, Gloria, but that's a first! Listen, it's been real nice chattin' with ya, but I have to run now. Bye!" And with that, Swindell had hung up the phone. Even now, as he replayed that conversation in his mind, Swindell rolled his eyes and shook his head in disbelief. Gloria Cheswick clearly had wandered far off 'the reservation.'

He shuddered at the thought that he might, one day, have the misfortune of facing Gloria in court. Unlike

Beverly West, who played the 'domestic violence' card frequently, but always in a cold, calculated way, Gloria Cheswick behaved erratically...and emotionally.

Gloria seemed to fancy herself as a true champion of oppressed and victimized women. For some unknown reason, all the domestic violence propaganda freely circulating within the legal community seemed to resonate with Gloria on a deeply personal level. Her passionate, warped perspective made her actions highly unpredictable and, on occasion, genuinely unprofessional. That, in turn, made her extremely dangerous in the courtroom. Whereas Swindell could deal with Beverly West, he had no idea how to read or strategize effectively against someone operating on Gloria Cheswick's private wavelength.

Gradually, things were starting to make sense to Swindell. He felt he was beginning to understand what it was about Martin that initially had awakened his sympathies. It was a combination of Martin's inherent decency and naïveté, coupled with Swindell's growing awareness of the size, scope and intensity of the hidden forces aligning themselves against his client. On reflection, Swindell thought Martin's situation was beginning to resemble that of a young buck suddenly caught in the glare of an onrushing tractor-trailer's headlights.

He realized Martin could have no more idea of the true nature of the legal juggernaut tearing his way than a deer would have had of the sophisticated mechanics propelling a Mack truck toward it at sixty-five miles an hour. Both would remain ignorant right up to the point of impact, when the fender and grille would crush and flatten them into fresh road kill.

Swindell could clearly see that truck bearing down on his client with a malevolent inevitability that was painful to watch. He could see diesel smoke coughing up out of the exhaust pipe above the cab and the cold, harsh headlights locking in on their prey. Meanwhile, Martin just stood there, alone, in the middle of the road, in his dark business suit, freshly pressed shirt, and power tie, his face frozen in dumb terror and framed by a full head of salt-and-pepper hair.

Unlike Martin, Swindell also could discern the four, bold letters painted straight and tall on the side of that truck. He knew what the "V-A-W-A" stood for. They were the initials of the "Violence against Women Act."

Congress had passed the Violence against Women Act back in 1994, and President Bill Clinton immediately signed it into law. On its face, the VAWA was supposed to protect women against a broad range of legitimate threats, including violent spousal abuse. But the law's vast, overreaching nature and its general disregard for due process and men's civil rights quickly turned it into something altogether different: It became enabling legislation for the radical feminist movement's takeover of the family law courts.

Swindell initially watched with alarm as the VAWA, backed by relentless lobbying from lawyers with the National Organization for Women, overturned centuries of carefully crafted common-law and due-process protections. It achieved this, primarily, by allowing women to bypass the criminal courts altogether to bring what were essentially criminal actions against their husbands. In the Civil Court, which tried these cases, both the legal protections for the accused and the standard of proof demanded of the accusers were far weaker. Swindell felt a great many of these cases were highly suspect, to say the least.

In civil court, under the VAWA, women could now level charges of "assault, aggravated assault, and battery" against their unsuspecting husbands through one-sided, and secret, *ex-parte* proceedings that were not even permitted in true criminal cases. A Civil Court petitioner only needed to show the judge a "preponderance of the evidence" to prove a case, while Criminal Court demanded proof "beyond a reasonable doubt."

In civil court, the alleged guilty parties had to provide, and pay for, their own counsel. They were not entitled, as they are, in criminal cases, to free legal representation from the Public Defender's Office, and this held true even if they had no money. Meanwhile, the term 'alleged' was never used, in the text of the VAWA, to refer to an "abuser." The law repeatedly referred, indirectly, to women as the 'victims' and to men as the 'abusers' (as if they already had been tried and convicted of the 'alleged' offenses.)

The VAWA also was funded legislation. Each year, it poured hundreds of millions of federal dollars into programs designed to document and aid female victims of domestic violence—and to indoctrinate judges on how to try the cases. Funding recipients immediately had a stake in portraying men as the perennial abusers and women as the eternal victims—despite a growing body of empirical evidence to the contrary.

For a brief time, Swindell and several of his cronies bemoaned the damage the VAWA was doing to family law, as heavy-handed tactics and unethical maneuverings quickly became the order of the day. But soon—surprisingly soon—the VAWA showed them another side: the positive effect the law was having on their practices' bottom lines, through the heightened conflict it generated between estranged spouses.

Marginal cases that would have settled quickly in the past were suddenly going to trial—with legal fees mounting all the while—as men fought either to get even with their wives or to avoid losing their children, their reputations, and their prior standards of living. Swindell and his fellow lawyers watched in amazement as this runaway tractor-trailer miraculously morphed into a big, fat, legal gravy train.

Swindell was 'old school' enough that he never exploited the VAWA for his own tactical advantage. But he never fought against its misuse by others, either. He had read the subtext in conversations with his peers. He had attended the government-funded Continuing Legal Education workshops that tirelessly beat the drum about the growing menace of male-initiated domestic violence. And he had reviewed his law firm's now permanently inflated balance sheet often enough to know better.

So, in the face of what his legal training and his own good sense told him to be a great and terrible wrong, Swindell remained silent. He resolved, simply, to give his clients his best efforts. He would 'fight the good fight' exclusively in the courtroom, where the odds grew increasingly long for the men he typically represented.

Meanwhile, like an oncologist treating a terminal patient, Swindell learned to manage the information he shared with his clients. He would withhold bad news as long as possible, in order to give them hope, to boost their spirits—and to keep his fees flowing.

As he watched his clients struggle, like so many lost souls, to climb out of the legal quicksand they found themselves in, to end the horrible nightmare and to break free of the vicious snare divorce court had become, Swindell assumed the role of quiet confidant. He was part philosopher, part silent witness to their misery. If he could not help them, he would try his best to *understand* them or to make them *feel* understood. That was the least he could do.

So long as he received his fee, Swindell, like a modern-day Charon, would calmly guide his clients across the deep and terrible waters of divorce, steadily rowing forward, ever forward, until they reached the far shore. Once in the shallows, he would lift his oar and allow the boat to glide forward the last, few remaining feet, as the awful mists cleared and his clients found themselves staring up at the dark, and foreboding, Gates of Hell.

Swindell took the cigar from his mouth and tapped it twice against the edge of his ashtray. Two inches of gray, spent tobacco ash fell away, revealing a glowing, orange core. He looked down at his case-management program.

The counter showed seven minutes had elapsed on his yet-to-be-placed call to Beverly West. Already, with the software's rounding-up feature, the call had cost his client sixty dollars. If he was efficient and could limit his actual time on the phone with West to less than five minutes, Swindell could prevent the 'meter' from adding yet a third, thirty-dollar increment to Martin's bill. Buoyed by this uncharacteristically altruistic thought, Swindell picked up the phone and threw himself back into his work.

Chapter 10

Beverly West bit her lower lip so hard that it bled, when Swindell called her just before noon, Wednesday, to say that Martin had completely rejected her client's settlement offer. Fortunately, she managed to keep her cool when it finally became her turn to speak.

"Your client," she said into the phone, with all the nonchalance and bravado she could muster, "is either a brave man or an ignoramus. Our offer is extremely generous. This case is a slam dunk."

"On the other hand," Swindell countered, "maybe you're the ignoramus, Bev, and your case is anythin' but–. Well, we'll all know soon enough."

"Don't forget to tell your client about the many risks associated with going to trial, Chester. I wouldn't want you to give him future grounds for suing you for malpractice."

Swindell chuckled. "Thanks for lookin' out for me, Bev. It's quite comfortin'."

"My pleasure, counselor. Call me if the 'lunatic' changes his mind."

"I certainly will, but I wouldn't hold my breath. He seems quite determined."

"That's splendid! I'll send my victory suit out to the dry cleaners this afternoon. You know, it's the one I wore for that last case of ours, the one that went all the way. See you in court."

"It sure looks that way."

As soon as the call ended, Beverly dialed Katie Silkwood's cell phone. "Katie," she said, "we've got a problem."

Katie, who was at a patient's bedside, cupped the phone with her hand and stepped away for some privacy. "What's the matter, Beverly?" she whispered.

"I presented our settlement offer to your husband's lawyer yesterday, and he just called me back." She paused. "Your husband has rejected it out of hand."

"Well," Katie said, stepping out into the hallway, "you told me it was just our opening position, so, I didn't expect him to accept it without some changes. What's his counter offer?"

"That's just it, Katie. There is no counter offer. Martin doesn't want to settle. We're going to trial."

"What?!" Katie shouted, as orderlies, visitors, and a few gowned patients, who were walking down the hall, towing their drip lines behind them, all suddenly turned their heads in her direction. Her voice quickly returned to a whisper. "You said Martin had way too much to lose to risk a hearing!"

"I know, Katie. And he does. As I told you, almost *all* my domestic violence cases settle at this point for precisely that reason. I must admit, your husband's response caught me completely off guard. I thought you said he was as an extremely conservative, deeply private, risk-averse man?"

"That's how I've always thought of him. He's certainly not a gambler, if that's what you mean."

"Well, my dear, you may want to dust off the old dossier. It appears 'hubby' has grown himself an impressive, new pair of balls."

"Wonderful! So, what do you intend to do about that?"

"Katie, 'gelding' is not a skill set you'll find listed anywhere on my resume."

"Well, after talking to your references, it probably *should* be."

"Really?"

Katie's tone became far more serious. "Listen, Beverly, you promised me this would all be over quickly and cleanly. I cannot afford a full-blown trial now. I mean, this isn't even the actual divorce case. I trusted you, when you said there would be no surprises. Now, you need to make this right."

"I understand how you feel, but as I have told you, repeatedly, Katie, there are no 'guarantees' in divorce cases.

As your lawyer, I can express my opinion about how things might turn out, but I can't promise or guarantee you anything."

"I don't know, Beverly. 'No surprises' sounds an awful lot like a guarantee to me."

"That's not a place you want to go with me, Katie."

Katie thought about that for a moment. "Fine, but I expect more from a lawyer with your reputation, and your hourly rate, than: 'Katie, we've got a problem.' I would think you would have a solution or two in mind before picking up the phone and ruining my day."

"Point taken, Katie."

"So, what can we do now? Should you go back to them with a more generous settlement offer, one that possibly gives Marty more time with the kids, but not nearly enough to approach joint custody?"

"No. To return to the bargaining table now with any revised offer, after we've been completely rebuffed like this, would make us appear desperate. That would only make matters worse."

"Great. So, what do you propose we do?"

Beverly considered the options. "For the moment, nothing."

Katie wanted to scream, but she held back. "How much extra could this little domestic violence hearing wind up costing me, Beverly?"

"It all depends. I don't see it lasting for more than a day, but then, there's considerable prep time involved. You're probably looking at costs of somewhere between $4,000 and $5,000. But, Katie, that's —"

"I know, 'not a guarantee?'"

"Right. In addition, a bad outcome in the domestic Violence case, while still a remote possibility, is something we must now consider. That could further complicate matters."

"Meaning it could cost me even more in legal fees?"

"I'm sorry, Katie, but that is how the system works."

Katie could now feel a panic attack coming on. Her head throbbed and her pulse quickened. She steadied herself against the hallway wall, as inconspicuously as possible, to counter her sudden light-headedness. Then, she made her way toward a small, rarely used family waiting area.

"Katie? Katie, are you still there?"

"Yes, Beverly. Hold on a minute, please."

Katie opened the door a crack and looked inside. The room was empty, so she went in, closed the door behind her, and took several deep breaths. "My plan—our plan," she said, slipping into a seat, "had been to use the money I withdrew from the household checking account to pay my divorce expenses. What am I supposed to do now? I'm not sure I can manage this, too."

"First of all, Katie, this is no time to panic. I know it may not seem like it, but next Monday is still five days off. That's an eternity in this kind of case. So, you need to get a grip on yourself. This probably is just a minor bump on the road. We have not driven into a sinkhole.

"You wanted to know what I think. I suggest we start by reassessing the situation. Right now, we know your husband is angry. OK, maybe this is just his way of blowing off steam. He already may have come to his senses—or he probably will soon. If his attorney, Mr. Swindell, does his job—and I have every reason to believe he will—he probably will push Martin to come up with some sort of counter offer. That way, Martin might be able to get most of what he wants without the added costs, and risks, of a trial. Believe me, Katie, this matter is far from over."

Katie's breathing had finally returned to normal.

Beverly continued. "I gave your husband's attorney plenty to think about, when he told me about Martin's decision. As a tactical matter, I think we need to give them a day or two to stew on this. Meanwhile, you probably should start working on our contingency plan."

"What is that, again?" Katie asked.

"The plan is for you to pass the hat around to family, friends and acquaintances and ask them to help underwrite your attempt to break free from an abusive marriage that now threatens you and your kids."

"I'm not sure I'm ready to start making those calls just yet, Beverly."

"That's OK. I just want you to start compiling your list of people *to* call."

"All right," Katie said. "I can certainly do that."

Chapter 11

Martin felt elated after his phone call with Swindell. Despite his attorney's renewed warnings about the risks of trying cases in the female-biased Family Courts, Martin had stuck to his guns. He cupped his hands behind his head, put his feet on top of his credenza and smiled. He had seized the initiative, rejected Katie's lopsided settlement offer and, more importantly, demanded that they go directly to trial.

The decision had been bold and gutsy. Katie would never expect it. He wished he could be there, like the proverbial 'fly on the wall,' to see the panic register on her face when she would hear the news. At least, Katie would now know that she had a fight on her hands. Her husband was not going to be a pushover.

On another level, Martin felt he had no choice but to reject Katie's proposal. Even if she had intended it merely as an opening gambit in their negotiations, her offer sought to marginalize Martin's role in his kids' lives, and he would have none of that. In marriage, Martin and Katie had been equal partners in parenting. He expected no less in divorce. After all, he reasoned, he loved his kids and they loved him. Why should a change in marital status suddenly affect that?

By reaffirming his commitment to his children and his principles, Martin also hoped to send a clear message to Katie. If she could be fair and reasonable regarding the divorce, then he would cooperate, but if she preferred to behave selfishly and without regard for his interests, or the best interests of their children, then he would oppose her with all the resources at his disposal.

The decision had re-energized Martin. For the first time in days, he walked with a spring in his step and a glint in his eye. He seemed more upbeat, more optimistic. But Martin's new-found confidence would not survive the afternoon.

At four o'clock, Monique buzzed Martin on the intercom and asked if he had time to meet, briefly, with Santori and Feldman, in Santori's office?"

"Sure. When?"

"Now, if possible."

"OK. Just give me a minute to finish what I'm doing, and I'll be right there."

Martin quickly wrapped up his work and, once more, headed for the hexagonal office at the south end of the building.

The scene that greeted him there bore little resemblance to the relaxed, congenial atmosphere he had experienced the previous day. When Martin came through the door, he found Santori and Feldman seated side-by-side in chairs, intently pouring over copies of some type of report. Rick Wainwright, the firm's long-time legal counsel and trusted advisor, sat across from them on the couch. His briefcase lay open beside him, and he held a third copy of the report in his hands.

At six-foot-four, with a rugged, stocky build, Wainwright still looked the part of a former all-American lacrosse player. Wainwright had paid his way through undergraduate school, by earning a full athletic scholarship to Johns Hopkins University. From there, he went on to Georgetown University Law School, where he ranked seventh in his class. His jet-black hair, now graying at the temples, and his ruddy complexion were the only hints of his mixed ancestry. Wainwright was third-generation Irish-American on his father's side and full-blooded Cherokee Indian on his mother's. Cratered scars from severe childhood acne added further character to an otherwise handsome, youthful face.

"You wanted to see me?" Martin asked.

Santori glanced up from his report with a pained look in his eyes. "Marty, glad you could make it," he said flatly. Then, he took a deep breath. "Lock the door behind you, please, and take a seat."

"Lock the door? What's going on, Joe? You look like someone's been putting the screws to you."

Martin and Wainwright exchanged quick nods of recognition. "No offense meant, Rick," Martin began, turning back to his partners, "but why is counsel here?"

"None taken," Wainwright said.

"We have a serious problem on our hands, Marty," Santori began, "with potentially grave implications for the firm...and for you, in particular."

"For me?" Martin frowned, as he sat down at the opposite end of the couch from Wainwright. "Why, me?"

"I'll get to that in a minute," Santori said.

"Rick's been briefing us," Feldman added.

"Briefing you on *what*?"

"'What' is not the operative word, Marty," Santori said. He paused and briefly closed his eyes, while he gathered his thoughts. "The correct word, in this instance, would be 'Who.' And, although I'm still trying to get my head around it, the 'who,' appears to be 'you.'"

"Me? What the hell did I do?"

Santori's eyes flashed rage. "It's really what you didn't do, Marty. It appears you didn't tell us the truth yesterday."

"I most certainly did," Martin said, straightening up in his seat. "I was incredibly forthcoming with you guys. In fact, I volunteered the information that Katie and I were separating and would likely be getting a divorce. And I was under no obligation to tell you anything. You said so yourself, Joe, when you told me how much you appreciated me coming forward."

Santori glared at Martin. "What do you take me for, Marty, a fool? Your divorce was never the issue."

"Then, what is?"

"When you left here yesterday," Santori said, "I was deeply concerned that serious trouble might lie ahead for you. Ironically, I did not want you to encounter any unpleasant 'surprises' along the way. I consider you a valued partner and friend, and I wanted to help. I knew you'd never contact Rick on your own, so I asked Dave to get in touch with him on your behalf."

"You did *what?*" Martin asked.

Wainwright cleared his throat. "Marty, your partners asked me, as corporate counsel, to dig around a little and check out the lawyers representing you and Kate. They wanted to know about their past success rates and the kind of tactics they typically employ. I sent one of our junior associates out to review the case filings in Circuit Court, in order to identify the attorneys of record. She called me a little while later concerned, because she couldn't find any paperwork about your divorce."

"Of course, not," Martin said. "Those papers haven't even been filed yet! That proves how early I brought you guys into the loop."

"Well," Wainwright continued, "to be thorough, and since she already was at the Courthouse, I asked her to swing by the district court on her way back. There, she found a filing for the only active *Silkwood v. Silkwood* case, in Montgomery County."

Martin swallowed hard.

"It was a petition for a Temporary Restraining Order against you, Marty, brought on charges stemming from four 'alleged' instances of domestic violence. And, as I assume you know, the petition was granted last Monday."

"That's right," Martin said.

Santori was seething. "How could you, Marty?" he asked. "I stood there at the door with you yesterday, and I asked you, man-to-man, if there was anything else related to your divorce that we should know about—anything that could potentially harm the firm. Do you remember that?"

"Yes, I do."

"And knowing about these charges, and the potential damage they could cause, you still looked me in the eye and said, 'No?'"

"That's right." Martin said.

"How is that even *possible*?"

"Well, to start with, Joe, the charges Katie made are completely false, and I intend to prove it."

"Who cares?!" Santori shouted, throwing his copy of Wainwright's report flying across the room. "True, false, it doesn't matter! The charges exist, don't they? They're now part of the public record. Don't you understand what that means?"

"Apparently not," Martin said.

"It means the charges are *out there*, Marty. A black mark on your character is now available for anyone with an Internet connection to see—including our potential clients. Any firm that performs due diligence prior to engaging us, and runs background checks on the partners, will be able to find it. Your prospective audit clients will see that you've been accused of domestic violence. How do you think that's going to sit with them?"

A silence fell over the room. Martin looked anxiously at Wainwright. "Is he right, Rick? Will these records remain out there even if I win in court?"

Wainwright seemed taken aback. "Even if you win, Marty?" he said, shaking his head in disbelief. "I hope you're not serious. If you fight this thing in court, and *lose*, it could destroy your career. As Joe just explained, you could become a major liability for the firm.

"You know," he added, "there's a whole HR side to this issue that we haven't even addressed yet, although it's in my report."

"What are you talking about?" Martin asked.

Feldman spoke up. "As lead auditor, Marty, you oversee teams of men and women—married and single—who travel with you out of town, often for several days at a time, right?"

"Yes."

"Now, suppose a woman who works for you proves to be incompetent. You let her go, as you should, but then, she, or her attorney, discovers that you've been named, publicly, as the aggressor in a domestic violence case. That might encourage her to retaliate by filing sexual harassment charges, or something equally unpleasant, against you. The mere threat to file would give her enormous leverage. We probably would have to settle."

"Is that a real possibility?" Martin asked Wainwright.

"I put it in the report, Marty. What do you think?"

Martin shook his head. "This thing is an absolute nightmare!"

"Now, he's starting to get it!" Santori said.

"Marty, would you like my opinion?" Wainwright asked.

"Yes."

"I think you need to make this case go away as quickly, and quietly, as possible. Settle with your wife. Get her attorney to withdraw her complaint, if possible. Who knows, you might even get the judge to remove the filing from the public record for the very reasons we've just discussed."

"Otherwise?" Martin asked.

"Otherwise?" Santori said mocking him. "Marty, there is no *'otherwise.'*"

"Are you guys telling me—no, *ordering* me—to give up my right to a hearing?"

"No," Santori said. "We are strongly encouraging you to be practical here, to consider your career and your continued involvement with this firm and to exercise sound judgment."

"Why would you want a trial anyway?" Feldman asked. "It's not like you'd have a chance of winning."

Martin glared at him. "How could you possibly know that?"

"Well," Wainwright, interjected, "if we go by your lawyer's track record, Dave's got a point. I looked it up. Swindell has faced Beverly West six times in domestic violence cases. He settled five of those cases before trial, and he lost the remaining one in court. That makes him 0 for 6 in terms of outright wins."

"He's batting a big goose egg against her," Feldman said.

"Were you aware of that, Marty?" Santori asked.

"No," Martin said. He was starting to feel nauseous.

"You've got other problems, too," Wainwright added. "You may have a strong case, and your wife's allegations may be completely false, but you still have to prove that in court."

"Right," Martin said, "because the judge already has ignored any presumption of innocence on my part?"

"That's correct," Wainwright said. "So, how do you expect to do that?"

"Well," Martin said, "each time Katie claims she called the police, I was out of town doing audits."

"Are you sure about that?" Wainwright asked.

"Yep."

"Your wife's got some nerve!" Feldman said, with genuine admiration.

"Perhaps," Wainwright said. "Or maybe she knows the odds of a case like this ever going to trial. Remember, her attorney, Beverly West, is a master strategist in these kinds of domestic violence cases.

"If you're right, Marty, and Katie made the whole thing up," Wainwright continued, "then one way to prove your innocence would be to show the judge that the police reports from her alleged 911 calls don't exist, right?"

Martin nodded agreement. "Yeah, I guess."

"Forget it," Wainwright said. "That's never going to happen."

"Why the Hell not?"

"Marty, your court date is set for next Monday, isn't it?"

"Yes."

"That's a legal requirement. The court must give you a hearing within seven days of issuing a Temporary Restraining Order against you. Sounds reasonable enough, right?"

"Yeah."

"The problem is, the law also gives the police ten business days, or two weeks, to respond to any evidence request. That means, they don't have to produce those police reports until a week or more after your hearing date."

Martin looked stunned. "That makes absolutely no sense."

"Welcome to my world, Marty. The legal system is sometimes as close as we may ever get to experiencing life in a parallel universe."

Santori spoke up. "Marty, perhaps I've judged you a bit harshly."

"You think?" Martin asked.

"Yeah. I mean, it's clear you didn't fully understand all the ramifications of this thing."

"Thank you," Martin said.

"I want you to know, that I, for one, have no doubts regarding your innocence."

"I'm still on the fence though," Feldman quipped.

Santori glared at him. "This is no time to joke around, Dave."

"OK, scratch that last remark."

"While we might like to force your hand on this," Santori added, "we would never actually try to dictate what you should do. That decision must remain yours."

"I appreciate that."

"But that said, we also have to protect the firm against any negative fallout. So, until this case is either settled, proven meritless, or the public record regarding it is cleared, we're going to have to officially limit you to a support role in all current and future audit assignments."

"What!?" Martin felt the bottom fall out of his already compromised world. "Joe, you can't be serious."

"Sadly, I am, Marty. We all discussed it. As far as your clients and staff are concerned, though, your status will not change. You will remain the team leader, but clients will think you're acting in an 'advisory, support capacity' on their projects to mentor more junior staff members in the leadership function."

"This won't affect the Great Plains audit, will it?" Martin asked, with sudden concern.

"I've asked my nephew, Tony, to take the lead on that one, Marty."

Martin looked stunned. "Shouldn't that have been my decision, Joe?"

"Too late. I discussed it with him this morning, unofficially, so that he could immediately start getting up to speed."

"You went behind my back and did that, knowing I was opposed to giving him that level of responsibility?" Martin asked. "You've got a lot of fucking nerve."

"At the time," Santori said, "whether fair or not, I really didn't care what you thought."

"Well, now you can deal with the consequences," Martin said, rising. "I suggest you buy a plane ticket, fly to Chicago next week, and do your best to manage the audit and mentor your nephew. And 'good luck', explaining all of this to Paul Miller, at Great Plains!

"Meanwhile, I think I'll stay back here and see what I can do to undermine *your* position." Martin started walking toward the door. "I'm out of here."

"Wait just a minute, Marty, *please!*" Santori said.

Martin already had unlocked the door and opened it a crack. "Why should I?" he asked, turning around. "How much more of your holier-than-thou bullshit do I have to take?"

"Listen, I didn't do anything to undermine you," Santori said. "Yes, I went behind your back, and I probably shouldn't have, but I told my nephew this was part of a new training initiative that we will be rolling out across the board. I didn't present it, in any way, Marty, as a knock to you."

"So?" Martin said, opening the door a few inches farther.

"So, first of all, I'm sorry. I will never do it again."

"Do I have your word on that?" Martin asked.

"Yes."

"And second?"

"From now on, you will decide who takes the lead and on which projects. Now, please," he said, gesturing toward the couch, "come back in here so we can wrap this up."

Martin shut the door. "OK," he said.

After Martin returned to his seat, Wainwright cleared his throat. "Marty, there's one more caveat I want to leave with you. If you decide to settle this matter, do not—I repeat, *do not*—sign a Consent Decree."

"What's that?"

"It is an agreement that, without any formal admission of guilt on your part, keeps you, for a period of time, under the judge's supervision. The closest corollary in criminal law would be 'probation before verdict.'"

"Why would I ever consider such a thing?" Martin asked. "I want the charges against me dropped."

"Precisely. You need the record to show that your wife's case was completely without merit. And for that to happen, the judge must either dismiss the case or rule in your favor. There's really no other option."

"Then, signing a Consent Decree is the last thing I would want to do?"

"Right," Wainwright said, "but that assumes you would be fully and properly informed."

"Are you suggesting that my lawyer, or any lawyer for that matter, would deliberately mislead a client about something that important?"

"You'd be surprised what happens," Wainwright said, as he slowly began returning papers to his brief case.

"What I just said, Marty, probably does not apply to your attorney. It appears local lawyers hold Swindell in fairly high regard."

Martin smiled. "At least that's good to know."

"But some of these judges take civil domestic violence charges extremely seriously, far more so than I think they should, given the current state of family law practice. The judge might insist that you sign a Consent Decree before he agrees to drop the charges against you—even if your wife's attorney has proposed dismissing the case.

"If that happens, Marty, *don't do it*. Hold your ground and, if you must, go to trial. You'll do better for yourself and your career by taking your chances and slugging it out in court. Remember, to clear your name you must either win this case or have the charges against you dropped, nothing less."

"Why are you telling me this, Rick?"

"Because once you sign a Consent Decree, your case cannot easily be removed from the record. Civil court doesn't operate the way criminal court does. The court has a completely different process for expunging charges...or convictions. What's more, should you wish to sue your wife for damages caused by the false domestic violence charges, you won't be able to remove anything negative from the court record for up to three years!"

Martin's eyes bulged. "Thanks for the heads up," he said.

"You're welcome." Wainwright stood up and sighed. "Gentlemen, I believe that concludes our meeting." He shook everyone's hand. Then, he turned to Martin. "I hope you come out of this thing whole, my friend."

Martin attempted a smile. "That makes two of us, Rick."

Chapter 12

Even before Martin had returned to his office, he could feel the shock and panic of the previous Monday night returning. Once more, he shook from an adrenalin-induced fight-or-flight response similar to what he had experienced when sheriff's deputies abruptly threw him out of his house.

This time, however, his partners had figuratively 'thrown him out' of his role as 'lead auditor.' He had feared that if they learned about the domestic violence charges they might have forced him to assign junior staff members as backups on most projects. But he had never expected this. They had cast him in the backup role—even if under the guise of mentoring his team in project leadership skills.

Martin desperately wanted to gain some perspective and to sort through what Wainwright had told him, because he now felt completely adrift, without any reliable plan or strategy, and because he suddenly had serious concerns about Swindell's judgment and forthrightness. He needed the advice and counsel of a good friend.

He decided he would to try to get Ted Gardner on the phone. Once back at his desk, Martin dialed Ted's work number, only to learn he was in a client meeting that would probably run through the dinner hour.

Martin deeply valued Ted's advice. Aside from being the successful founder of a commercial construction company, Ted was, at heart, a pragmatist who had a great head for business and a knack for quickly isolating the essential points of any argument or situation. Martin also appreciated Ted's straightforward communication style. Ted did not mince words or sugarcoat the facts. You always knew where he stood on an issue, and that helped Martin maintain his own bearings. Most of all, though, Martin valued Ted's advice because he knew it was rooted in their deep, and enduring, friendship. He considered himself lucky to have such a friend.

It was now slightly past five o'clock. While he consciously wrestled with what his next move should be, Martin watched his left arm reach for the phone and his right hand begin pressing keys. He entered Swindell's direct number and was more than a little surprised, a moment later, when Swindell answered the phone.

"Chester Swindell speakin'. How may I help you?"

"Mr. Swindell? This is Martin Silkwood."

"Mahr-tin, how are you?"

"Not too good."

"What's the matter?"

"What isn't? I just got ambushed by my partners and our firm's attorney. Somehow, they found out about the domestic violence charges."

"I see," Swindell said. "What happened?"

"Well, for starters, they told me this domestic violence case could ruin my career if it succeeds in creating a permanent public record of the charges against me. And they said that's true regardless of the outcome of the case. They want me to settle with my wife, expunge the public record, if possible, and put the whole thing behind me as soon as possible."

"Really?"

"Yeah. They think going to court at this point would be *insane* and that I should only consider it as a last resort. All of which begs the question, why didn't I hear any of this from you? Don't you have a responsibility to advise me against taking such a reckless course of action?"

Swindell considered what Martin said as he tried to formulate an appropriate response. He decided to buy himself a little more time. "Mahr-tin," he asked, "is your firm's attorney well-versed in family law?"

"Not personally," Martin said. "But he comes from a large firm with associates who *are* experts on the subject, and I'm sure he consulted with them before speaking to me."

"So, in other words," Swindell added, "you'll give him the benefit of the doubt, but not me? I find that very troublin'."

Martin could barely believe his ears. "That's pretty presumptuous of you, Mr. Swindell. I've known you now for what, a couple of days? On the other hand, Rick Wainwright has represented my firm for years. I know how he operates. This is not a matter of me blindly trusting a stranger, while second-guessing you. I don't blindly trust anyone. If you want my trust, you're going to have to earn it, and the sooner you start, the better."

"You're right, Mahr-tin," Swindell said, back pedaling furiously. "I do apologize. I guess that did sound rather smug of me. In my defense, I can only say that I have been practicin' law in this area for decades, and I've built an excellent professional reputation. Still, I shouldn't assume that you would be aware of my reputation, or unduly influenced by it, even though you said you found me through the referral of a trusted friend.

"Let me try to address some of the points you have raised."

"Please do," Martin said.

"Somethin' I try to do, as an attorney, Mahr-tin, and I may not have done it well enough in your case, is to gauge each client's temperament at the outset of an engagement and then adjust my communication style accordin'ly.

"Some clients like to have everythin' explained to them in advance. Others prefer that I simply tell them what they need to know when they need to know it. The former approach, while offerin' maximum guidance and disclosure, can be tedious, inefficient and unnecessarily costly. In your case, the decisive way you rejected your wife's settlement offer this mornin' may have caused me to misread you. In addition, it appears I may have allowed my pride to influence me as well.

"I initially considered callin' you back after we spoke about the settlement offer, but then I thought better of it."

"Why?" Martin asked.

"Well, Mahr-tin, the practice of law, as I do it, involves considerable gamesmanship at times, and by that, I mean strategic maneuverin', posturin'—even bluffin', if you will. I can act strategically on your behalf, in negotiations and such, because the actions we take and the decisions we make are rarely final. We can generally reverse, rescind or amend them.

"At the same time, my status as an attorney also makes me an officer of the court and that sets ethical limits on me. For instance, I am not supposed to collude with clients to achieve certain ends. So, I prefer to use whatever leverage the moment provides."

"I'm not sure I follow you," Martin said.

"Hang on, Mahr-tin, I'm gettin' there! Whether I thought your decision this mornin' was sound or not, it gave me an openin' to honestly press the other side for some additional concessions.

"I called Beverly West and told her precisely what you had told me, and I could do that because I had not yet tried to talk you out of that particular decision.

"Now, she pretended not to care, but I've been dealin' with these types of cases long enough to know that your response was both unexpected and unwelcome news. It put them off-balance and improved our bargainin' position."

"OK," Martin said. "I get it. Have they revised their offer, yet?"

"Well, not yet Mahr-tin. We need to allow a little time for that hand to play itself out. In the next day or so, if I mention that I might be able to get you to reconsider a settlement, provided they sweeten the pot a bit, they might then come back with enough additional concessions that a settlement suddenly becomes attractive."

"I see," Martin said.

"Did any other developments come out of that ambush that I should know about?" Swindell asked.

"Yeah. I think, in part, to motivate me to drop this, they have effectively demoted me from audit team *leader* to audit team *trainer*.

"They are worried that I may not be able to make this thing go away, Mr. Swindell, even if I don't fight the case in court. And if they're right, I probably am screwed."

Chapter 13

At twenty past five, Martin left work in a state of near panic. Just hours earlier, he had been ready to fight the domestic violence charges in court. Now, he cowered at the thought. He hoped there might still be time in which to reach a settlement with Katie.

The covert group remained the one unknown. Did they really have the power, and the capabilities, to level the playing field? Were they a serious option? If so, their involvement could change everything, provided they did not expect too much in return.

But where were they? Nearly two days had passed— forty-five hours of the allotted forty-eight-hour follow-up period—and, still, no one from the group had reached out to him. For all practical purposes, the organization had gone dark. Had it given up on him for some reason and discarded his case in favor of another? As Martin left his office building, he scanned the street in both directions, looking for operatives. He was constantly on the lookout now and permanently on edge.

It had taken a great deal of mental energy for him to maintain this perpetually heightened state of alert for the previous two days, and at this point, he felt beaten and emotionally drained. That's why, when he saw the Sign of the Dolphin pub, Martin veered off course. He opened the door, drawn in by the promise of alcohol-induced escape that lay just a few feet beyond. The thought of killing off a few million over-active brain cells suddenly seemed irresistible.

The Sign of the Dolphin was a rare cross between an urban pickup bar and a serious drinking hole. A long, wooden, saloon-style bar ran the length of the establishment, from just inside the front door to the small kitchen in the rear. Some of the stools along the bar were reserved for the pub's regulars. You could find these men and women at their designated perches at virtually any hour of the day. But most nights, they preferred to drink alone, at home. The bar's primary concession to the singles crowd was a considerable amount of permanent, open mingling space between the stools to the left and a single row of dining booths on the far right.

To enhance the Pub's appeal, the owners had recently added several dartboards, a snooker table and two card tables in back. As usual, The Dolphin also promoted more than a dozen microbrew beers that were always cold and always on tap.

At this hour, the Pub was nearly empty. Most of the daytime crowd had gone, and the city's young, urban professionals, still hard at work at their desks, would not put in appearances for at least another hour. Martin grabbed an empty bar stool and flagged a bartender who was standing near the cash register, drying off freshly washed shot glasses. He ordered an extremely dry vodka martini and began drumming his fingers on the edge of the bar, as he waited for his drink to arrive.

The first sip was cold, wet, and tangy. Martin closed his eyes to savor its full effect, as the liquor slowly slid down his throat. Sometime between consuming the olive and completing the final gulp, he failed to notice the new figure stepping behind the counter and donning an apron.

"Just about given up on us, I bet?" she asked as she laid a cloth towel down on the bar to Martin's right.

Martin looked up and saw a young, attractive African-American woman smiling at him. She was in her late twenties and wore a black leotard that showed off her sleek, classic figure, rich, brown skin tones and fresh, girl-next-door looks. Her long, brown hair hung loosely in a ponytail that draped over one shoulder. Martin wondered if she were a theatre major or a dancer, working part-time to pay the rent.

"Are you referring to the service here?" he asked.

"No, I'm talking about the video disk you received the other night."

"What?!" Martin bolted up in his seat. He leaned forward. "Are you with the——?"

The woman quickly raised a finger to her lips and feigned a frown. "Don't shake my hand!" she added a second later, as she shooed away Martin's suddenly outstretched arm. He immediately withdrew it.

She looked at him quizzically, and smiled. "You're surprised I'm a woman, aren't you?"

"No," Martin said, shaking his head. "Well, maybe a little. I think I'm just relieved that I'm finally talking to *someone*."

"Martin," she said, "let me explain how this works. We are going to have a quick chat together while I clean up the bar for the evening trade. OK?"

"Sure," Martin said. "But please, call me Marty."

"OK, Marty."

"And your name is…?"

"Teresa."

"Great. So, Teresa, I'm curious, how did you know to look for me in here?"

"That's easy," she said. "Hand me your brief case." Martin lifted it up onto the counter and Teresa ran the palm of her hand over its surface. Suddenly, she stopped and peeled away a small black plastic bar that was about a half-inch long and a quarter inch thick. Then, she slipped it in her apron pocket. "We've had you under surveillance for quite some time now, Marty, but since last Monday night, this small transmitter has been keeping tabs on your movements. Its battery is about to expire."

"Did the guy on the subway plant that on me?" Martin asked.

Teresa nodded, *yes.*

"So, tell me, how does this organization of yours work?"

"Sorry," she said. "That's 'top secret' information, available strictly on a 'need to know' basis, and you, quite simply, don't need to know. But you do need this." She slid the bill across the bar to Martin. "You'll find your instructions handwritten on the back of the tear-off slip. Just do what it says."

"Since you brought it up, Teresa, how did a nice girl like you get involved in this business?"

"You really want to know?"

"Yeah."

"I do it to honor the memory of my big brother, Brian," she said. "He died in a car crash a few years back, after he lost his business and his ex- suddenly pulled up stakes and moved across country with their three kids.

"Brian was a devoted dad—and like a second father to me," she said. "He deserved better."

"I'm sorry," Martin said.

"Thanks. That's very sweet."

"Can I ask you another question?" Martin asked, as he paid the bill and slipped the receipt into his pocket.

"Sure."

"Am I buying trouble, here?"

"Not from us. We are strictly in the trouble-mitigation business. Whether you realize it or not, Marty, our involvement means you're a very lucky guy."

"I'm sorry, Teresa," Martin said, smiling. "But did you just say that I'm going to get 'lucky'?"

"Not that kind of 'lucky,'" she laughed, "but, for someone in your situation, lucky enough."

Just then, a customer passed by. Teresa lowered her voice. "Just follow the instructions!" she whispered. Then louder, "Come back again, soon, sir—and thanks for the tip!"

"Sure thing," Martin said, getting up. He left the bar feeling soothed, elated and more hopeful than he'd been in days.

Once seated on the metro, Martin took the receipt out of his pocket and examined it. On its back, he found the following message: "Harkins Tours, Suite #221, 3745 Diamond Court Center, Gaithersburg, MD. Appointment: 8:00 p.m., tonight."

Chapter 14

"How's production going?" Dave Clancy, CEO of Quadratic Sound Studios, in Bethesda, MD, asked his chief programming engineer, Jay Liu, during a rare evening coffee break.

"Awesome, man," Liu said excitedly. "I've been toying, for some time, with the idea of building multiple subliminal redundancies into the audio feeds, to enhance the recording's suggestive power and to help the brain make more vivid images during REM."

"And," his boss asked, "any progress?"

"Oh yeah," Liu continued. "I've actually got programs now to automate sublim production. I've even used them to lay down tracks for the current job."

"Have you tested it?"

"Oh, it works great! We applied it to the last series of audies we ran for Hypno Health Associates, and Brimmer, the head guy over there, man, loves it. He said it's more than doubled the depth of trance states. (Did you know he runs biofeedback on every one of his subjects...just to avoid lawsuits?) Anyway, he told me it will probably prolong the effectiveness of a routine hypno session by twenty percent."

"I like where you're going with this," Clancy said. "It's got possibilities."

"Oh, you have no idea, man!"

Clancy could see Liu was now ready to burst. He started a mental countdown, 'three, two—.'

"You see," Liu began, jumping the gun, "my theory was that if the mind heard the audie in a hypnotic state, then every detail would be remembered—even those subliminal messages that we do not take conscious notice of. No two people are alike, you know, so each of us responds better to different thought suggestions. Therefore, the more suggestions we provide, the more universally powerful the experience. And now, with this layering effect, I've found a way to add limitless bandwidth and power to the audies."

Clancy was all smiles.

"Oh, and that new head juice is awesome, too, boss," Liu added. "I stuck myself once before listening to the hypno audie, "You're the Stud Your Momma Said You Never Could Be," and then I went home and made love to Melinda for two solid hours—and I mean *solid*."

"Well, I guess that's conclusive proof of efficacy," Clancy said, laughing. "By the way, have you got a copy of the sublim script?"

"Sure."

"Good. Email me one when you get back to your desk. I want to check the quality of the selections. Nice work, Jay."

"Thanks, man."

Clancy returned to his office and fired off a quick email to his 'silent partners' to let them know the status of the current project and to share Jay Liu's latest stroke of genius.

He told them, based on the enhancements Jay had outlined, that the ten-minute dream narrative sequence they had ordered probably would occupy about one-half a gigabyte of data storage space compressed rather than the standard one-hundred-megabyte file. He also mentioned Jay's personal experience with the 'head juice' that they had sent along for testing. He concluded by saying the new audie would be ready for transmission to them within the hour.

Clancy knew they would be extremely pleased. Initially, five years earlier, when he was short on cash and they offered to become his financial "angels"—for a piece of the action, of course—he had been concerned that they might be a front for organized crime. But, gradually, 'little things' had convinced him that they were somehow hooked into the intelligence community. That's when any remaining qualms he might have had completely disappeared.

Chapter 15

Martin pulled up to 3745 Diamond Court Center at 7:50 p.m., his heart pounding. The building, which was dark, except for its lobby, appeared to be the typical, nondescript suburban office complex. It had lots of glass, lots of steel, fake polished-onyx flooring, and a generous assortment of tall indoor trees and ubiquitous potted plants.

At this time of day, the building and its parking lot were nearly empty. Martin entered the lobby and took the elevator up to the second floor. When he stepped off, he saw a law firm to his left and a mixed-use executive office suite to his right. Its glass door read, "Suites 201 to 235." The door was locked, and only a few security lights lit up the reception area behind it.

Martin walked over and pressed the bell. Moments later a buzzer sounded, and he entered. Lights illuminated only one of the two hallways opening onto the reception area, so Martin headed in that direction. Toward the end of the hall, past several offices and conference rooms, he found Suite 221. The door was slightly ajar. He could see lights shining inside, so he entered.

Harkins Tours' reception area contained all the obligatory destination posters for a regional bus tour company. These included: A composite poster of Washington, D.C. destinations; a fiery, mid-autumn shot of Skyline Drive as well as scenes of historic Williamsburg; wild ponies at dusk on Assateague Island; Marlin fishing off Maryland's Atlantic coast; a composite photo of historic Annapolis, MD; and a breathtaking view of the Greenbrier Resort, once the favored retreat of presidents and railroad tycoons.

The company had tastefully decorated the room with Persian rugs, black leather sofas and chairs and sparkling chrome-and-glass tables. Harkins' Tours brochures beckoned from acrylic display holders on each end table, and several of the day's finest travel, dining and lifestyle magazines sat neatly on the coffee table. Martin also noticed the tiny red power light glowing on the small security camera perched in the far corner of the room.

Just then, a strikingly attractive young woman appeared in the doorway leading to the back offices. She was dressed, professionally, in a navy pinstripe jacket, white blouse, and skirt. Her pocket book hung down from her left shoulder, and she carried a soft, black leather satchel in her right hand. She stopped abruptly upon seeing Martin. "Oh, hello," she said, looking somewhat surprised. "Have you been waiting long?"

"Just got here," Martin said, returning her smile.

She came forward and shook his hand. "Hi, I'm Lacey."

"Martin Silkwood."

"I was just on my way out," she said, brushing her sandy, brown bangs away from her hazel eyes. Martin looked at her and smiled. She was dazzling, he thought, with her butterscotch complexion and her understated makeup.

"You must be here to see Robert," she said. "He's the only one of us who routinely works eighteen-hour days. I'll just buzz him to say you're here."

"That won't be necessary, Lacey," said a man, emerging from the doorway where she had been moments before.

"Oh," she said, smiling, and putting down the phone. She quickly gathered up her bags. "You're in good hands, Mr. Silkwood," she said, giving Martin a final smile. "I'm sure Robert will help your group put together a fantastic tour!" And with that, she left.

"Mr. Silkwood," Robert said, stepping forward and extending his hand. He was a tall, lean, clean-shaven man in his late thirties, conservatively dressed in a blue and white pinstripe oxford shirt, a red and blue striped tie, and a pair of charcoal gray slacks. "I've been expecting you," he said, shaking Martin's hand. "I'm Robert Brooks."

"Nice to meet you."

Brooks walked over to the front door, closed it quietly and then carefully turned the lock. "Lacey is new," he said. "She's a real go-getter, in addition to being easy on the eyes.

"Normally, this place clears out at six, but now I may have to start moving my evening hours back a bit. Come in," he said, taking Martin by the elbow and leading him out of the reception area. "We've got a lot of ground to cover in a very short time."

Brook's office was located at the back of the suite and was considerably larger than the others they passed along the way. Once inside, he led Martin past his formal desk and sitting area and over to a small round table by the window. Brooks then poured two mugs of hot coffee and fetched a laptop computer, which was already running. He sat down and pushed his Harkins Tours business card over to Martin. "This is for you," he said. It listed him as 'Senior Vice President, Sales.'

Brooks got right to the point. "Martin, tonight, you're going to learn some highly sensitive information about our little enterprise. For starters, you already know my real name and my place of business. That, however, is about as far as your knowledge of our personnel will go. I have been chosen to be your primary contact, the only operative you will work with directly. From now on, I will be your sole link to the organization. And it will stay that way unless something happens to me. That's how we operate. We maintain everyone's anonymity, and safety, by keeping contact points to a minimum.

"Martin," he continued, "everything we discuss here tonight must remain strictly confidential, understand?"

"Yes."

"I want to be clear about this. You are agreeing never to mention this to anyone, not even to your closest friends and relations."

"I understand."

"OK, then. When I'm done, it will be your turn to make some decisions."

"Such as?"

"Well, first, you will need to decide if you really want our help."

"Why wouldn't I?" Martin asked. "You aren't about to spring some kind of outrageous fee on me, are you?"

"No," Brooks said, with a chuckle. "Believe me, Martin, we neither want, nor need, your money. But we do operate within strict parameters, and we have certain expectations."

"Expectations? I'm not sure I like the sound of that."

"You may not. That just underscores my point. It's also why we've instituted the following rule: You must formally request our help to get it. Now, what do you say we get started?"

"Sure."

Brooks opened the laptop computer and turned it so Martin would have a clear view of the screen. "Let's begin by reviewing your case."

Martin nodded as the computer screen sprang to life. He could immediately tell, by its rapid operating speed, that Brooks' laptop was not something you could buy on the street. Moreover, it appeared linked to a remote computer platform of extraordinary size and power. Brooks rapidly keyed in some numbers and, instantly, up came Martin's case file. He clicked a link and the screen filled up with the image of a woman Martin had never seen before.

"That's Beverly West," Brooks said. "She's the reason we became aware of your case."

"That's my wife's attorney?" Martin asked.

"Correct."

West appeared to be in her early fifties. The photograph captured her from the waist up. She sat with her body facing away from the camera, but she had rotated her upper torso so that she was staring down, imperially, into the lens, challenging it with defiant gray-green eyes.

Fit and trim for someone her age, she appeared to pay meticulous attention to every aspect of her physical appearance. Nothing looked haphazard or out of place.

She was wearing a custom-tailored gray, herringbone suit jacket over a beige silk top. A short necklace of cultured pearls hung around her neck, complemented by a matching pair of pearl-and-diamond stud earrings. West's dirty blonde hair, heavily frosted and worn in a pageboy, framed an attractive, but determined, face that seemed disturbingly lifeless, and cold, as if its taut skin and delicate, refined features were chiseled in stone. A layer of concealer, which West had used to hide her endless freckles, added to the illusion, by lending her skin, the subtle, mottled appearance of granite. Only her thin, frosted lips, which projected the tiniest hint of a smile, suggested otherwise.

Brooks continued, "West is a high-powered divorce attorney, from Rockville, MD, who is known to push the ethical envelope to extremes. She will do whatever it takes to give her clients the upper hand in divorce cases.

"Her practice generates *ex-parte* domestic violence petitions the way most law firms crank out subpoenas and document requests. She's her own cottage industry! That behavior brought her to our attention long ago. Now, she heads a nationwide list of 3,521 unethical attorneys whom we monitor constantly.

"Every time a new client retains her for a divorce proceeding, our system flags us," Brooks said, proudly. "Your wife hired her nine months ago, in late August."

"No, that's impossible!" Martin protested. "Katie and I only started having marital problems this winter."

"Then, your wife must be psychic!" Brooks continued. "Here, look at this." He clicked on an icon, and immediately, the image of one of Katie's personal checks filled the screen. The check's date line read: "August 23, 2018." It was written for $2,500 and Katie had made it payable to "Beverly West, Esq." The memo line read, "Retainer for legal services, divorce."

"How do you explain that?" Brooks asked.

Martin stared at the screen, trying to comprehend what he was seeing. "I-I can't," he said, still smarting from the news. "How did you get a copy of this? Have you hacked the banks?"

"I can't comment on that, Martin. But, I can assure you, the check is real."

"I don't doubt it," Martin said, swallowing hard. "It appears to confirm my worst suspicions—even if my timing was way off."

"Your suspicions?"

"Yes," he said. "West called my attorney yesterday to present my wife's settlement offer. Among other things, it stipulated that we could start dating other people immediately. When I saw that, I realized Katie probably had been having an affair. I guess it's been going on a lot longer than I ever imagined."

"Sorry," Brooks said.

"Hey, what's done is done," Martin said dismissively. He continued to study the screen, unable to take his eyes off it. He didn't want Brooks, a stranger, to see how troubled he was by this news. Only the pained look on his face, and the sudden shakiness in his voice, hinted at the powerful feelings of betrayal and hurt that were welling up inside him.

Oblivious, Brooks plowed ahead. He clicked on another icon and a new screen appeared. This one contained a spreadsheet titled, "Domestic Violence Case Disposition Report: Beverly West." The document showed stats detailing every time one of West's clients had sought a Temporary Restraining Order before filing for divorce. This chart covered the previous ten-year period, when fifty-two of West's seventy-eight female clients had obtained at least one TRO as part of a 'preemptive strike.' A graph on the following page clearly showed the numbers trending upward.

Brooks hit some keys and highlighted several columns under the general label 'Disposition.' They showed that out of West's clients' fifty-two domestic violence cases, only three (six percent), ever led to permanent restraining orders. Judges dismissed ten cases at trial (twenty percent of the total). And West managed to settle all the remaining thirty-six cases (seventy-four percent of the total) while awaiting trial.

"Based on these numbers, it appears that only one-in-ten of West's petitions have merit," Brooks said. "But here's the really sad part, Martin: The legal profession only disciplined West once in all these years, and that action barely amounted to a 'slap on the wrist.' Her tactics work. They have helped her clients get the edge eighty percent of the time. And they've kept her completely out of trouble ninety-eight percent of the time."

"How does she get away with it?" Martin asked.

Brooks smiled sympathetically. "You don't know, do you?"

"Know what?"

"That the legal profession is self-regulated, with enforcement taking place at the local level, where political clout, personal relationships, and financial contributions have the most influence. As a result, in most states—Maryland being one—anything goes, because the foxes literally are guarding the hen houses."

Martin nodded. "I'm beginning to see that. But Robert, with all this information at your disposal, why did your group wait so long to contact me?"

Brooks took a sip of his coffee. "Two reasons."

"First, we needed to make sure you were not an abusive person, because, as you've seen, Martin, at least some of West's TROs seem to have had merit. If we had concluded you were abusive," Brooks added, "we never would have offered our help.

"To find out, we checked police records going all the way back to when you were eighteen, and except for a few speeding tickets, your record was clean. Zero arrests and zero violence. And when it comes to violent behavior, past violent acts are often major indicators of future behavior.

"In other words, violent people commit violent acts. Non-violent people, particularly non-violent people without any prior history of drug or alcohol abuse, rarely do."

While he was talking, Brooks called up all the police report searches the organization had ever run on Martin. The details of every parking ticket and traffic citation he ever received suddenly flashed by on the screen.

"Still," he said, "timing is everything. We also have learned, from experience, that the best time to approach a husband is shortly—very shortly—before his wife hits him with a TRO. Otherwise, we find most husbands dismiss us as a bunch of lunatics and never seek our help."

"That makes sense to me," Martin said, recalling how he had felt immediately after viewing the video disk. "By the way, who was that guy on your video?"

"All I can tell you," Brooks said, "is that sometime in the past, several top people in the intelligence community (military and civilian) were put through the same meat grinder that's now preparing to turn you into sausage.

"They didn't like it any more than you will. While they lacked political influence, these men more than made up for that through their access to power. I'm talking about the kind of raw power you get with control of billions of dollars in state-of-the-art intelligence-gathering equipment, command and control of highly disciplined special ops units, global satellite networks, secret offshore accounts, and classified technologies.

"Eventually, they got together and quietly devised a way to use the resources at their disposal to help anyone being victimized by 'the system': legal, judicial, banking—whatever—and to help set things right."

"That's incredible," Martin said. "And they've been able to operate undetected the whole time?"

"Of course. Why do you think we call them 'spooks'?"

"Does this organization of yours have a name?" Martin asked.

Brooks smiled. "I call it the 'home office,' but there really is no official name. And again, that's deliberate. Our founders were not looking to draw attention."

"Listen, Martin," he continued, "we want to help you out of your current predicament, and we can because our resources are considerable. We have access to people and assets you can scarcely imagine. The point is we can be extremely effective. Even so, we will only help you up to a point, and I want to be perfectly clear about this.

"Our goal is to reestablish a level playing field for you with the court. We believe in the justice system. We just want it to work properly: free from bias and corruption. So, that's as far as our interference goes. Despite what you may think, we are not subversives. Although some might call us 'terrorists'—if they even knew we existed—we think of ourselves as reform artists."

Martin looked puzzled. "Reform artists? I don't get it."

"We call ourselves 'reform artists,'" Brooks continued, "because we effect systemic change through actions taken on an individual level. That's not easy to do. It requires great sophistication and delicacy. When we get involved on someone's behalf, such as in your case, we take precautions to make sure no one gets seriously hurt, no one gets killed, no one gets threatened, and no one's property gets damaged or destroyed.

"Instead of blowing up buildings and terrorizing people, we achieve our aims peacefully, by bringing institutions back into balance. It's a subtle, disciplined approach to maintaining the social order.

"Sometimes our efforts produce permanent changes in people. Other times, the effects are just temporary. But gradually, we move society in a better direction. You could easily compare our work to continental drift. Its effects may seem miniscule in the moment, but when compounded often enough, over time, it can change the face of the world."

Martin considered everything Brooks had said. "What you do sounds impressive, Robert, I'll give you that. But I don't have millions of years in which to see meaningful results. My case goes before the judge in just five days. And everything I care about—my relationship with my kids, my position with my firm and my reputation—it's all on the line. Everyone keeps urging me to just settle the damned thing and make it go away. I don't like the idea of rewarding my wife for lying. And I'm sure that, if I settle, I probably won't like the terms I get, either.

"But more importantly, I don't want my kids blaming me for breaking up the family. I don't want them believing, for one instant, that their father ever abused them or their mother. I also don't want anything left in the public record that might lead people to conclude that these domestic violence charges ever had merit.

"Robert, what assurance can you give me that, if I do ask for your assistance, your plan will work?"

"I can't guarantee anything, Martin," Robert said. "No one can. All I can say is that we will do everything in our power to 'level the playing field' for you. What happens after that is largely out of our control."

Martin frowned. "That's not what I would call a compelling sales argument."

"Maybe not," Brooks said. "But what's your alternative? If you go to trial without our help, you're pretty much guaranteed to get screwed."

"I could settle," Martin said.

"Really? If you thought that was a viable option, I doubt we'd be having this conversation."

Martin thought for a moment. "How soon would I need to give you an answer?"

Brooks looked him squarely in the eyes. "I need your decision right now, Martin. Tonight. We barely have time to plan and execute the operation."

"Whose fault is that?" Martin asked. "You guys had forty-eight hours in which to contact me. What the hell were you waiting for?!"

"I don't know," Brooks said. "That's not my call. But I am sure whoever was responsible had a good reason. Regardless, I need your answer now."

Martin put his left elbow on the table and, leaning forward, began rubbing his temples with his left hand. As he did, he closed his eyes. "I've got to think this through," he said. Then, he looked up. "Can you, at least, give me until morning?"

"Impossible," Brooks said.

Martin glared at him. "You've got to be kidding me! I can't do this now!"

"Why not?"

"I don't know!" he said. "I'm just not ready."

Brooks quietly exited the database and shut down the laptop. Then, he looked at Martin, who was still leaning over the table, rubbing his temples. "We're done here," he said, indifferently, closing the laptop and returning it to its case. "I'm sorry," he said, standing up.

Martin's heart was pounding and he had started to sweat. "That's it?" he asked, "After all your months of research and preparation?"

"It happens," Brooks said. He walked over to the coffee pot and turned the power off. Then, he gestured toward the door. "You ready?"

Martin's pulse was racing. "All right, all right!" he blurted out. "Let's do it!"

"Are you sure?"

"Yes, damn it! Do it! Do it!" he said, wringing his hands. "I think you're right. I really don't see any other options. You guys are it."

Brooks sat back down. "Martin, if you give us the go ahead now, I need you to understand —"

"What? What else is there, Robert?"

"Your decision must be final. There's no going back on it."

"Why the hell not?" Martin demanded.

"Because as soon as we leave here, our group will begin committing considerable manpower and resources to run your covert op, resources that could just as easily be used to help someone else. We'll also be asking certain people to break the law in order to help you. We cannot ask them to do that in vain.

"Considering that, are you still prepared to go forward?"

Martin teetered at the edge of panic. He knew that, if he said 'Yes,' to Brooks, he would forfeit any chance of settling the case before trial, something he had been eager to do only hours earlier. Now, he would be 'locked in' to a trial, no matter how appealing his wife's final settlement offer might be.

"If I say 'yes' now," Martin asked, "does that mean I must see the trial through to a final verdict?"

Brooks looked puzzled. "No one's ever asked me that before."

"Well?"

"Here's what I think," he said. "You'd be agreeing not to entertain settling the case at least until after your attorney rests. From that point on, you'd be free to settle, on the advice of counsel."

Martin took a deep breath and relaxed. "Okay, then," he said. "Yes. I'm all in."

Brooks smiled, and the two shook hands. Then, he softly cleared his throat. "There is one final matter we need to discuss, Martin. I believe I mentioned at the start of our conversation that we have certain 'expectations.'"

Here it comes, Martin thought.

"In addition to requiring that you tell no one about our organization's existence, we also will need your solemn pledge that you will assist us—without hesitation—if we ever ask."

He looked Martin squarely in the eyes again. "Are you comfortable with those conditions?"

"Yes," Martin said.

"Good. Then, roll up your sleeve and extend your arm."

"What for?"

"It's necessary, Martin," Brooks said. He waited as Martin rolled up his right sleeve and laid his exposed arm down on the table. Brooks quickly applied rubbing alcohol to a small area toward the outside of Martin's upturned arm, just below the elbow. Then, as he held Martin's arm down with his left hand, he revealed a small syringe in his right.

"Whoa! What's that?" Martin asked with more than a little concern.

"It's just a small, sub-dermal tracking device," Brooks said as he removed the cap with his teeth and then plunged the needle under Martin's skin.

"Hey!" Martin said, but it was too late.

Brooks tossed the empty syringe into a nearby trashcan. "The tracking device is non-negotiable," he said. "It allows us to determine your whereabouts on a moment's notice, and that's critical if we are to operate effectively as an organization."

"What is it, exactly?" Martin asked, rubbing the injection site.

"It's a crystal-based micro transmitter that runs on wireless Tesla power," Brooks said. "It represents the next generation in ultra-high-frequency, passive transmission technology. Officially, it's only in the testing stages—and authorized for use in rare instances. But, for us, it's standard issue.

"Its primary value comes from its tiny size and its evasiveness. This transmitter can clear metal detectors, x-ray scans and other popular security devices."

"How does it work?"

"The transmitter remains dormant under your skin, until activated."

"And how do you activate it?" Martin asked.

"That's the beauty of it," Brooks said. "The unit contains a tiny electrical induction coil set to receive near-field wireless electrical power transmissions. We set them to operate at the same frequencies that run wireless inventory control RFID-tag systems and Smart Cards. So, throughout the day, whenever you come in range of these devices — at retail establishments, banks, and gas stations — your device powers up temporarily and listens for its unique ultra-high frequency pulse.

"The technology is perfectly suited to our purposes. For instance, we only need to know your whereabouts, or the whereabouts of any operative, when we have a specific assignment for them."

"To find you, we simply transmit the appropriate ultra-high-frequency pulse through our global network until we get a response. When you and your transmitter come into range, our signal activates your transmitter's resonant harmonics, triggering a high-frequency return signal burst. The process is similar, in concept, to echo-location on demand."

"So, it's safe?" Martin asked.

"Perfectly," Brooks said. "The device produces virtually no heat, and it's all based on highly efficient, low-energy output."

(Of course, Martin also realized, this newly installed device now meant Brooks and his 'associates' would always be able to find him, further assuring his continued loyalty and compliance.) "How do I know you haven't installed a little cyanide dispenser in it?" he asked.

"You don't," Brooks said, putting on his best poker face. Instantly, he regretted it as Martin's eyes bulged in horror. "But we didn't," he continued, smiling. "Remember, Martin, we are a non-violent group."

"You'd better be!" Martin said, a little annoyed with Brooks, but also intrigued. He was once more feeling the renewed confidence that comes from making a bold decision and from committing himself to a new, promising, course of action. "So, what's next?" he asked.

"That's simple," Brooks said. "Between now and your hearing next Monday, we will implement a covert plan to make sure that Judge Farnsworth, the judge presiding over your case, behaves more even-handedly at your hearing."

"How do you intend to do that?"

"I could tell you, Martin," Brooks said, smiling, "but then, as the saying goes, I'd have to kill you."

Martin laughed nervously.

"Well, I think that concludes our business," Brooks said. He extended his hand. "What do you say we call it a night?"

"Sounds good to me," Martin said.

The two shook hands. Then, Brooks locked up for the night and escorted Martin back to his car.

Chapter 16

Roger Hannah bought a small cup of coffee and instinctively took a seat in the far corner of the nearly deserted McDonald's® restaurant. From this vantage point, he could see through the store's large, front windows and quickly spot anyone approaching. Outside, car headlights flickered intermittently through the hedges as late-night shoppers entered and exited the adjoining shopping center. Inside, the night shift busied itself behind the counter, shouting out drive-through order details and words of encouragement to each other, while the inviting smell of sizzling burgers and fries wafted through the dining area.

In his Naval Academy windbreaker, Under Armor® jogging slacks and white running shoes, Hannah looked like he had just completed a routine, nighttime run. He unzipped his windbreaker and sat down revealing a drab, gray t-shirt stretched tight across his muscular chest. He looked fit enough to be in his mid-to-late forties. Only his gray, military-issue haircut, his tan, weathered, deeply lined face, and tired gray eyes hinted at his true age and at the lifetime of classified work that had helped shape his character and outlook.

Hannah glanced at his wristwatch: 9:42 p.m. At ten, the restaurant would close its doors for the night, and staff members would start cleaning up and restocking the dine-in area for the morning rush. About thirty minutes later, the assistant manager, Leanna, would politely ask him to leave. That meant he had nearly an hour in which to surf the Internet over the restaurant's public, and personally untraceable, wireless access network. With his powerful, 256K data encryption software scrambling his communications and a random I.P. address generator program masking his computer's identity, Hannah would be able to do his 'extra-curricular' work in relative secrecy while physically hiding in plain sight. The sixty-four-year-old NSA deputy administrator knew it was foolish to expect any more privacy than that. After all, his own agency had been illegally intercepting, analyzing, and storing virtually all domestic and international online communications, as well as voice and data transmissions, for the better part of two decades.

Hannah took out his laptop and plugged in an additional layer of security: A tiny, USB memory stick "boot drive" that contained a covert operating system. He pressed the power button and the laptop sprang to life, booting directly from the thumb drive, and bypassing its regular operating system altogether. Now, any activity logs this new work session might generate, and any information Hannah might choose to download, would reside exclusively on the tiny, password-protected USB drive—leaving nothing incriminating on his NSA-issued computer.

As an added precaution, Hannah launched a tunnel browser program that covertly routed his online session through a string of far-flung, remote servers, changing his computer's IP address several additional times.

Hannah brought the Quadratic Sound Studios website up on his browser and then opened a "lock box" program located on the thumb drive. He scanned the list of accounts. When he found the entry for the "Quadratic Sound Studios, of Bethesda," website, he keyed in the information and hit Enter, logging in as Dave Clancy.

Hannah lifted the coffee cup to take a sip. His hand shook excessively—a reminder of his recently diagnosed Parkinson's disease and the fact that, at this late hour, his medication was starting to wear off. He used his left hand to help steady the cup, took a quick sip, and hastily returned it to the table.

Hannah went to Clancy's "sent mail" folder where he found, and opened, a new email addressed to him at one of his many online depository accounts. The email mentioned a promising, new technical breakthrough and included two attachments. The first was a compressed copy of a new

'Hypnotic Dream Sequence' audio file. Hannah had ordered the file several days earlier just in case Martin Silkwood decided to give his team the green light. The second file contained a transcript of the Hypnotic Dream Sequence narration. Liu's latest discovery, Clancy reported, had made the HDS file several times larger, and many times more powerful, than before. Hannah smiled as the laptop began downloading the files.

Earlier that evening, Hannah had received an email announcing a new post on Robert Brook's Mid-Atlantic travel blog. He had followed the link to the post, where he had found the encoded message, 'It's a go,' buried in the copy. Now, he could get started doing the work he loved most: formulating and orchestrating high-risk covert operations.

By now, the Silkwood Project had survived its first three operational hurdles. Phase One, 'Target Acquisition,' had occurred nine months earlier, when the group's automated Legal Watch system first flagged Katie Silkwood as Beverly West's newest divorce client. Within two weeks, routine background checks gave Martin Silkwood an 'extremely low risk' domestic violence score, clearing the way for the Silkwood case to move into the organization's Covert Ops holding queue. There it sat until the previous Friday, when Katie Silkwood filed for a Temporary Restraining Order against her husband, in Montgomery County, Maryland, District Court. The filing activated the Silkwood case and led, in rapid succession, to Phase Two, 'The Face Off' on the subway, when an agent slipped the introductory DVD into Martin's pants pocket and tagged his brief case with a small, discreet tracking device. Phase Three, 'The handshake,' began earlier that night when the second agent contacted Martin in the bar. It ended in Martin's face-to-face meeting with his handler, Robert Brooks.

Each phase involved a heightened level of organizational exposure and risk. Each also required more prolonged, direct contact between the target and the group's covert operatives. But they all paled, in terms of risk, to the next step: Phase Four, the hostile action they would take on behalf of their new client. Phase Four demanded a coordinated effort, involving multiple operatives, and typically targeting at least one, possibly more, 'high value' individuals: government officials or powerful businesspeople. Phase Four also nearly always required the group to engage in some form of 'extra-legal' activity.

This operation would be no different. Hannah intended to use Quadratic's dream manipulation technology to temporarily, if not permanently, alter District Court Judge Michael J. Farnsworth's thought patterns and behavior. Farnsworth was the presiding judge in the Silkwood v. Silkwood domestic violence case as well as the Chief Administrative Judge for Maryland's twelve district courts.

If all went according to plan, the operation would succeed in making Judge Farnsworth more sensitive to the rights of 'respondents' (in this case, Martin Silkwood) and less biased toward the claims of the 'petitioners' (such as Martin's wife, Katie.)

To pull it off, Hannah's agents would need to gain access to the Judge in an isolated, contained environment. Everything had to occur without raising the judge's suspicions and without exposing him to any serious physical danger.

Typical ops sites included the target's home, workplace, or such third-party locations as a neighbor's home or a medical or dental office. Hannah's group had used any number of third-party locations with success in the past. He preferred them, because they usually presented him with the least number of variables and unknowns to control. By far, the easiest ops his group had ever run took place in temporary, out-of-town accommodations, when his crews had followed targets on trips to professional conferences and workshops. Posing as room-service, they had quickly gained entry to their targets' hotel and motel rooms, where they completed their assignments effortlessly, in relative secrecy.

Hannah knew that the ideal spot for carrying out a covert operation against Judge Farnsworth, or any sitting judge for that matter, was inside the judge's chambers, where the need for complete privacy, and discretion, overrode normal security concerns. The county may have blanketed the courthouse with security cameras and listening devices, and bailiffs, sheriff's deputies, and other support staff may have roamed the halls freely, but both official and casual snooping stopped abruptly at the judges' chamber doors. Security cameras continuously monitored entry and exit points only, and no court employee wishing to keep his or her job would ever consider entering a judge's chambers unannounced...or uninvited.

The substance of any negotiations or discussions that occurred inside that 'holy of holies' remained sacrosanct, known only to the judge and the other participants.

The problem from Hannah's perspective lay in obtaining a 'free pass' into the judge's chambers. Access normally came exclusively through judicial invitation. If an unauthorized person even attempted to gain entry, he or she would immediately draw attention. At best, guards would appear and escort him or her out of the building. At worst, they could detain the individual for questioning and file criminal trespass charges.

Hannah's researchers had been busy, since the Silkwood *ex-parte* hearing, gathering intelligence about the judge, his habits, movements, and contacts. One went to his house, swapped out his trash bags, and took them to a secluded place where she methodically combed through the items, seeking any useful information. She pulled details off the judge's empty pill bottle labels; phone, cell phone and cable bills; medical bills; credit card statements, and more.

Another, an NSA employee, requested a 'data dump' of intelligence gathered through the agency's illegal Sentinel mass domestic-surveillance program. The requested files covered data from all households located in a few randomly generated census tracts — including, in this case, the one where Judge Farnsworth lived. The data ostensibly was being used to run systems simulations and data integrity checks. Although the coded files included no names, the agent could quickly cross-reference the data against the judge's home address and phone number and retrieve his social security number, bank account numbers, driver's license number, credit card numbers, email account user names and passwords, income tax data, and much more.

A third had hacked into the court's website and downloaded the previous week's security camera tapes. He then ran the tapes through a facial recognition program, tagging and tracing the judge's daily movements within the courthouse and identifying everyone with whom he came in contact. Agents then cross-referenced those identities against the organization's database of operatives, looking for potential matches to exploit.

One final agent had performed sophisticated data mining on the internet, using meta-search engines to cull any information that mentioned the judge by name. Afterward, he downloaded the file and fed it into a filtering tool that eliminated duplicate records and sorted and ranked 'hits' according to their potential value and relevance.

By now, the agents had finished their investigations and had run their reports. Hannah logged into the organization's top-secret website and downloaded those files onto his thumb drive.

He then took several sips of coffee as he waited for an additional 'fetch' bot he had created to make the rounds of a handful of online depository accounts he had set up as extra drop points. At each stop, the program would download any newly deposited files and then delete all traces of them from the site directory. When it had completed its rounds, the program downloaded the retrieved files to the open folder on Hannah's thumb drive.

With all the ops data now in hand, Hannah loaded a name extraction program and pointed it at the folder containing the downloaded files. The program rapidly scanned the contents of all the intel reports, isolating, copying, and exporting any common names it found, along with any associated identifying data. Hannah then accessed the organization's secret website again, where he uploaded the processed file and ran it through a program specifically designed to cross-reference its names against his group's entire roster of operatives. Moments later, he downloaded the results: A report listing each extracted name on a separate page, along with a list of likely internal 'hits.' The report returned a separate line for each potential match, identifying the operative by name and ID number and appending a four-digit fraction estimating the probability that the two names were, in fact, an exact match. (Hannah would use the list to identify operatives who might have useful connections, or access, to the judge.)

Next, he uploaded the remaining files from the folder and fed them into a powerful data analysis app that his team had adapted from the NSA's famed 'Thin Thread' software, created in the late 1990s. Several years after 9/11, the NSA had secretly modified and expanded 'Thin Thread' to drive a highly invasive, and illegal, domestic surveillance program that served as a precursor to Sentinel.

To run 'Thin Thread' efficiently, Hannah configured the website with a series of parallel processors that could crunch data with all the processing power and speed of a super computer. Within a minute, the program completed its analysis and produced a detailed report, identifying opportunities and associations buried within the data.

Hannah downloaded the report and went immediately to the summary page. As expected, the report had failed to identify any suitable third-party locations, owing to the incredibly short time window. That meant Hannah might have no choice but to stage the operation at the judge's home, where his wife would most likely be present, further complicating matters. Hannah found homes to be among the least desirable sites for running special ops, and he actively tried to avoid them. Family, friends, or neighbors could stop by, unannounced, at almost any time, disrupting his carefully laid plans and greatly increasing the risk of exposure or out-and-out failure. (Hannah's typical approach, in homes, was to have one or two operatives pose as service technicians, from either the power or the cable company. Once inside the home, they would discreetly dose the residents with a short-acting aerosol anesthesia such as Twilight, complete their operation and then exit as quickly as possible.)

Hannah jumped to the back of the report where he found pages of links to the most promising support documents. As he scanned down the columns of entries, one immediately piqued his curiosity. It referenced a Montgomery County *Journal* news story whose headline read, "Local Barber Holds World Record for District Court Appearances."

Hannah clicked the link, and an October 5, 2013 newspaper article immediately filled the screen. It contained a picture of Judge Farnsworth receiving a haircut at his desk, in chambers. The caption identified the barber as the judge's life-long friend, Tony Sands. It seems Tony Sands and the Judge had a standing appointment every Friday at 1 p.m. Sands, the article reported, had been clipping the judge's hair in court for nearly five years and had just completed his 250th "court appearance."

Hannah's pulse quickened as he entertained the unlikely notion that this tradition might have continued for another five years and that he might now somehow find a way to take advantage of it.

He opened the video surveillance logs and scanned through the Friday afternoon records. While they showed Judge Farnsworth entering and exiting his chambers several times each Friday, they made no mention of Tony Sands. To be thorough, he checked the Monday through Thursday afternoon records as well, just to make sure they hadn't switched the designated day. Still nothing.

All this proved, Hannah realized, was that the video cameras had never captured the judge and the barber together, at any point, outside the judge's chambers. That did not mean, however, that Tony Sands had stopped visiting the courthouse. If he had been to the courthouse during the previous month, Hannah reasoned, then the facial recognition software should have identified him from the security camera footage, and his name would appear somewhere in the name extraction report.

Hannah opened the report and entered "Sands" as a search term. The search produced a single result: the one he wanted. Tony Sands had been to the courthouse the previous month.

Now, he needed to determine if "Tony Sands" was an operative. (Based on Sand's age, Hannah thought, the odds were unlikely.) He opened the report that had cross-referenced the extracted names against the organization's database of operatives. "Sands" sounded like it might be a common name. At least, he hoped so.

He keyed "Tony Sands" into the search field and hit Enter. Immediately, the computer displayed the results: a single page with the name "Tony Sands" listed at the top and a single matching "Sands" from the list of operatives printed out below. Then, Hannah saw the probability score and his eyes bulged. The program had returned a score of "0.0000," meaning it had determined, with complete certainty, that the two "Tony Sands" did not represent the same person.

This was the first-time Hannah had ever seen the program return a zero-correlation score, and he was flabbergasted.

He quickly recovered and decided to probe deeper. Hannah opened the organization's "Tony Sands" file in search of an answer. He found what he was looking for almost immediately, in the form of an all-too-common set of initials trailing after the operative's name, and it made his stalwart face momentarily soften into a broad, satisfied smile.

Chapter 17

Swindell arrived at work shortly after 7:30 a.m. Thursday to find the message light blinking on his telephone console. *Someone got off to an early start, today,* he thought as he sat down and pressed it.

"Hi Chester, this is Beverly West. Please call me at your earliest convenience. I need to ask a very small favor."

Interestin', he thought. For the two decades Swindell had known her, Beverly West had never asked him to do anything 'small' let alone 'very small.' But at moments like this, when she did need something from him, he could always count on her to cast her request in the most diminutive terms possible. *Requestin' a favor puts her in my debt,* he reasoned, *so she's just tryin' to set the lowest possible exchange rate for any future reciprocation.*

He smiled. West was, indeed, a worthy opponent: always calculating, always plotting, always thinking several steps ahead.

Despite the value of thinking strategically, Swindell could not bring himself to do it habitually or in as compulsive a manner as West. He found the mere thought of it exhausting. Instead, he only strategized about matters of great importance, such as planning a deposition or building a case.

Swindell chuckled as he fantasized about what the inside of Beverly West's strategically hyperactive brain might look like. He envisioned an enormous warehouse filled with thousands of gerbil cages crammed end-to-end atop endless rows of narrow tables. Each gerbil was running itself silly on a squeaky exercise wheel-generator that powered small, decision-making logic circuits. Meanwhile, white-coated lab technicians, with clipboards in their hands, continuously patrolled the rows, making observations, and taking notes on the status of each data display.

Swindell picked up the phone, pressed West's speed dial and waited for her to pick up. "Beverly," he said, at last, "this is Chester Swindell, returnin' your call."

"Thanks for getting back to me so quickly," West said. She paused before continuing. "Chester, everything I'm about to tell you has to be treated as privileged information—and it must stay that way. OK?"

"Sure, Bev."

"Last night, I got a call from my client. She's very concerned about the Silkwood's six-year-old son, Justin. He has become increasingly belligerent and distraught over the approach of his seventh birthday, this Saturday."

"I'd say he's a bit young to be havin' those kinds of age-related concerns, Bev."

"Cute, Chester. Justin is upset because he doesn't understand why his father cannot attend his birthday party."

"Frankly, Bev, we don't understand why, either. Are you now proposin' that we actually take the 'best interests of the child' into account and allow my client to attend?"

"No."

"Why the hell not? That certainly would qualify as a 'very small' favor."

"We are not prepared to defy the judge's order in such a blatant, and disrespectful, manner, Chester."

"Fine. Have you explained your reasonin' to the boy? I'm sure he'll understand."

"Chester, I need you to be serious for a moment, OK?"

"All right."

"Justin wants to talk with his father, and my client said she is willing to arrange a 15-minute phone call this evening, but it's contingent on your client agreeing to certain conditions."

"Such as?"

"Well, first: No new information gained during the phone call may be mentioned, or otherwise introduced into evidence, at the hearing—and that includes any details of the phone call itself."

"Accepted. What else?"

"Your client must not disparage either my client or the judge, during the call."

"Bev, I understand your concerns, here, but I cannot agree to that."

"Why not?"

"Well, it's just too darn broad and subjective."

"In what way?"

"Well, Bev, suppose your client misrepresented or, in our opinion, misinterpreted, the court's decision, its intent, or its role in this matter, when she explained it to Justin. Or suppose my client wished to clarify any disparagin' inferences his son may have drawn, independently, based on his own, limited understandin' of the court's actions? If my client were to address such issues, you might be able to construe disparagement. I cannot voluntarily expose him to that."

"OK. Then, what would you suggest?"

"We'll agree to tell the truth and to do our best not to assign disparagin' traits or motives to either the court or your client. Will that work?"

"Yes."

"Now, Bev, can you give me some off-the-record specifics about how this issue has affected young Justin, so that my client will understand both the necessity for this phone call and any issues that he might wish to address?

"Of course. Katie said her son has had severe temper tantrums. He has thrown and broken things, refused to eat his meals, told his mother he hates her and the 'dumb judge.' He also has threatened not to go to his own birthday party. Worse, he has had trouble sleeping. Several nights this week, he woke up after midnight, crying for his father. He wants to know when his father is coming home, and he has asked his mother if his father is angry with him."

"OK. Thank you." Swindell said. "So, Bev, to sum up: Your client wants my client to help her with her parentin' responsibilities. What does my client get out of this?"

"You mean, besides helping his son?"

"Well, yes, of course."

"I would have thought that was obvious, Chester: He gets fifteen minutes on the phone with his son, personal contact that is currently forbidden."

"Well, that's certainly true," Swindell said, pondering whether he should push further. Instead, he decided to introduce a new issue. "Bev, has anyone told Justin that you're tryin' to arrange a phone call between him and his dad?"

"No."

"Good, because I also have certain conditions. One of them is that you and your client must agree not to discuss any plans for a phone call with the boy until after I've had a chance to speak with my client and finalize the details. If, for any reason, the call doesn't happen, or it doesn't happen as quickly as you'd like, I don't want the boy, or his mother, to blame that on my client."

"That seems quite reasonable," West said.

"You sound surprised?"

"Well, I—"

"May I make an observation, Beverly?"

"Of course."

"On one level, the need for this 'tiny favor' of yours suggests that your client has realized that she cannot raise the children, effectively, all by herself and that the kids need their father in their lives as a co-parent. In the best interests of the children, Bev, do you think she might now allow you to stipulate that fact in court?"

"Fuck you, Chester."

"Well, it was worth a try."

"*Really?*" West said. "That's why anything reasonable that comes out of your mouth catches me off-guard."

"Humph," Swindell snorted.

"Shall I go ahead and write up an agreement, Chester, so that we'll have it ready for the parties to sign?"

"Yes. Fax me a review copy. Meanwhile, I'll speak with my client and get back to you as soon as I have somethin' definite."

"That sounds great. Bye."

"Bye."

Swindell called Martin's cell phone and was immediately routed to his voicemail. "Mahr-tin," he said, "this is Chester Swindell callin'. It's early Thursday mornin'. Please give me a call as soon as you get this message. Your son's havin' a hard time comin' to terms with your separation and with your exclusion from his birthday party. Consequently, your wife is now offerin' to let you speak with him, briefly, by phone, this evenin'. We just need to finalize arrangements. I'll fill you in when you call."

Chapter 18

Chester Swindell sat behind his mahogany desk, scrawling notes on a yellow legal pad. One of his better Honduran cigars smoldered in a nearby ashtray, and his office door was conspicuously closed. Swindell had cleared his desk of all "debris" immediately after his 7:30 a.m. phone call with Beverly West. He had decided to spend several hours this morning focused on pressing matters that demanded his undivided attention.

"Debris" was his administrative aide, Nancy's, term for the seemingly endless piles of case folders bulging with pleadings, stacks of correspondence, law review articles, case summaries, client-provided background materials, newspapers, trade magazines, and partially spent legal pads that steadily accumulated on Swindell's desk. They grew, and spread around him as he worked, like snow drifts.

Swindell had carefully stacked these items in yard-high piles on two leather-bound, black, wooden library chairs positioned discretely, against a far wall. In their place, he had arranged a small stack of casefile folders, several fresh legal pads, and a plastic cup that Nancy had filled with a dozen newly sharpened pencils.

Swindell preferred to work in longhand and in pencil whenever he did "thinkin' work." He would log each activity into his case management program, which he accessed and tracked through a wireless keyboard and flat-screen monitor kept atop a small computer stand at his left.

When he finished an assignment, Swindell would tear off the relevant pages, staple them together, and then place them in a folder labeled with the client's name and case number. Later, Nancy would transcribe and save a copy of each folder on the office network's hard drive and place a printed version in the appropriate permanent file.

Swindell's first order of business that morning had been to write out a counter-offer settlement plan for Martin. Even though Martin ultimately had accepted Swindell's 'wait-and-see' attitude regarding a potential settlement, he wanted to show his client that he was actively "on the job," looking out for his best interests. He felt compelled to do so after their last conversation.

Martin's comments still burned in Swindell's ears. "They want me to settle with my wife, expunge the public record, if possible, and put the whole thing behind me as soon as possible," Martin had said about the pending domestic violence hearing.

Far more painful, however, had been what his client had said next. "They think going to court, at this point, would be *insane* and that I should only consider it as a last resort. All of which begs the question: Why didn't I hear any of this from you?"

Swindell bristled as he recalled those biting words. He could feel the heat and color rushing back to his cheeks just thinking about it. He had spent a half hour outlining a set of demands, opening gambits, and fallback positions for Martin to consider, and he looked forward to presenting them to his client at the earliest opportunity.

On reflection, Swindell realized that the other side's initial settlement offer had been exceptionally stingy in nature—a typical Beverly West trial balloon, designed to test his and his client's expectations and resolve. *I should have dismissed it immediately, without ever passing it on to Martin.*

Fortunately, his client had rejected it out of hand. Bev sure underestimated him! Perhaps her arrogance is finally startin' to take a toll.

Swindell knew West could not afford to be rejected outright twice. That, he had concluded, was why she had yet to mention anything to him about revising or revisiting the initial settlement offer. West, he realized, also could have been playing "chicken" with him. Like Swindell, she knew that the first attorney to bring up the subject of a "settlement" would be in the weaker bargaining position.

At 10:15 a.m., the light on Swindell's private line began blinking, and he picked it up, only to discover Martin Silkwood on the other end.

"Mahr-tin, how are you?"

"Fine, Mr. Swindell. I got your message about a chance to speak with my son tonight."

"And?"

"I'm in, of course!"

"Great."

Swindell spent several minutes reviewing the background details that Beverly West had shared with him, along with the ground rules the two attorneys had hammered out regarding what Martin should and should not say to his son.

"Are you comfortable workin' within these guidelines, Mahr-tin?"

"Sure. It all seems reasonable enough. What time will Justin and I be talking?"

"Your wife's goin' to call you at about a quarter-to-seven," Swindell said, "and she would like you to limit the call to no more than fifteen minutes."

"Why?" Martin asked, suddenly annoyed by Katie's new power and her willingness to use it.

"I don't know, Mahr-tin. Maybe because she can."

"Well—"

"Look, I get that you don't like it, but it's fifteen minutes you wouldn't otherwise have. In fact, if the judge ever got wind of it—"

"OK, OK." Martin said. "You're right. It's not worth fighting about."

"Correct. Now that we've gotten that out of the way," Swindell continued, "I want you to know, Mahr-tin, that I took very seriously what you said yesterday, about settlin' this case as soon as possible."

"Oh...really?"

"Yes. So, this mornin', I roughed out a counter offer we could present, along with a strategy to use in any negotiations. I'm prepared to go over it with you right now, if you like."

Martin glanced at the tracking device's injection site just below his right elbow. The area still appeared slightly pink.

"No, that won't be necessary, Mr. Swindell." He paused for a moment, recalling their earlier conversation. "Besides, didn't we decide to let Katie and her attorney make the first move? I thought that was where we left things?"

"Well—yes—" Swindell stammered, "but, at the time, you seemed quite concerned about potential negative fallout from a trial. So, I thought, at the very least, I should prepare a contingency plan just in case they don't come back with anythin'."

"Do you think that's a possibility?" Martin asked.

Swindell thought his client sounded surprisingly indifferent. "Anythin's possible, Mahr-tin. And, as you know, time is runnin' out. The trial is scheduled to begin at nine o'clock, Monday mornin'. That's less than one business day away."

"That's certainly true," Martin conceded. "I appreciate that you took the initiative on this, too, but, I think I'm going to pass."

Swindell was stunned. "Mahr-tin, has somethin' happened since we last spoke, somethin' you're not tellin' me about?"

"No."

"I ask because, quite frankly, I felt like I had to 'talk you off the ledge' yesterday and now—"

"Now, what?" Martin asked.

"Now, it's almost as if that entire conversation never took place. I don't sense any concern or urgency at all, on your part."

Martin's end of the line went silent.

"Mahr-tin? Mahr-tin, are you still there?"

"Yes."

"Good. For a moment, there, I thought I lost you."

"No, I was just thinking about what you said."

"And?"

"I guess...after sleeping on it, I realized that my partners were being extremely selfish and alarmist. Their comments scared the hell out of me, too. I admit it. But now that I've had time to think it over, I find myself in agreement with your original position. We should wait and let them make the first move!"

Swindell moved the phone receiver away from his ear, frowned and looked at it sideways. He wanted to scream at his client.

"Are you sure, Mahr-tin?" he asked, trying to keep his frustration in check. "Don't you think we should at least discuss what I've put together? Where's the harm in that? Besides, the situation has changed materially. Both sides are now workin' together to address Justin's behavioral issues. That may give us a new openin' to try and settle."

"Doesn't that give them the same opening, Mr. Swindell?"

"Of course, but—"

"You do still think Katie wants, very much, to avoid the costs of a trial?"

"Yes, I do, because I don't think she ever imagined the case goin' this far."

"Good. Then, we're in agreement. Let them sweat it out...right up to the start of the hearing, Monday, if necessary. Who knows? Maybe Katie will get so desperate that she'll offer to restore everything she took."

Swindell frowned. "Well, Mahr-tin, I don't know about that—"

Martin breathed deeply and sighed. "Do what you can to get them back to the table, then, Mr. Swindell. But, if I were you, I'd concentrate most of my efforts and energy on preparing for, and winning, this case."

Chapter 19

Tony Sands Jr. sat in the waiting area of Dr. Harold Merritt's Silver Spring, Maryland, dental office, nervously tapping his fingers on the wooden arms of his seat. He was excited, agitated, even slightly terrified, after having received 'the call' at ten o'clock that morning.

"Dr. Merritt has cleared a half hour, this afternoon, to see you about your toothache," the office manager had said.

Sands didn't have a toothache. "What time?" he had asked.

"He can squeeze you in at the end of the day today: four-thirty sharp?"

"I'll be there."

And now, there he was, on a seemingly ordinary Thursday afternoon, waiting for his first assignment. It had been so long in coming—more than three years since they had helped him out with his divorce—that Sands had almost completely forgotten about the "tag," as he called it, that they had slipped under the skin of his right forearm.

Now he wondered what it was that they would ask him to do? He had never thought about it before. He hoped he would be up to the challenge.

From across the room, the young receptionist stared, wide-eyed, at him. He smiled at her, but when her steely expression remained unchanged, he realized she was fixated on his exposed, and bulging, left biceps, where the tattoo of a bloody knife tip was exposed beneath his rolled-up shirt sleeve.

He quickly unrolled the sleeves on both sides of his shirt and buttoned them. Then, he flashed a sheepish grin in her direction and shrugged apologetically. She blushed and immediately turned her eyes downward. Once more, he made a mental note to get that tattoo removed. It had become a permanent and increasingly awkward reminder of his brief, teenage involvement in a neighborhood street gang.

"Mr. Sands?" a young dental hygienist said, as she poked her mane of sandy blonde hair into the reception area and then opened the hall door wider. She appeared to be in her mid-twenties, had a pleasant smile and a trim, full figure that was surprisingly well-accentuated by her dental uniform: a floral-patterned shirt and solid purple pants above a pair of white leather nurse's shoes.

Sands stood up and walked over.

"Dr. Merritt will see you now," she said. "Follow me."

Sands walked down the hall several steps behind her, smelling the typical dental office aroma: toothpaste accented by just the slightest hint of burned, drilled enamel. As he walked he wondered about who came up with the patterns and color schemes dental hygienists wore. *Is there any point, or reason, to it?*

They passed several closed doors on either side of the hall, then a room where another dental hygienist was busy bending over a seated patient, cleaning his teeth.

His guide stopped just ahead of him and opened a door on the left, gesturing for him to come inside. "Please, have a seat in the dental chair and make yourself comfortable," she said. "Dr. Merritt will join you in just a moment." Then, she smiled and left.

It had been in another room just like this one, three years earlier, that Sands had met Dr. Merritt for the first time. That was when he had learned the scant details Dr. Merritt had been authorized to tell him about the shadowy, underground group that was then offering to help him in his divorce case.

Sands remembered that he had felt sick to his stomach with dread and had wanted to bolt. The thought of putting his fate in the hands of a group of total strangers would have been hard enough under any circumstances. But these guys? They seemed to be a paramilitary, covert fifth column of some sort. The fact that he had shown up for his appointment underscored just how desperate and scared he had been.

Back then, he had had every reason to be desperate. Sands had returned home to an empty, gutted apartment after a weekend fishing trip with his dad.

Renée had moved out, taking their six-month-old daughter and everything else with her. She not only took all the furniture, she took every scrap of paper and most of his belongings—even his socks. *Well,* he thought, correcting himself, *Renée hadn't taken every scrap of paper. She did leave a large manila envelope (on the hardwood floor, next to the phone) filled with every unpaid bill she could find...after she had first called around to all the companies and had them take her name off the accounts.*

Later, he learned that she also had cleaned out all their checking and savings accounts—to the tune of nearly $18,000.

Still later, he got the other bad financial news: He discovered that Renée had filed her tax returns as a *single head of household* (which wasn't even accurate) instead of filing jointly with him, as had been their custom. (They always had taken zero exemptions on Renée's marketing executive's salary, in order to cover her withholding taxes and his quarterly estimated taxes as a self-employed barbershop owner. Then, they had lived off his income.

As a result, Renée had a huge tax refund coming her way, while Sands was left holding-the-bag—a conspicuously empty one—for his entire tax bill, plus interest and penalties.

Renée's thievery eventually drove Sands into bankruptcy, but that wasn't what devastated him.

What stung the most were the child molestation charges Renée had made against him. She filed the papers immediately before disappearing to St. Kitts for several days of rehabilitative sun worshipping. Renée had accused him, specifically, of fondling their infant daughter. The charges were civil, not criminal, but she had made them without a shred of supporting evidence.

Sands recalled asking his attorney why Renée would do such a thing, and the attorney had looked at him, briefly, as if he had two heads.

"Well, if you didn't do it—" the attorney had said feebly, as Sands glared at him, "then to get total custody of your daughter. With full custody, she could take your daughter across country—or around the world, for that matter— without ever having to notify you."

Thanks to Dr. Merritt and company, Renée's plan backfired and Sands got joint custody of Samantha, his pride and joy! (Renée never had to pay back a cent of what she stole, but Sands considered it to be a bargain, because he had salvaged his reputation, kept his daughter in his life *and* had rid himself of Renée—all at the same time!)

Sands heard a light rapping on the door and turned around just in time to see Dr. Merritt step inside. He looked the same as he remembered him: short with curly gray hair, butterscotch, tanning-bed complexion and a jovial, yet humble, countenance.

Dr. Merritt was in his mid-forties and seemed to slump a little, when he walked, which Sands attributed to days spent bending over dental patients.

"Hi, Tony," he said, smiling.

"Doc, so you finally missed me?"

"Hardly," Dr. Merritt grinned. "But someone else clearly did. I'd love to reminisce with you, but we just don't have time."

"Don't sweat it, Doc."

Dr. Merritt walked over to one of the credenzas with dental models on top and gestured for Sands to join him. He opened a drawer and took out a plain, manila envelope.

"What's my assignment?"

"Shhh!" Dr. Merritt raised a finger to his lips and frowned. Then, he flipped a switch and the sound of a whirring dental drill filled the room. "Better safe than sorry."

Dr. Merritt pulled a sheet of paper out of the envelope. It contained a diagram of a side view of a man's neck. "We have an intriguing assignment for you, which will require precision and skill with your hands."

"Using a scissors?" Sands asked, pretending to snip at imaginary hair.

"No," Dr. Merritt said, opening the credenza drawer. He withdrew a beige plastic box and slid the lid open. Inside, embedded in foam, were a plastic-tipped syringe, a vial containing a clear liquid, and some form of tiny aerosol pump. He removed the syringe. "Using this."

"What's the liquid?" Sands asked, as he felt that familiar queasy feeling overtaking him again.

"A psychotropic solution designed to heighten the power of mental suggestions."

"Oh, you mean something like liquid LSD, then?"

Dr. Merritt shrugged noncommittally.

"Anything else?"

"Yes, a tiny Nano-sized navigational device and neural implant that will enter the body with the fluid."

"Neural implant?" Sands asked, surprised. "Neural, as in 'brain'? You want me to mess with someone's brain?"

"Yeah," Dr. Merritt said.

"Whose?"

"I'm going to tell you, but does it really matter?" Dr. Merritt asked. "It's someone who's playing a role in a divorce-related hearing, not unlike yours. Remember?"

Sands thought about his case. "Look, I want to help and all, but I'm not crazy. I want to know just how much shit I'm getting myself into, before I commit."

"You should have thought about that before you accepted our help, Tony. You're already committed."

"All the same," Sands said, folding his arms, and staring at Dr. Merritt intently, "who's the target?"

Dr. Merritt paused. Sands thought he saw him stiffen and grow tense, but that might just have been his imagination.

"Well, of course, you need know who we're targeting. The target's the most critical part of the whole assignment. It's also non-negotiable, understand?"

Sands nodded.

"Your target is a Montgomery County District Court judge."

"A what?!" Sands' eyes registered shock and rage.

"Do you know how much trouble I could get into if this little plan of yours backfires?"

Dr. Merritt looked at Sands, then down at the floor. He shook his head and shrugged. "Can't be helped."

Before Dr. Merritt knew what hit him, Sands grabbed the needle out of his left hand and wrapped his right arm tightly around the startled dentist's neck and jaw in a headlock. Then, he pressed the blunt end of the needle against Dr. Merritt's exposed neck.

"Careful with that," Dr. Merritt rasped.

"Careful? Like your plans for me? You want me to fuck with a sitting judge's brain, with *this*," he said, pressing the blunt end of the needle into Dr. Merritt's flesh for emphasis. "Why not just strap one of those 'suicide bombs' to my chest?"

"No other way," Dr. Merritt gasped. "You have access...through your dad."

"Oh, no!" Sands said, further tightening his grip. "I'm not dragging Pops into this, or harming his friend." He pressed the syringe handle even tighter against the dentist's neck. "You can forget it!"

"Didn't complain when we...did it...for you."

"What?" Sands continued the headlock, but stopped pressing the syringe against Merritt's throat. "For me? Is that what you said?"

"Yes!" Dr. Merritt hissed. "Now, let me go!"

Sands hesitated for a moment, letting the information sink in.

"Now!" Merritt ordered.

Sands released his grip and Merritt pushed him away. He rubbed his neck and scowled at Sands. "What the hell's wrong with you?"

"I- I didn't—"

"Right. You didn't. You didn't know! You're not supposed to know." Then, he saw that Sands was holding the syringe backwards. "At least you didn't contaminate our only syringe."

"No, I—"

"Forget it," Dr. Merritt said, rubbing his neck, and shaking his head in disgust. "We're running out of time, and I need to tell you what you have to do."

Dr. Merritt stared intently at Sands. "Are you going to honor your commitment, or not?"

Sands just stood there with a blank look on his face.

"So, that's how it is? Merritt asked. "All right, I'm going to tell you something that should make this more palatable for you. I want to assure you that the Nano probe you will inject into Judge Farnsworth's bloodstream is a molecular-sized, temporary-acting, non-lethal device.

"I cannot go into further detail, because the technology is classified and, quite frankly, I don't understand it all. But the judge should be in no real physical danger—aside from the effects associated with having a very bad dream."

Sands shrugged. "Well, that's good to know," he said. "Sorry about your neck, Doc."

"Forget it."

Dr. Merritt quickly became all business once more. "The good news, Tony, is that you know how to react decisively, in a crisis, and you are good with your hands."

Sands made a feeble attempt at a smile.

"That could prove helpful, if something were to go wrong. But don't let it. This isn't rocket science.

"You're going to take your father's place this Friday, when he normally goes to court and cuts Judge Farnsworth's hair in his chambers."

"How am I supposed to do that?"

Dr. Merritt again opened the drawer. This time, he withdrew a plain number-ten envelope. "You're going to give your dad an early birthday present: a one-day, chartered-fishing-trip-for-two, on the Chesapeake Bay. He goes with a friend and you cover for him at the shop."

Sands nodded. He opened the envelope and pulled out a brochure containing the tickets. "Captain Sculley's Charters," he said. "That's a first-class operation. He'll love it, but he'll wonder where I found the money."

"Tell him you won $500 on Power Ball."

"You guys know I play the lottery?"

"No," Dr. Merritt chuckled. "It's just simple addition: Italian, divorced and short on cash!"

Then, he moved the beige box to one side, revealing the drawing of the right side of a man's head. "We have a proven methodology for helping 'reorient' people's thinking. It's complicated, and I'm not going to go into detail except to say, this is not brain washing.

"I guess you could call it a form of dream manipulation. It's designed to give the judge, who's been conditioned to think favorably about the 'petitioner' in *ex-parte* cases, a new, vivid, and compelling experience that should make him more sensitive to the 'respondent's' point-of-view."

"And how is that not brain washing?"

"If anything, it's designed to temporarily counteract the brainwashing that's already occurred."

Sands' right eyelid rose, skeptically.

"Here's what has to happen," Dr. Merritt said. "We're going to give you a music CD. You'll have to get the judge to listen to it through a set of headphones, while you inject the needle into his jugular vein and cut his hair.

"The tape contains subliminal messages that will relax him and give him suggestions for the dreams."

"What if he doesn't want to listen to it?"

"He has to," Dr. Merritt said.

"Is the CD ready?"

"No. We'll send it, along with the CD player, by messenger, to your shop tomorrow morning."

"Listen," Sands said. "I'll check with my dad and see if he knows what type of music the Judge can't resist. I'll call you as soon as I know."

"OK," Dr. Merritt said, "but you will need to call me tonight."

"How risky is the operation...for me?" Sands asked.

Dr. Merritt considered that for a moment and smiled. "We haven't lost anyone yet, if that's what you mean."

"It is."

"So, Tony—," Merritt began.

"What, Doc?"

"Don't be the first!"

"Yeah. Right. I'll keep that in mind!"

Tony leaned back against the dental office wall and folded his arms. "So, now that I know what's expected of me, how am I supposed to pull it off? How am I going to inject him without arousing his suspicions?"

Dr. Merritt pulled out a small pump sprayer. "This contains a vanilla-scented spray that's also a topical anesthetic. You'll tell him it's aroma therapy and a muscle relaxer.

"Spray a little around his head and spray the rest in the general area of the injection site. Then, use one of those scalp and neck massagers on his neck before injecting him.

"Now, let me show you how to find the jugular vein."

Sands smiled. "No need, Doc. You forget; I'm a barber. They taught us anatomy from the neck up, in barber school."

Dr. Merritt smiled. "Right! That's normally the trickiest part of this. Just remember, to apply pressure on the inside of the collar bone and palpate the skin above it to root out the vein for injection purposes."

"Got it," Sands said. "That'll be much easier to do once I've applied the spray."

"I've got one more item for you," Dr. Merritt said, again, opening the drawer. This time he brought out a brand new, black barber's bag.

"All the additional tools you'll need for our operation have been made of a highly rigid polymer that will not show up on the court-security, x-ray scanners. But just in case the guards inspect your bag, we want you to use this one. It has a false bottom where you can hide the syringe and pump sprayer."

"What about the solution for the syringe?" Sands asked.

Dr. Merritt took the syringe and drew all the fluid from the vial into it. Then, he reapplied the cap and placed it securely in the foam, along with the pump sprayer and slipped them under the case's false bottom. He tossed the empty vial, with its metal rim, into his office trash can.

"That does it," he said, patting Sands on the back and showing him to the door. "Now, it's time you let me get back to earning a living!"

"See you in another three years, Doc?" Sands asked.

Dr. Merritt rubbed his neck where Sands had pressed the syringe. "Not if I see you first!"

Chapter 20

At five o'clock Thursday afternoon, on the way to her car, Katie Silkwood called Beverly West for a progress report.

"Beverly," she said, "I've only got a minute, but I wanted to check in with you. Is the phone call with Justin on for tonight?"

"Yes, Katie. I just received a text message from your husband's attorney. Martin will be available to speak with Justin at six forty-five tonight. You should call him on his cell phone."

Katie sighed. "Thank God. Maybe Marty can get somewhere with that boy. Justin's behavior is driving me crazy!"

"Let's hope," West said. She knew what was coming next, and she braced herself.

"Have you received a counter-offer from them yet?"

"No, Katie. In fact, the subject never even came up during the call this morning."

Katie thought about that for a moment. "How long were you two on the phone?"

"About ten minutes." West said. She sighed softly, "I'm sorry, Katie, but settling just doesn't seem to be a priority for them at this point."

Katie could feel her heart start to race. "Then, what do you think is a priority for them, Beverly?"

"I think they're busy preparing for trial."

Katie wanted to scream. "This is terrible! I can't afford this."

"I know. I know," West said. "I wish I had better news…"

"What should we do?"

"For now, we only have one option, Katie. We wait."

At the other end of the line, Katie scrunched her hands into fists and shook them violently. "I just want to scream!"

West tried to change the subject. "How are you coming along with your list of potential financial angels?"

"I-I finished it, Beverly," Katie said, her voice sounding a bit shaky, "but – I will need their help to pay for the divorce trial. I don't want to tap any of them now."

West wanted to keep her client's spirits up. "I've been getting ready for another round of negotiations," West said. "I've worked up a revised settlement offer. Let me fax you a copy. You can review it, when you get home tonight. Then, we should talk."

Katie sighed. "Thanks Beverly. That would be nice."

"Meanwhile," West said, "we'll wait and see what happens."

"We can't wait too much longer, Beverly," Katie said. "After all, the trial starts Monday!"

At her end of the line, West shook her head slowly. "I know, Katie. I know. Please be patient."

Katie wanted to scream. She felt cornered and desperate. "All right, Beverly," she said at last, trying to present a calm front. "I'll try."

Chapter 21

Tony Sands left Dr. Merritt's dental office and called his father on his way to his car. "Hey Pops. Sorry. I'm running about ten minutes late. But good news: I've got a surprise for you! Yeah. No, not telling. Great, I'll be right over!"

His 2012 Mazda Miata purred to life, despite its seventy-six-thousand odd miles, and he quickly completed the five-mile trip back up Wisconsin Avenue to the barbershop in downtown Rockville. The Miata was the only "luxury" item Sands had purchased since his divorce. It had seventy-one thousand miles on it when he bought it, so "luxury" was a bit of an overstatement. But with no money to his name, a rundown apartment, and debts galore, he needed some form of "chick magnet" or, he figured, he'd never get laid again.

Sands had bought shrewdly, casing the online classifieds for weeks until he found the right car and the motivated buyer he needed. Then, he completely refurbished the car and rebuilt the engine, leaning heavily on what he had learned in his high-school shop classes.

On the way to the barber shop, Sands called his father's best friend and fishing buddy. "Sam? Hi, this is Tony, Tony Sand's son. You doing anything tomorrow? Great, I'm treating Pops to a charter fishing trip on the bay—with Captain Sculley, out of St. Mary's county.

"That's right! And you're invited to keep him company. No, I'm not shitting you! And I'm footing the bill. Yeah, I guess you have been living right! But, listen. It's a surprise, so don't go calling him about it. Wait for him to call *you*. I'm on my way to tell him now.

"They leave the dock early: at five o'clock in the morning, so I'll bring him by your place no later than four, OK? Can you drive? Great!"

Sands pulled up to the barbershop just as Tony Sr. was drawing down the front-door shade that announced "Closed" in large, red letters. Under it he had printed the store's general hours and phone number. It was 5:12 p.m. and none of the other barbers was anywhere in sight. His father was holding a blue, zipped canvass cash bag in his left hand as he slipped the key in the lock and worked it shut.

Then, he drew the wrought iron gates from the left and right side of the store front, slipped their footings into the holes drilled into the sidewalk in front of the door, and reached into his pocket for the large padlock. He opened it, slipped it in place, and then snapped it shut.

Sands studied his old man with admiration. He was turning sixty-three in several weeks, with a head of thick gray hair, but he still looked every bit as fit and trim as he had been when he was in his mid-thirties. Tony Sr. worked at it: walking three miles, three times a week and spending a half hour each night working out with weights and a bench press that he kept in the basement. He also got help from Angie Sands, who ruled the kitchen and carefully regulated how much bread, pasta, fat, and sweets her husband consumed.

His father walked with a decided spring in his step as he crossed the sidewalk to Tony Jr.'s car. "Another day, another dollar!" he announced as he hopped in the front bucket seat next to his son. "I need you to stop by the bank, on the way to the house, so I can deposit our 'small' fortune!"

"Dad," Sands said, as he steered the car into traffic, "how many times have I asked you not to carry that cash bag out in the open? Slip it under your jacket, for Christ sake. You don't have to be so damned obvious about it, do you?"

Tony Sr. looked at his son, squinted, then smiled. "Come on Junior, get serious. Yeah, we make a living, but it's an *honest* living. No self-respecting thief is gonna want to do a smash-and-grab on your old man! They'd get accused of thinking too small.

"Now, if we operated a Seven-Eleven® that would be different. They'd get more cash, and they could bring home slushies and pizza slices for everyone! 'Course those places are often crawling with cameras...and cops."

"Right, Dad. You're the easier target of opportunity. If they snatch the cash bag from you, they may get less money, even a few stray hairs on their clothes, but they won't get caught!"

"All right," Tony Sr. said. "It's touching. You care. I get it. But, remember, I'm not some weak, senile old dude. I'm still in the game. I could probably beat you if we arm wrestled for a beer. Stick around for dinner, and we'll see."

"In your dreams, old man," Sands said, smiling. "In your dreams."

"So, what's this about a surprise you have for me, Junior?" his father asked.

Tony reached into the left side of his wind breaker and withdrew an envelope. "Here it is, Pops. Enjoy!"

His dad eagerly opened the envelope and studied the brochure. "Wow! Sculley! He's a first-rate operation. I know a couple of guys who've used him before. They raved about it! But they also said it cost a small fortune."

"Yeah?"

"Well, no offense, son, but where'd you get the *do-re-mi*?"

"Pick three."

"You don't say? Nice picking!"

They had arrived at the bank. Tony Sr. got out of the car and made his night deposit.

"So, when do we go?" he asked, as he slipped back into his seat.

"Not we; you. Happy Birthday! You leave first thing in the morning! Sam's going to keep you company. I'm supposed to deliver you to his place at four o'clock, sharp."

"Well, that's great!" Tony Sr. said, smiling. Then, almost as quickly, a frown appeared. "Wait a minute. Tomorrow's Friday!"

"Yeah?"

"I can't do it."

"What are you talking about? I'll manage the shop for you, Dad. This is your day. Enjoy!"

"But ——"

"But, what?"

"Mickey Farnsworth. I have a standing appointment to cut his hair every Friday, at one, in his chambers at district court."

"So?"

"So, he's expecting me! I've been cutting his hair in court for *ten years*, and I've never missed a date. I'm not about to start now."

"What's the matter, Pops? You afraid he'll think you're slipping?"

Tony Sr. waved his hand at his son, as if he were chasing off a fly. "Hardly. It's difficult to explain, but we go way back, that's all."

"OK, so tell me what he likes and I'll stand in for you."

"It's just not the same, Junior. No offense. The man has his routine and I'm part of it."

Tony glanced over at his dad and saw the troubled look on his face.

"Dad, what's the last time you took a day off from work?"

"I don't know…. The last time I caught the flu, I guess."

"That doesn't count. I mean the last time you took a day off from work to do something for yourself?"

"Beats me, and what's your point, anyway?"

"I don't think you've missed a day the whole time I've been working with you. You're due."

Tony Sr. crossed his arms and stared ahead. "You're not putting me out to pasture, Junior, not even for a day. You're just going to have to reschedule this trip with Sculley."

Tony shook his head. The old guy could be stubborn, but he hadn't expected this. "I can't do that, Dad."

"Why the *hell* not?"

"Sculley gave me a special rate, for tomorrow only. He had a last-minute cancellation to fill. So, if you don't go tomorrow, that's it. I'm out five C-notes, and you and Sam will have to pay your own way to go another time."

Tony Sr. sat quietly, letting his son's comments sink in. "That sucks."

"Yeah," Tony Jr. said, "sure does. But what's all this about being 'put out to pasture?' Where'd that come from?"

His father squirmed in his seat. "That's how it starts. A day here. A day there. Then, half a week. I've talked with some of my gang. I know."

"You've got nothing to worry about on that score, Pops," Tony Jr. said. "You've got more stamina than me!"

Tony Sr. smiled. "You got that right, boy!" he said, letting out a sigh. After another moment, he continued. "So, were you serious about filling in for me tomorrow, with Farnsworth?"

"Sure."

"Really? Because, it's a big schlep over there from the shop, and, now that you mention it, you *do* look a bit out of shape. You don't think you'll get too winded, do you?"

Tony Jr. smiled. "I think I'll survive, Pops."

"OK, then. No point in ruining your surprise and blowing all your dough. As for the haircut, it's pretty simple, really. Razor cut. Take off no more than a week's growth. He also likes a bracer of Vitalis®, for some ungodly reason, and a neck and scalp massage. "Think you can remember all of that?"

"I'll do my best, Dad. Listen, I'd like to do something extra special for the judge, to make up for the fact that he won't get to spend time with you. I thought I'd bring him a CD to listen to, while I cut his hair. After all, he and I probably won't have much to talk about. Any thoughts about what music he'd find irresistible?"

"That's easy: *La traviata.*"

"The opera?"

"Yep. He first got smitten, when he was visiting our house as a kid."

Tony Jr. made a mental note to call the title in to Dr. Merritt, as soon as he dropped his father off at home.

"How far back do you and the judge go, Pops, if you don't mind me asking?"

"Quite a way. I met Mickey Farnsworth a lifetime ago, in Little League. I was thirteen and Mickey had just turned twelve. Coach Richards assigned him to play second base."

"What was the name of your team, Dad? I always forget."

"The Silver Spring Tigers: We had a near-perfect record that year. I was starting my second season as the first-string catcher and team captain. And Mickey," he said, with a chuckle, "he was a complete mess: tall, gawky, extremely gung-ho... a real nerd. (We just didn't call them that, then.) He had a $64 vocabulary, which he couldn't turn off to save his life. He'd spout his big words at the coach, and you could just see them sailing right over his head, like frozen ropes lined over the pitcher's head and into center field. Every time he opened his mouth, the coach felt like a dummy. Not good.

"Mickey was a misfit, no way around it, and I've always had a soft spot in my heart for misfits. I took him under my wing, so to speak, showed him the ropes, introduced him around the clubhouse and filled him in on each teammate.

"We were about as different as two kids could be. Mickey came from an old, 'up county' family of doctors, lawyers, accountants, and landowners. Meanwhile, as you know, I came from the streets—albeit the 'not-so-mean' streets—of Silver Spring."

"Getting a bit overly dramatic, there, aren't you?"

"I don't know what you're talking about," Tony Sr. said. Then, he continued, "Mickey was the older of the two Farnsworth kids. He and his sister, Penny, and their parents, lived with a parakeet and a golden retriever in a gargantuan, wood-framed Georgian-style mansion on New Hampshire Avenue, extended. Their annual Christmas photo looked like a Norman Rockwell painting.

"Mickey's dad was a surgeon at the Walter Reed Army Medical Center. He had Mickey focused on getting into an Ivy League college even back then."

"That was another big difference between you two, huh?" Sands said, with a grunt.

"Sure. Your grandad wasn't sending the six Sands boys to community college, let alone to an Ivy League school. He was a small-time residential contractor, who ran a crew of 'Paisans' as he called them. He did single-family home renovations and, occasionally, a small apartment complex or two. He supported us while your grandma, Roberta, took care of the home, volunteered as a Cub Scout den mother for each of us, in turn; prepared my dad's company's books; and provided him with 'unofficial' marketing consulting services.

"My dad had simple ambitions for me," Tony Sr. said. "He wanted me to go to barber school. He was proud that I would be earning a living, still with my hands, but indoors, out of the burning sun and with refined tools and schooling, rather than with hammers, saws, and heavy lifting."

"I think Mickey had a not-too-secret crush on your granny. She was quite a looker, back then. She could have passed for a slightly older version of Annette Funicello. Remember her?

"Not really, Pops."

"Wow, what a body! She was a Disney Mouseketeer, who eventually grew up, filled out and starred in the movie, 'Beach Blanket Bingo.' You should rent it sometime."

Sands looked ahead, smiled and rolled his eyes.

Tony Sr. continued. "Mickey used to have an odd sense of humor. Perhaps you'll see it in action, but I think he's toned it down since becoming a judge."

"Wasn't that like thirty years ago, or something?"

"Somewhere in that neighborhood. Mickey had been practicing law for eight years — we both had moved back to the area by then, and his career, as a litigator, was going nowhere fast. At thirty-four, he started campaigning for an open spot on the district court bench. He made the rounds to his friends' and colleagues' law offices and country clubs, and soon he had his judgeship. He owes many of them favors, too. He's told me as much."

"So, how did you get the weekly gig at the courthouse?"

Tony Sr. smiled. "For twenty years, he'd come in the shop every other week. Then, ten years ago, when they made him administrative judge he said it was too much. He couldn't take the time off. He called the shop. 'How about cutting my hair each week, in the courthouse?' he asked. I remember hesitating because of the time and the long walk, you know."

"'Come on,'" he said. 'We can reminisce. The walk will do you good. I'll give you a good tip, and I'll introduce you around the courthouse, like you introduced me around the club house. You'll pick up lots of business! Besides,' he added, 'no one holds a candle to you!'"

They had arrived at Tony Sr.'s house. He opened the car door a crack and then turned to face his son. "What could I say?" he shrugged. "I agreed to do it. After all, the man was right!"

Chapter 22

At precisely six forty-five Thursday night, as planned, the phone in Martin's extended stay motel room began ringing. He picked it up.

"Hello?"

"Daddy!" Justin said.

"Hi, buddy! Boy, it's good to hear your voice! How have you been?"

"I've missed you, Daddy."

"I know. I've missed you, too. Terribly. I'm so sorry I haven't been able to see or talk with you."

"Where are you?"

"I'm staying in a motel nearby. Do you know what a motel is?"

"Unh uh."

"Well, it's a building full of rooms for people to sleep in when they're traveling."

"But you're not traveling."

"You're right."

"So, why don't you just come home?"

"I wish I could, Justin, but I can't for now."

"Why not, Daddy? Don't you want to be with us anymore?"

"Of course, I do, buddy. But it's complicated. Did Mommy tell you about the judge?"

"Yes."

"What did she say?"

"She said the judge is very wise, and he thinks it would be best if we were apart for a while. She said the judge won't let you see us or even talk with us until after Monday. But he made a 'ception and let me talk with you tonight."

"That's right."

"Mommy says the judge wants to keep us safe. Daddy, would you ever hurt me or Monica or Mommy?"

Martin swallowed hard. "What do you think, buddy?"

"No."

"That's right, son. I love all of you – including Maxie. I would never hurt you guys. You mean the world to me."

"Will you be at my party tomorrow?"

"No, son. I'm in a kind of grown up time out. I can't see you until it's over."

"Did you do something bad to get time out, Daddy?"

"I don't think so. The judge is very busy, so he put me in it for a few days, until he and I can meet and talk. That's what we're going to do on Monday.

"Tell me about your party, son."

"No! I don't want to talk about it if you can't come!"

"Please, Justin?"

"No."

"I have a special surprise for you – sort of a birthday present."

"You do?!"

"Yep. Tell me about your party, and I'll tell you what it is. OK?"

"All right."

"I heard the party's going to be at the Cider Mill farm. Is that right?"

"Yeah."

"And there will be animals to pet – and pony rides?"

"Yeah."

"That really sounds like fun."

"I know."

"Which friends of yours did you invite?"

"Petey and Jeffrey and Mikey and Dougy and some other guys. Petey's getting me a baseball bat. He told me."

"Wow. That's a great present! We can use it when we practice your Tee Ball swing together. Won't that be fun?"

"Yes!"

"A lot of special people will be there for you tomorrow; do you know that?"

"Who?"

"Well, Grandma Es and Grandma Phyllis! Uncle Jeb and Aunt Neenah, too."

"They're not special people, Daddy. They're family!"

"That's right, but you don't get to see them every day, do you?"

"No."

"So, that makes them kind of special, doesn't it?"

"Maybe …. Are they bringing the baby, Daddy?"

"Yes, baby Suzy will be there, too."

"Good. She's funny!"

"Yes, she is, buddy."

"Daddy, do I have to go if you won't be there?"

"Yes, son. It's a very special day, for a very special guy. You're going to be seven years old! That's so amazing, do you know that?"

"Yeah!" Justin said, giggling.

"Everybody's coming to see you blow out the candles – and they're bringing you presents, too."

"You won't see me blow them out, Daddy. I don't feel like cel'brating, if you can't come!"

"I've got an idea. How about if I talk to Mommy and arrange to call you tomorrow, on Skype®, just as you are about to blow them out? That way, I can join everyone else and sing 'Happy Birthday,' and you can see and hear me do it. It will almost be like I'm there!"

"That would be great, Daddy. Will you?"

"I'll ask her, buddy. I think we can make that happen."

"Daddy," Justin said, "I'm so happy now. I feel like crying. Isn't that silly?"

"No," Martin said, trying to hold back his own tears. "It isn't silly at all. And Justin?"

"Yes, Daddy?"

"You need to listen better to Mommy. OK?"

"I'll try."

"It's important, because you're going to be seven years old. You're a big boy. And you need to behave like one. OK?"

"I guess."

"You know, you forgot to ask me something."

"I did?"

"Yes. Remember, I told you I had a surprise for you?"

"Oh, yeah. What kind of surprise?"

"Well, as soon as I can, I am going to come visit you and Monica and Mommy and Maxie, and when I do, I am going out take you out for a special father-son birthday celebration!"

"Really?!"

"Uh huh. Just us guys. And guess where we're going to go?"

"Where?"

"We're going to Baltimore to watch your favorite team, the Orioles, play ball. We'll make a day of it."

"Really?"

"Yes siree."

"And we can eat hot dogs together?"

"Yep. And Coke and Crackerjacks, too!"

"I love you, Daddy."

"I love you too, Justin. Happy Birthday! And I'll speak with you tomorrow!"

"OK, Daddy. Bye!"

"Bye."

Martin sat on the side of the bed for a moment, sighing. He wiped the tears from his eyes. Then, he dialed Swindell's number and left a message on the answering machine, explaining that he had figured out what 'tiny' reciprocal favor Swindell should now request from Katie's attorney.

Chapter 23

Beverly West sat at her antique French provincial writing desk, in her Rockville law office, sipping tea, nibbling at a stale cheese Danish, and staring, uncomfortably, at the telephone. It was now nearly nine o'clock Friday morning and, for the past ten minutes, West had been trying to motivate herself to call Chester Swindell and offer to meet with him and his client to discuss settling the case.

West leaned forward, arms bent at the elbows and head resting on the backs of her hands. She was out of options and she knew it. She sighed as she stared at the lifeless device. On some level, she knew she was stalling, in the hope that a last-minute call from Swindell, with a similar request, might rescue her.

West had hoped she would never have to make this call, but twenty minutes earlier, Katie Silkwood had made the decision for her. Katie had called, ostensibly, to thank West for getting Martin to speak with their son. Justin, she had said, was now "back onboard" for his birthday party, but she added, that was not the real reason for her call.

"Beverly, I'm out of time. I need you to call Martin's attorney *today* and offer to settle the case. We need to make Monday's hearing go away. I'm sorry, but I just can't afford it!"

West swallowed hard as her hand inched toward the receiver. Like any lawyer, she preferred to deal from a position of strength, but her present reluctance ran deeper than that. For years, she had struggled to be taken seriously by those closest to her and that had made her hate feeling even the slightest bit vulnerable.

When she had first expressed an interest in the law more than thirty years earlier, the men in West's family had belittled her. Skilled tradesmen and small business owners, they thought she was "putting on airs." In ways both real and imagined, she felt they had hindered her legal ambitions.

The jokes subsided when West made law review at the University of Maryland, and later, she thought they had ended altogether when she passed the Maryland state bar exam on her first try. But her decision to specialize in family law, strangely enough, had inspired new taunts. Why, they had asked her, was she willing to squander her hard-won legal skills to pursue such a shallow, insignificant branch of the law? It took her stunning record of wins representing female divorce clients, and her conspicuously affluent lifestyle, to finally shut them up.

West pushed Swindell's speed dial number and waited. When he answered, she gently eased into her topic.

"Chester, I've got good news for you. Whatever your client said to young Justin last night really helped. Katie Silkwood called me earlier today and said his behavior is much improved. He's once more looking forward to attending his birthday party tomorrow."

"That's great, Bev. Just goes to show you how important co-parentin' is, wouldn't you agree?"

"In this case, Chester, I would have to say, 'yes'. I was quite impressed with the way the Silkwoods came together, for Justin's sake. I think this may give them a new foundation upon which to build."

Swindell, who had been slouching at his desk, sat up straight in his chair. "What are you gettin' at, Bev?"

"Well, Chester," West said, hesitantly, "I think now might be the time to take another look at settling this case. I think we should try to preserve this positive, new momentum. It would be a real tragedy if we allowed the Silkwoods to return to a state of acrimony. What do you think?"

At the other end of the line, Swindell smiled and pumped his right fist up and down several times, in a silent, victory salute.

"I don't know, Bev" he continued. "Your last attempt to settle didn't turn out all that well. What makes you think this time will be better?"

West felt blood rushing to her cheeks. "Chester, you know that first offer was nothing more than a trial balloon. The process never should have ended there."

"But it did, Bev, and at my client's insistence. Want to know why?"

"Sure."

"It ended because my client, who is a decent man, did not like being robbed of his parental rights and falsely charged with domestic violence in a one-sided trial. What you call a 'trial balloon' he considered to be insult heaped upon injury."

"So, what are you saying, Chester? Your client wants to go to trial? Potentially, he still has a lot to lose."

"That may be, Bev," Swindell said, smiling, and shaking his head. "But he doesn't seem to care! The man, pardon the expression, has balls. I don't think he wants to go to trial any more than he wants a divorce. But he also won't beg to have what he considers to be stolen property returned. Please tell me how I can assure him this won't be another waste of his time."

West cleared her throat. "We are prepared, Chester, to put virtually everything on the table. No sacred cows."

Swindell considered that for a moment. "You said 'virtually everythin',' Bev. Precisely what does 'virtually' mean?"

"It means *nearly* everything, Chester. My client does have a few non-negotiable items, but I assure you, they do not include anything that a normal, rational human being, in your client's position, would consider to be a deal breaker."

"I sure hope you're right, Bev."

"Then, you're willing to give this a try?" West asked.

"Yes."

"Good." West felt a wave of relief. "How about if you, your client, and I meet Saturday morning, at eleven o'clock, at your office?"

"That should work," Swindell said. "I'll check with Mahr-tin. If you don't hear anythin' different from me, we're on."

"Great. Now Chester," West said, "I also need your reassurance about something."

"What's that, Bev?"

"After having been rebuffed once, by your client, I would like to know that I won't be wasting my time again. A girl doesn't like to be turned down once, let alone twice! How serious do you think Mr. Silkwood will be about settling this matter?"

Swindell stroked his chin as he pondered just how forthcoming he should be. "That's a tough one, Bev. He's been a bit hard to read, lately, on that subject. One minute, he seems eager to resolve the matter out-of-court; the next, he seems to have dug in his heels the other way.

"Well …" West sighed.

"Bev, I think he was very hurt by what he considers to be his wife's false allegations, so I think you'll need to be a bit contrite and extremely generous and flexible right out of the gate. Be prepared to bend over to make your offer as appealin' as possible."

West smiled. "Chester, I think you meant to say, be prepared to 'bend over backwards' not 'bend over.' I don't need reassurance in *that* department."

Swindell laughed, "I should hope not, counselor!" He paused a moment before continuing. "Uh Bev, there's another small matter that's come up that I need your help on."

"What's that, Chester?"

"Mr. Silkwood wants to attend his son's birthday party tomorrow – virtually, via Skype," he clarified, "and only long enough to sing 'Happy Birthday' and watch the boy blow out the candles."

"I think that should be doable."

"Great, Bev. Please let me know the details, so I can pass them along to him. I think he'll consider that to be a nice pre-settlement conference goodwill gesture.

"You also should know that my influence with my client, in this area, may be a bit more limited than you might think."

"I'm sure you're understating that a bit," West said. "But I hear you."

"Good. See you tomorrow, counselor, at eleven sharp."

"Right."

Chapter 24

Rockville was baking in the Friday, midday sun as the temperature climbed to 89 degrees. Tony Sands Jr., turned left on the sidewalk at MD Rte. 28 and saw the district court building looming dead ahead.

He licked the corner of his lips, removing a bit of tomato sauce left over from the slice of pizza he had picked up, on his way from the barber shop. He carried his brand-new barber's bag in his right hand and a cup of diet soda in his left.

Sands took another sip of soda through the straw and smiled as he remembered how excited his dad had been earlier that morning, when he had called his son about the fishing trip.

The call came at 3:18 a.m. "Huh?" he had said, still half asleep.

"Junior, where the Hell are you?" his dad had bellowed. "I can hear those bluefish and rockfish flapping their fins in the water!"

"Calm down, Pops. I'm only five minutes away from you, and Sam isn't expecting you until four."

"I'm calling him next. Otherwise, we'll get there and he'll still be sawing away! You said the boat leaves at five, right?"

"Yep."

"Well, let's not cut it too close, son. Traffic could be heavy."

"At four o'clock in the morning? I don't think so, Pops. Why don't you ask Mom for one of her pills? It'll calm you down."

"Calm me down? Whose side are you on, the bluefishes'?"

Tony laughed, just thinking about it.

But now as he advanced toward the district courthouse, each new step seemed to bring him down a little further. He was thinking about the bag in his right hand, its contents – including the tape recording of *La traviata*, that a courier had delivered to him just before seven thirty in the morning. He also was worried about the security checkpoint he would have to clear inside the courthouse in just a matter of minutes. Suddenly, the barber bag handle began to feel sweaty.

Sand's imagination had been running wild with scenarios.

In one, he was at the checkpoint and had removed all the metal objects in the bag, but when he passed it through the metal detector, the alarm tripped anyway. Instantly, the sheriff's deputies turned on him with their guns at the ready! He raised his hands. "OK, OK. You got me. Don't shoot!"

They flipped him around, pressed him against the conveyor belt, spread his legs, and handcuffed his hands behind his back.

"You have the right to remain silent," one of the sheriff's deputies said. "Anything you say can and will be used against you in a court of law…"

"Jeeze!" Sands moaned, annoyed at his inability to control his thoughts. Real sweat was now pouring down his face. He pulled out a couple of paper napkins he had grabbed at the pizza parlor and began wiping his brow. He willed his brain to shut down and prayed his handlers knew what they were doing.

It was 12:35 p.m. when he pressed the large, polished stainless-steel door handle and slowly pushed open the courthouse's tall glass door. A frigid blast of air hit him like a Maui wave.

Inside the lobby, lighting was minimal. He saw a sign directly ahead that read, "Please have your driver's ID ready. Remove all metal objects from your person, and open your bags for inspection."

A line of well-dressed men and women had formed ahead of him – attorneys, he figured – with an occasional, less formally attired person – a client, perhaps? – interspersed between them.

Ahead three guards – two men and a woman – manned the scanners. The woman waved a wand up and down the female visitors while the male guard screened the men.

A thin, Latin-looking man in his early twenties, wearing a loose-fitting, patterned Caribbean shirt, walked briskly under the scanner arch, and triggered a loud "bleep."

"Hold on," the third guard said. He stepped forward and cut the man off from his attorney.

"Empty your pockets."

"I already did," the young man said.

"Did you take off your belt?" the guard asked.

"Whaaat?"

"Lose the belt, sir."

"Ahh, that's mean, man," the young man said as he undid his belt and handed it to the guard. A large pen knife was attached in the center of the back of the belt.

The guard smiled. "Say 'goodbye' to your little friend. You're never going to see it, or the belt, again."

"Say, what?" the young man said, stamping his feet. "How am I going to keep my pants up?"

The attorney had moved around the guard and was now standing at his client's side. "Shut up, Rodriguez, before he charges you with carrying a concealed weapon. Use your hands."

After what felt like hours, Sand's turn finally came. The larger of the two guards, an African American man in his late thirties, asked for his ID.

"I'm Tony Sands, the barber's, son," he said, handing the guard his driver's license. "I treated Pops to a charter fishing trip today, so I'm here to give Judge Farnsworth his weekly haircut."

"OK," the guard said. "Take off your belt and put it in one of these little trays, along with all of your metal items."

He handed a tray to Sands, so that he could begin emptying his pockets. Afterward, Sands took off his shoes and put them on the conveyor belt as well, along with his barber's bag. "Should I take the metal objects out, or just leave them all together?" he asked.

"Yes. Take them out."

Sands emptied the bag into one of the larger trays. The guard glanced, momentarily, at the tools. Then, to Sand's horror, he asked for the bag.

He opened the top, looked inside and examined the outside. "Wow, some nice bag!" he said. "Your dad's rundown old thing looks like hell, in comparison." Then, he noticed that the bag's interior stopped two inches short of the bottom.

He frowned. "What's this about?"

Sands suddenly felt lightheaded and scared. *What was he supposed to say?* He decided to live dangerously.

"It's a cushioned bottom," he said. "To make sure we don't break anything, like aftershave bottles, or damage equipment by setting it down too hard."

The guard looked at him skeptically.

"Hey," Sands continued. "You've seen my dad's bag. It didn't get like that without a lot of help from him! We barbers are notorious for banging them up."

The guard considered that for a moment and smiled. "Makes sense to me. Here," he added, picking up the bag and tossing it back to Sands. "Put it on the conveyor belt, and then walk through the arch."

Sands did as he was told, but when he was halfway through the arch, the buzzer went off. "Oh, shit" he muttered to himself.

He stretched his arms out, waiting for the guard with the wand to come over and scan him again. When the guard reached him, he smiled and shook his head, as if to say, 'Gotcha, fool!' Then, to Sands' surprise, he reached his arm out and unfastened Tony's wrist watch. "A bit absent-minded today, huh?"

"I sure seem to be," Sands sighed.

"Gather your stuff together and Jack will escort you to the judge's chambers."

Sands smiled "Thanks. Will do."

Moments later, Sands had all his items back together, and Jack, the guard who had checked his belongings, took him to Judge Farnsworth's chambers on the second floor. When they arrived, he opened the door with a key and led Sands inside. "The judge likes to have his hair cut in this chair," he said, tapping a leather-lined and padded black wooden chair.

"You can put your floor cover underneath it and use these outlets," he said, pointing to a bank of sockets on the lower wall. "The judge will be in here any minute."

"OK. Thanks," Sands said.

"No problem."

When the guard left the room, Sands crossed himself once and breathed a heavy sigh of relief.

Chapter 25

At 1:00 p.m., as he always did, Judge Farnsworth declared a one-hour lunch recess. When he arrived back in chambers, he thought, for a moment, that he had been transported back thirty years in time. There, standing before him, was his good friend Tony, looking half his age! Sands saw the confused look on the judge's face and, smiled, extending his hand.

"Hi, Your Honor," he said, "I'm Tony Jr. I treated Pops and a friend to a charter fishing trip today, so he asked me to fill in. I hope you don't mind."

"No, no. Not at all," Judge Farnsworth said, shaking his hand warmly. "It's a pleasure to meet you! You know, you are the spitting image of your dad at your age."

"Yeah, I know," Sands said, smiling, as he showed Judge Farnsworth to his seat. "It's uncanny, Pops says. But I always tell him I'm a lot better looking than he was. I say, 'You may have looked good, back then, Pops, but not *this* good!'"

The two shared a good laugh.

Sands fluffed the plastic smock, spread it out in front of the judge and then fastened the collar around his neck. "Don't worry, Your Honor," he said. "I know exactly what you like. Dad gave me detailed instructions—right down to the Vitalis®."

"Are you working with your dad now?" Judge Farnsworth asked.

"Yeah," I used to have my own place downtown. But I sold it several years ago." Tony Jr. brushed the Judge's hair and sprayed it with water in preparation for the razor cut.

"What happened?" the judge asked, "Did the neighborhood change?"

"No, my wife and I split up, and it wasn't pretty. Big custody fight. I ran up a lot of legal bills, and they had to be paid."

"I'm sorry to hear that," the Judge said. "Who represented you?"

"Jerry Doyle, of Doyle, Dubney and Fastow," Tony Jr. said, starting to lightly apply the razor blade to the tips of the judge's hair, as instructed.

"What kind of fees did you run up with him?" the judge asked.

"Thirty-five thou."

"Wow, that's a lot of money! How did he do by you?"

"Not too bad. I had a complicated case and we did all right in the end. I got joint custody of my little girl, and that meant a lot.

Sands kept cutting and combing the Judge's hair. In a few minutes, he was done. He pulled out a mirror and gave the judge a good look.

"Just like your old man," Judge Farnsworth said.

"Thanks."

Now, Sands opened his bag again and brought out the Vitalis and the scalp-massaging unit. "I've got a special treat for you today, Your Honor," Sands said. He waved a small pump sprayer around the judge's head and Farnsworth smelled a refreshing burst of vanilla.

"What's that?" he asked.

"Aroma therapy, to heighten the relaxing effects of the massage. It's also a muscle relaxant. I'm going to spray some on your neck to make the massage even more soothing. OK?"

"Sure," Judge Farnsworth said, as Sands spritzed the solution all over his neck.

"Pops told me you're an opera buff?"

"Sure am."

"He said your favorite opera is La traviata. Did I get that right?"

"Yeah."

"Well, I've got a special, Quadraplex recording of it that you're gonna love. I'll put the head phones on you while I massage your scalp and shoulders. It's incredible—extremely relaxing."

"Great," the Judge said with a smile. He closed his eyes as Sands placed the headphones over his ears. The music began with a richness he had never heard before.

"This is wonderful," the judge said. "Your dad's going to have to step up his game!" Then, he felt a slight pinch at his neck. "Ouch!"

"Oh, sorry, Your Honor," Sands said, putting the cap back on the syringe and burying it in his pocket. "I think the massage unit must have pinched you."

"That's all right," the judge said. "I'm fine now."

Slowly the music grew even deeper and richer in intensity as the massage unit began working the judge's shoulders. Then, a soothing voice spoke to him out of the music, a voice he didn't recognize, but a voice he enjoyed listening to, nonetheless. The voice promised to take him on a brief, refreshing journey to a wonderful place created by the music. It told him many things. And it promised he would remember none of them. But it also told him he would be making the journey again, very soon, and that it would seem as real as real could be.

Sands released the paper neck guard and began applying powder to the judge's neck with the whisk brush. Judge Farnsworth opened his eyes brightly.

"My God," he said, "that was refreshing! What an excellent rendition of La traviata. It was extraordinary!"

"You fell asleep," Sands said. "I wasn't sure you liked it."

"Oh, no, it was marvelous," the Judge said, as Sands brushed the rest of his cut hair off the smock and onto the floor. He removed the smock, splashed the judge's cheeks with a little aftershave, and then began sweeping up.

Judge Farnsworth picked up the mirror and looked his haircut over once more.

"You're definitely your father's son," Farnsworth said, primping a little. "Be sure to give him my best."

"I will, Your Honor."

Then, the judge stood up, slipped twenty-five dollars into Sand's hand, and walked to where his judicial robe was hanging next to the door. He put it back on and smiled. "I haven't felt this refreshed in ages," he said. "It's like I just slept eight hours!"

Then, he opened the door to return to the courtroom. "Tell your dad next Friday, same time, same place, OK?"

"You bet, Your Honor." he said.

After Farnsworth left, Sands emptied his dustpan into the trash, put away his remaining tools, zipped up his bag and was on his way.

Chapter 26

Martin, as requested, arrived at Swindell's office ten minutes early for the Saturday morning settlement conference. Swindell greeted him at the door. He was dressed, informally, in khaki trousers, loafers, and a navy-blue polo shirt, and he was smoking a Meerschaum pipe rather than one of his customary cigars.

Swindell smiled broadly at the sight of his client and ushered him inside. "Mahr-tin, thanks for gettin' here early," he said, vigorously shaking Martin's hand. Then, with a twinkle in his eye, he added. "I think we may be in the home stretch."

Swindell led Martin to a small conference room toward the back of the office's first floor. "Sit anywhere you like," he said. "I'm makin' coffee. Want some?"

"Yeah," Martin said. "That would be nice."

"They blinked first!" Swindell had proclaimed in the message he had left on Martin's cell phone the previous day. "Your wife's attorney would like to meet with us tomorrow, at eleven, in my office, to discuss a new settlement offer! This is huge, Mahr-tin! Call me as soon as you get this message."

Martin had replayed Swindell's message several times while he sat in his motel room, considering his options.... He had wondered why Swindell sounded so excited on the phone. *I have to go. Otherwise, it would look suspicious. But I can't seriously entertain settling the case – not now – not after accepting Brooks' group's help.*

Martin wasn't looking forward to the meeting for another reason: He didn't expect Katie's attorney to propose any 'major' concessions. *Katie has behaved poorly and tried to take advantage of me from the beginning. Why should that change now?*

When Swindell returned to the conference room, he held two mugs of coffee in his hands. Each had a metal spoon sticking out over the top. He placed one down at his seat and the other in front of Martin. Then, he emptied his pockets, tossing assorted sweeteners, napkins, and powdered cream packets in a pile in the center of the table.

"Help yourself, Mahr-tin," he said, taking a long sip of his coffee. "Here's where I think we stand. Beverly West says she wants to save all of us the cost of litigatin' this case by comin' up with a reasonable settlement package. She also commented on how 'nicely' she thought you and your estranged wife had worked together regardin' young Justin's birthday. She said it could be a 'foundation' for buildin' a new spirit of cooperation.

"In other words," he added, adjusting his seat to a more comfortable height, "your wife's worried about suddenly havin' to pay to litigate the domestic violence case, a cost she never anticipated.

"And since you took such an extreme stand," he smiled, raised his eyebrows, and nodded, "and we never stepped in with an offer of our own, they're getting' desperate.

"This case could be over by Noon today. You may get a much better deal than they originally offered and a better outcome than we could hope for, even if we were to try the case and prevail. I take my hat off to you, Mahr-tin Silkwood!"

Martin smiled noncommittally.

Swindell was particularly eager to settle the case after learning, earlier that morning, about the existence of some potentially damaging new evidence that his paralegal had picked up on a visit to the police department. He hadn't seen the documents yet, so he saw no reason to share that information with his client. *"Besides, I don't want him second-guessin' himself today. It could undermine his perceived bargainin' power."*

Swindell leaned forward in his chair and looked Martin dead in the eye. "So, Mahr-tin, what's it gonna take to get you to sign off on a deal today?"

Martin stared back and shrugged. "I have no idea, Mr. Swindell. I guess I'd like to be treated fairly, that's all."

Swindell grimaced. "Well, what does that mean? What is fair treatment, in your opinion?"

"Why don't we just wait and see what she's prepared to offer?"

Swindell tilted his head and studied his client, while Martin took a long sip from his coffee mug. "In my experience, Mahr-tin, it's always best to enter a negotiation knowin' what you want – or, at least, what you will accept."

"You're probably right, but I'm still trying to figure that out. I think we should just give her a chance to make her case and then take it from there."

At that moment, Swindell's doorbell buzzed. "I guess that will have to do," he said, standing up, "as it appears she's here."

Swindell excused himself and went to the front door to greet his guest. Moments later, he returned, following behind West.

She was a trim, heavily made up woman, in her early fifties, with frosted blonde hair, worn in a page-boy style, and cold gray eyes. The eyes, Martin thought, looked even more intimidating than they had in the picture on Brook's computer screen. West wore a pale blue running suit. Her jacket was partially unzipped, revealing a white cotton shirt and a pearl necklace. She carried a black leather satchel over

her left shoulder and a matching, pale blue leather Coach®
bag in her right hand.

"Bev," Swindell said, once they were both inside the
conference room, "this is Mahr-tin Silkwood. Mahr-tin,
Beverly West, your wife's attorney.

Martin stood up and extended his hand. "Ms. West," he
said.

She flashed him the briefest of smiles. "Mr. Silkwood.
Pleased to make your acquaintance."

Her handshake was firm – perhaps a little too firm.

"Have a seat Bev, and make yourself comfortable,"
Swindell said, as he placed a mug of hot tea in front of her.
"It's Earl Grey, your favorite."

"Thank you, Chester." West surveyed the table with its
clutter of sugar and artificial sweetener packets, napkins and
powdered creamer and the slightest hint of a smirk formed
on her lips. She sat down at the head of the table, with
Swindell to her left and Martin to her right. She looked at
them both, in turn.

"First, I want to thank you gentlemen for agreeing to
meet with me this morning. I also want to apologize for my
outfit, but it is Saturday and my next stop is the gym!"

"Don't be silly," Swindell said. "You look just fine,
Bev."

Beverly West lifted and dunked her tea bag several
times. Then, she squeezed out any remaining tea by placing
the tea bag on the spoon and wrapping the string tightly
around it. Afterward, she placed the spoon and the spent

bag on one of the available napkins that she had slid beside her mug. She closed her eyes and took a sip.

"Mmm. Very good, Chester," she said. Then, she turned and stared wide-eyed at Martin. "I imagine, Mr. Silkwood, that Chester has informed you about the reason for this meeting, today?"

"Yes," Martin said.

"Good. Let me start by setting some ground rules that your attorney and I have gone over. Everything discussed in this room, today, Mr. Silkwood, will be considered 'privileged' information, meaning no party to this law suit can use anything revealed in our discussions as evidence in court, should this case still go to trial. Do you understand?"

Martin nodded.

"Good," West said. "As I told your attorney yesterday, I was impressed...and inspired...by how well you and your wife worked together, these past couple of days, to help your son with his birthday party and behavioral issues.

"Consequently, I now think it would be counter-productive and, quite possibly, inappropriate to litigate this matter—especially if that might undo some of the newly established goodwill that seems to exist between the two of you."

"I'm surprised to hear you say that," Martin said.

Swindell raised an eyebrow.

"Really?" West asked.

"Yes, because Katie and I always have gotten along well, particularly in matters involving our children and their welfare."

West took a deep breath. "Well, I'm sure you have at various points in the past, Mr. Silkwood, but—"

"No, Ms. West. That has not changed. At least, it hasn't changed where I am concerned. Has Katie told you anything different?"

West's expression went blank and Swindell stepped in. "Mahr-tin, I know you were offended by the nature of some of the charges brought against you in this case, but now is not the time to air your grievances, and Ms. West is not allowed – and quite frankly, would be ill-advised – to disclose the nature of her conversations with your wife to you.

"I suggest that we let her get to the heart of the matter: the proposed settlement that she has come to discuss with us this mornin'. O.K?"

"OK," Martin grunted.

"Fine," West said, regaining her composure. "As you both know, our original offer was to give Mr. Silkwood dinner with the children one night a week and visitation every other weekend. We are now prepared to alter that arrangement and, in addition, to offer him up to one week's visitation a month during the school year and up to five weeks with the kids over the course of the summer."

Swindell perked up. "Well, that's certainly a step in the right direction, Mahr-tin, wouldn't you agree?"

Martin stared at West. "What about vacations during the school year? Right now, it sounds like Katie would have the kids for all their vacations. Are you willing to split those up evenly?"

West smiled. "You've raised a valid point. That was an oversight on our part, I'm sure. I would be happy to work out something along those lines with your wife. I could even call her and get her agreement to specific terms before we break up this meeting, today, if that's what it will take to get us all on the same page."

Swindell nodded. "I think that's the kind of gesture that could go a long way toward helpin' us reach an agreement. Mahr-tin, what do you think?"

Martin continued to stare at West. "What about the other stipulations contained in your original proposal?" he asked. "Are you still expecting me to pay the full mortgage, and must I still agree not to 'set foot in the house, for any reason,' over the course of the next three years?'"

West cleared her throat. "Well, Mr. Silkwood, as far as the mortgage goes, you *are* the primary breadwinner in the family, are you not? So, I don't think that will be changing. In addition, your wife still wants you to agree not to enter the house, at any time or for any reason, during the next three years."

"If we work all these issues out," Martin continued, "then is Katie prepared to drop all the domestic violence and abuse charges?"

"Yes," West said.

"So, why would she continue to insist on a stipulation that implies she's afraid of me and that I'm a danger to her and the kids, when I'm not? I don't understand the logic behind that."

"I think your assumption may be wrong, in this instance," West explained. "I think Katie put that item in the original agreement, not out of fear of you, but because she wants to move on with her life without any interference from you."

Martin stared at West, letting what she had just said sink in. "Well, I'm not going to agree to such terms if I'm paying the full cost of the mortgage, including the part that covers her accommodations."

"He's got a point, Bev," Swindell interjected. "After all, Mrs. Silkwood is a nurse. She has a good job, and she certainly should be capable of paying her own share of the housing costs."

West had removed a pad and pen from her satchel and was now busily writing down notes. "I can certainly bring that up to her before I leave here today," she said.

"What about the stipulation that Katie and I agree that it's OK to start seeing other people immediately?" Martin asked.

West looked up from her pad and smiled. "I would think you would embrace that idea, Mr. Silkwood. Don't you want to move on with your life?"

"I'm not the one who wants a divorce, Ms. West; Katie is. I wanted us to see a marriage counselor and to work out our differences."

"Oh, I see."

"So," Martin continued, "I'm not really inclined to agree to that term."

"I think that's something you and Mr. Swindell should discuss among yourselves," West said. "But I don't believe your wife is prepared to concede that point."

"I have three additional issues I'd like to see addressed in any agreement I'd be willing to sign," Martin said.

West looked surprised and forced a smile. "OK," she said, glancing at Swindell, who looked puzzled and was now leaning forward, intently, in his seat.

"First, I want all of my custodial rights restored. The judge, in his *ex-parte* ruling, gave Katie sole custody of the children, isn't that right?"

West jotted down a few notes on her pad and then looked up. "Yes. That is correct, Mr. Silkwood. But, and Chester, please help me out here, we could state, in our agreement, which the judge ultimately must agree to, that a primary condition for settling the case would be that both parents share legal custody of the children. I think that's what you really mean. That would give you both an equal voice, and standing, in resolving any major issues regarding your children's lives. You would both have to agree, in each instance, before any definitive action could be taken, such as: changing schools, permitting certain medical treatments and making any significant changes of address. (Another way of saying this is that you would share full and equal parenting rights.) To share joint physical custody, however, would require that you both agree to have the children live with you approximately fifty percent of the time. I'm not even sure that would be possible, given the travel-related demands of your work."

"Actually," Martin said, "I'm only out of town twenty to twenty-five percent of the time. It could work."

Swindell interjected. "So, Bev, if I'm hearin' you correctly, you and your client are now willin' to have my client's legal custody restored. Is that correct?"

"Yes, Chester, I feel comfortable speaking on Katie's behalf on that one."

"Why not joint physical custody as well?" Martin insisted. "I love my kids every bit as much as Katie does, and I want to be able to see them as often as possible. Why should I accept a secondary role in their lives?"

West sat up straight in her seat and cupped her hands. "Well, Mr. Silkwood the degree of shared physical custody has other ramifications—"

"You mean, it could affect how much child support Katie would receive, right?" Martin asked, bristling.

"Yes."

Swindell cleared his throat. "Well, Bev, suppose my client was willin' to state that he would pay full child support, based on his proportionate share of the parent's combined income. Wouldn't that solve the problem?"

Even under a liberally applied layer of concealer, West's face was starting to show some color. "Well, Chester, as you know, those conditions could change…."

"So, it all comes down to money. Is that it?" Martin glared.

"No, of course not," West faltered. "But that is a consideration, Mr. Silkwood. I mean the children's best interests—"

"Do you really believe my wife is the only one who cares about what's best for our kids?" Martin's voice had suddenly grown loud. "I'm not stupid, Ms. West. I understand that Katie wants me to pay for her upkeep, in the form of her fair share of the monthly mortgage payment, even while she continues to see some guy behind my back.

"She wants to have her cake and to eat it, too. Well, she's not going to get everything she wants, unless she can convince a judge to give it to her after a full and fair hearing, in open court."

West stared at Martin, sizing him up. "A court case, as I'm sure Mr. Swindell has told you," she said firmly and deliberately, "is a costly and not always fair undertaking with results that can prove to be far from just or certain. I requested this meeting, this morning, Mr. Silkwood, in an attempt to spare you and your wife the need to bear those costs and from dealing with the uncertainty of how the court might rule. It goes without saying," she continued, her voice growing steadily louder, "that you are free to reject our offer at any time and to take your chances in court."

"I just may have to do that," Martin said, staring her in the eye.

After a moment of uncomfortable silence, Swindell spoke up. "Well, let's not make any hasty decisions, Mahr-tin. I think Ms. West and your wife are bein' surprisin'ly flexible, so far. We may have a few points that we need to hammer out further, but let's not abandon all the progress we've made just because every single item doesn't line up precisely the way you want.

"You said you had three issues that you needed resolved to settle this matter, but so far, we have heard only one. What are the other two?"

Martin took a deep breath. "The second is relatively simple and doable, I think. I want all of the domestic violence and abuse charges that I face expunged from the court record and for that to be accomplished without me having to sign a Consent Decree."

"We certainly can request that," West said, "but the judge has to agree. Consequently, there's no guarantee that he will agree or that you will ultimately get what you want."

"But what if we make the settlement agreement contingent on the judge satisfying that condition?" Martin asked, as he turned to face Swindell.

"Why yes, Mahr-tin," Swindell said. "We certainly could do that."

"That's problematic for us," West said, "because both parties would still need to come to court fully prepared to try the case. That means you and your wife, Mr. Silkwood, would still incur a large portion of the projected court costs. If the judge refuses to accept any of those pre-conditions, we also would have to go forward with the trial."

"Bev, haven't you already incurred most of those prep costs?" Swindell asked. "I mean, the trial date is fast upon us. I don't see how what my client is askin' for affects either party's pocketbook. What it *could* do is save them both a full day of litigation costs, but that's it. The only thin' the contingency clause does require is for all of us to make a court appearance."

"I would have to consult with my client on that point and get back to you," West said.

"What's your final issue, Mahr-tin?" Swindell asked.

"The final item is personal," Martin said, turning left to look West in the eye. "I want Katie to write a formal letter of apology to me for having wrongfully brought domestic violence and spousal abuse charges against me."

West looked aghast. "You mean you want that written into the settlement agreement?"

Swindell looked at Martin, frowned and subtly shook his head from side to side.

"Yes, I do."

"That is NOT going to happen!" West said, slamming her fists down on the table and turning to face Swindell. "Is he serious, Chester? Did you know about this? He wants my client, in essence, to declare publicly that she has lied about him in bringing this court action. And he wants her to agree to do that in a document that the court *must* review. He's asking her to violate her Fifth Amendment protection against self-incrimination and to invite the court to formally charge her with perjury!"

Now, Swindell was blushing. "No, I—Mahr-tin, are you serious?"

Martin sat at the table with his arms folded and slowly nodded his head.

"I'm sure he's kiddin' Beverly," Swindell insisted. Then, he raised his voice. "Mahr-tin, tell Miss West you're not serious about this!"

Martin sat perfectly still. "But I am," he said.

"I've had enough," West said. She stood up abruptly, gathered her pad and pen and threw them into her satchel. Then, she picked up her bags and took one step toward the door.

"Now, Bev—" Swindell stammered.

She turned, locked eyes with him and cut him off. "This is the last straw, Chester. I came here in good faith, *in good faith,* to attempt to settle this matter. I was willing to compromise further to give this man most of what he wanted. And this is the thanks I get? I should have known better!"

Swindell's jaw dropped. He looked up at her forlornly, not sure of what to say.

West sneered and turned away. She walked over to the conference room door, opened it a crack and then paused for a second, turning to look at them both one last time. "I hope you know what you've done, Mr. Silkwood. I'll see you gentlemen in court!" Then, she slammed the door behind her and was gone.

No one spoke for what seemed like minutes. Martin took another sip of coffee and avoided making eye contact with Swindell, who sat opposite him glaring and shaking his head in disbelief.

"What in God's name is wrong with you?" he finally asked.

"Pardon me?" Martin said, barely hiding his scorn.

"You heard me," Swindell continued. "Beverly West just offered you every domestic violence respondent's version of a wet dream: no trial, joint legal custody, a fairly generous visitation schedule with room to expand it, reduced child and spousal support costs, and a possible agreement to make expungin' the charges against you a pre-condition for settlin' the case.

"That's a grand slam home run outcome for most respondent cases like yours – even the ones that go to trial and find for the respondent. She was offerin' all of that to you without the expense, bother or worry, of goin' before a judge. And what did you do? You gave her a resoundin' slap in the face! She didn't leave here disheartened and demoralized, Mahr-tin; she left angry and pissed off...at *you!* She's back in the fight, now, and that just makes my job even tougher."

"I'm sorry," Martin said, "but I can't get over the fact that my wife got the upper hand in this case by lying, and that the system allows it. I cannot pretend to feel grateful to her for giving me back things that she unfairly took in the first place!"

"You put your hurt feelin's and pride above reason and pragmatism, Mahr-tin. And that's never a wise course of action. The result: In this case, a golden opportunity —a pre-trial settlement package unlike any I've ever seen before—has been lost to you, forever."

Martin recoiled at the finality of Swindell's remark, as a familiar, but unpleasant, queasy feeling began to overtake him. "Forever? Aren't you exaggerating a bit, Mr. Swindell? We can still settle this case. I understand cases can settle even after both sides rest, right up to the moment before the judge or jury delivers its verdict!"

Swindell shook his head in disgust. "You should stick to what you know, Mahr-tin: accountin' work. Yes, cases *can* settle late, but it takes two to tango. Settlements only occur when both sides have an interest in settlin'. The closer you get to the conclusion of a trial the less reason there usually is.

"Consider what was motivatin' your wife and her attorney today: They wanted to avoid the costs associated with a trial. With each passin' hour of a court case, that motivation disappears as the real court costs are incurred.

"The other reason for settlin' is the uncertainty of the outcome. Your wife's attorney already offered you ninety percent of all the positive outcomes you could ever hope to achieve in a case like this, and you said 'No!'"

"In court, the reality is that the worse the case looks for one side, the better it usually looks for the other. Where's the motivation to settle in that? There is none!"

Swindell shook his head, looking like he had just bitten into a lemon. "When you arrived here this mornin', Mahr-tin, I was ready to break out the champagne and celebrate your incredible good fortune. Now," he said, looking squarely at his client, "I'm thinkin' sacramental wine might be more appropriate. We can drink it while we pray we don't get fucked."

Chapter 27

The Cider Mill Farms party room was a scene of pure chaos as Justin, his friends, his little sister, Monica, and several other guests' younger siblings ran around in circles in the open center of the room, screeching and screaming at each other.

At the far end, opposite the door, Gloria Cheswick, Dougy's mom, and Esther Finch busied themselves around picnic benches draped in red-and-white checkered table cloths. They were placing plastic forks and spoons, soda cups, and paper dessert plates at each seat.

"My God," Esther said, stopping to clasp her ears. "What a racket! Can you imagine what this place will sound like when the kids get done eating their ice cream and cake?"

"Sure can," Gloria said, as she placed her final plate down. It was blue-trimmed, like all the others. A curved blue headline above a picture of two prancing ponies boldly announced, 'Happy Birthday, Justin!'

Then, Gloria pulled a pair of Styrofoam ear plugs out of her pocket and held them up for Esther to see. "That's why I brought these babies with me."

"Smart lady. How much for the pair?"

Gloria shook her head. "Unh uh. I wouldn't part with these for a year's income. Right now, it's every girl for herself!"

"I'll remember that," Esther said. "And next time, I'll bring my own!"

"That a girl!"

The two chuckled to themselves.

The Cider Mill Farm staff had configured the party tables so that they formed an enormous "u" at the head of the room. Justin and his guests shared the seats in the center, while parents, family and siblings sat on either flank. Esther and Gloria stood in the center of the "u" and surveyed the scene. At a kitchen counter on the far-right hand side of the room, Katie and Eddie were methodically scooping chocolate and vanilla ice cream into plastic bowls.

"I'm so proud of Katie," Gloria said, watching them.

"Oh? Why?"

"Just look at her. I'm amazed at how well she's holding up under all this stress."

"What stress, honey?"

"Well," Gloria said, suddenly stammering and glancing sideways at Esther, "her brave step in seeking the restraining order against Marty, for one. He's such a hothead!"

"Really?"

Gloria turned and looked Esther in the eye. "Well, certainly *you* know. You're her mother."

"I know nothing of the kind. Right now, I wouldn't be putting too much stock in what Katie says."

Gloria scoffed. "That Marty has sure got you fooled!"

"No. I'm not saying he's perfect. Who among us is? But he is no wife beater, and he is no bully, either."

"Esther, you take my breath away!"

"Marty's a decent man and a loving father. Do you know what he did to help out today?"

Gloria scrunched her face and turned away. "Nothing that I can see. But look at Eddie, over there. He's so helpful. Such a good, caring friend to Katie."

"The only thing Eddie's been doing is helping himself to Katie. Big, generous scoops of her."

"How can you talk that way about your own daughter?"

"My problem: I can spot a lie at thirty paces."

Gloria folded her arms and shook her head. "I can't listen to you defending Marty like this, particularly in light of his recent behavior."

Esther crossed in front of her. "Gloria, there wouldn't even be a party today, if it weren't for Marty. Amid all these allegations Katie has hurled at him, he agreed to speak with Justin last night, to calm him down. The boy misses his daddy terribly. He had been acting out and he threatened not to come to his own birthday party unless Marty could be here."

"Katie told me he only spoke to Justin so he could wangle his way into today's party. She said he gets to spend ten minutes talking to Justin by Skype and watching him blow out the candles. He's trying to steal the show and make himself the center of attention."

Esther raised her eyebrows and shook her head. "I need some fresh air," she said. Then she started to walk toward the door.

"Esther," Gloria called after her. "Forgive me, but you're the one who has been bamboozled. Katie's attorney proposed an incredibly generous settlement to Marty this very morning, and your darling son-in-law sent her packing!"

"What?" Esther turned around. She had a concerned look on her face. She took a hesitant step toward Gloria. "How generous are we talking about?"

"Based on my personal experience," Gloria said, "It was unprecedented."

The two were now standing toe-to-toe.

"Katie told me in confidence. I'm really not supposed to discuss this with *anyone,* but I'll tell you, Esther, if you promise not to repeat a word of it to anyone, including Katie."

Esther nodded.

"Beverly West gave Marty everything he could have hoped for...and more: joint-legal custody, reduced child support, and an offer to make expunging his record of the abuse charges a requirement of the settlement. To me it sounded like a complete capitulation."

"And Marty's reaction?"

Gloria knitted her brow in annoyance. "I don't know the specifics. He made more demands, things that Beverly West would not even consider agreeing to, and when he couldn't get his way on everything, Marty apparently said, 'No deal.' Beverly is livid. And, when your daughter called me earlier today, she was a total wreck. That's really what I'm so impressed with: her ability to keep it all together, today, for Justin."

"I don't understand," Esther said, a puzzled look on her face. "The other day, Katie told me she and her attorney had worked out a very generous settlement offer for Marty and that there would be no trial."

Gloria smiled when she saw the confused look on Esther's face. "You've been out of the loop then, haven't you? Marty apparently didn't think that offer was all that generous. He rejected it on the spot, and he said he'd see them in court. And his side never came back with a counter offer."

Esther stood there, wide-eyed, as she tried to absorb everything she had just heard. Tears started to well in her eyes, so she looked down for a moment and slowly bobbed her head, as she tried to marshal her strength. When she had regained her composure, she looked up and smiled, faintly at her daughter's friend.

"Gloria, this is deeply troubling news. Deeply. I'm just so disappointed...in them both." Then, she lifted her head a notch higher. "But Marty did not start this; Katie did. And situations like this are why we warn children not to play with matches: They just might get burned!"

Chapter 28

Martin sat at his laptop in his hotel room at 1:55 p.m. Saturday, with his Skype account open. He was waiting for Katie's call.

Before the blow up with Beverly West that morning, Swindell had told him the good news: Katie had agreed to honor Martin's request. Swindell said that Justin would be blowing out the candles at around 2:00 p.m. and that Katie would call him a few minutes before. She also had insisted that the call not last beyond ten minutes.

"I don't want this to become a side show and take the attention off Justin on his big day," she had warned.

Within a minute, the Skype account began ringing. Martin forced a smile and clicked on the link for a video conversation. The screen instantly filled with Katie's image. Her smile immediately shifted into an angry scowl.

"Hello," Martin said.

"Oh," Katie said, with a marked lack of enthusiasm, as she knitted her brow. "Hi, Marty." She continued sternly, under her breath, as she shook her head from side to side. "Beverly West told me about your awful, insane behavior this morning. I hope you're proud of yourself!" Then, she raised her voice loud enough for everyone to hear, "It's so nice to see you!"

"Yeah," he said.

Katie held the computer to her face as she walked through a crowd of family members and friends, some of whom waived awkwardly at Martin, when they saw him on the screen. He waved back.

"Justin," Katie said with feigned enthusiasm, "guess who's waiting to talk with you on Skype?"

"Daddy?!" Justin exclaimed.

"That's right!" she said, as she turned the laptop away from her and placed it on top of a red-and-white checkered table cloth, facing a brightly lit cake. Justin was seated behind it. His face glimmered in the yellow light of a handful of birthday candles dancing before him.

Justin broke into an enormous smile at the sight of his father.

"Hi, Mr. Birthday Boy!" Martin said. "Having fun?"

"Yes, now that you're here, Daddy!" Justin announced.

Just then, Martin heard a familiar, high-pitched squeal. "Daddy, Daddy! Me, too!"

A tall, muscular man with hairy arms and a black moustache, who was standing to one side behind Justin, bent down and picked Monica up. "Here you go, honey," he said, lifting her up behind Justin. "Can you see your daddy now?"

Monica beamed. "Oh, Daddy!" she said. "I love you!"

"I love you, too, honey!" Martin said, returning her smile. "Don't you look, pretty! Who's the nice man holding you up, dear?"

The room suddenly grew quiet.

"That's Mommy's friend, Uncle Eddie."

So, Martin thought, steaming. This is the other guy, the reason I'm in a motel room on Skype, instead of at Cider Mill Farms, celebrating my son's birthday with his friends and my family. Katie has no shame!

Martin wanted to tell Eddie to 'get the hell out of there,' but he wasn't about to give Katie the satisfaction...or ruin Justin's day.

"That was a very nice thing for him to do," he said flatly.

Uncle Eddie smiled awkwardly and nodded.

At that, Katie rushed over and lifted Monica out of Eddie's hands. She gave him a stern glance and moved Monica to the side until she was just out of camera range.

"OK, everyone," she said, regrouping. "It's time to sing Happy Birthday!"

Everyone, including Martin, serenaded Justin. When the song was over, Justin took a deep breath and prepared to blow out his candles.

"Hold on, tiger," Katie said. "Don't you want to make a wish?"

Justin stopped in his tracks and looked right at his father. "Yes," he said. "I want Daddy to come home now and never go away again!"

Martin smiled and held a finger to his lips. "You're not supposed to say your wish out loud, Son. Just whisper it quietly to yourself, OK?"

"Sure, Daddy," Justin said. He closed his eyes for a moment, deep in thought, as his lips moved ever so slightly. Then, he opened them again.

"All right," Martin said, "go for it!"

Justin took a deep, deep breath and blew, moving his head from candle to candle. Six of the seven candles went out right away, but the one closest to him did not. He found some extra wind and blew hard, turning almost red, as the candle flickered several times and then died.

Everyone erupted into a big cheer as Justin's smile returned to his face. He crossed his fingers. "Daddy, I hope my wish comes true!"

Martin smiled back and wiped away a tear. "Me, too, Son. Me, too!"

Chapter 29

At ten thirty-five Sunday night, Judge Farnsworth squeezed his wife, Alice's, hand lightly and rose from the couch. The baseball game was now in the bottom of the seventh inning, and the Orioles were beating the Angels five-to-two at Camden Yards.

"Going up, dear?" Alice Farnsworth asked. She was sitting in her nightgown with one eye still fixed on the game.

"Yep, I've got a full caseload tomorrow."

"OK, sweetie. I'll be up soon."

The judge smiled at this fifty-eight-year-old died-in-the-wool Orioles fan, a woman who only discovered the game after their boys went off to college. "It soothes me at night," she had told him several years earlier. "It's so slow paced, most of the time, like watching grass grow. But then, look out! Someone gets something started and, wow, everything changes!"

He was glad they could enjoy this activity together.

The judge walked up the steps to bed and thought the same thoughts he mused upon every evening at this time. *How lucky I am to be sixty-two years old and still to be able to sleep the sleep of the just.* He was glad he had taken their offer thirty years earlier and moved over to the bench – and proud that he had been elevated, twenty years later, to administrative judge, overseeing the entire Maryland District Court system. He thought about all the cases he had tried—all the people he had helped. And he looked forward to the next day's excitement, when the husbands of the women he had protected the previous week would come before him to explain themselves.

Thank God, Alice and I have created a good home for our sons and us. And, thank God, we made it through the tough years and have always managed to treat each other with respect. He wondered why it had become so difficult for his sons' generation to live together in peace, and why married couples today seemed so incapable of controlling their anger and honoring their commitments. He continued to think about this while he brushed his teeth, gargled, and washed his face with a cold washcloth. When he was done, he knelt by the side of his bed, said his prayers, and then, as usual, fell fast asleep almost as soon as his head hit the pillow.

At about 4:45 a.m., an image of terror flashed through Judge Farnsworth's mind. For a brief instant, he dreamed that he was peering over the south lip of the Grand Canyon and had found an abyss, where he had expected to see a gradually descending donkey trail. The image was triggered by the Nano probe that Tony Jr. had injected into the judge's neck two days earlier. Since then, the probe had made its way through his heart and then onward to the Amygdala, a small, almond-shaped ganglion located at the base of his brain. Once there, it drove a single Nano fiber deep into the nerves, enabling it to tap, control and recall some of the brain's most powerful—and vivid— emotionally charged experiences. The probe was now initiating a scheduled level-eight terror-impulse cascade. Each time it fired, Judge Farnsworth briefly saw himself staring over, and then falling into, the abyss. And with each repetition, the experience grew more intense. The third time, the judge's eyes began moving rapidly back and forth under his eyelids as his mind's eye exploded with pre-programmed sounds and images that rapidly assembled themselves into a vivid and compelling dream narrative.

He was terrified. The knocking continued: Three times loudly on the front door, then silence. Then, three times more. Judge Farnsworth could feel the door hinges rattle. He could hear the doorframe creak. He could feel tiny, microscopic pieces of wood splintering on the face of the door under the constant pounding...from the hand...with the flashlight...the black metal flashlight...crashing down....shattering the silence of sleep.

He was up now, barefoot on the cold floor panels, feeling his way toward the bedroom door. He turned to look back at the bed, to make sure Alice was OK, but Alice wasn't there.

Only his side of the bed had been disturbed. Hers remained folded down tight. Her pillows were fluffed and untouched. For some reason, the sight of her unused bed made him angry. Why? Where was she? He thought he should know the answer, but, if he did, he couldn't remember. Try! he said to himself. Try! Try! But no recollection came. He simply felt anger, fear, and confusion.

Farnsworth slowly descended the steps, the front door always in sight. As he reached the door, the pounding resumed. He felt the vibrations through his toes. The door buckled with each blow. Then, it returned to normal. With each blow, frost crept in from underneath. He was wearing his robe, even though he didn't remember putting it on. He wrapped it tightly around him as the pounding resumed.

"Open up, Your Honor!" a cold, harsh voice shouted. "Open up! It's time. It's time!" More frost rushed in under the door, chilling the tops of his feet.

"Who's there?" he asked, fearing Death. "Who's there?"

"Open up, Your Honor. You have to go!"

Eye to the peephole, the judge saw the image of Deputy Bert Taylor's distorted beefy cheeks and swollen belly. He turned the latch and drew back the door. In came the cold, rushing through him like a mountain stream, cutting him in half like a great steel sword, burning his hands like dry ice.

Deputy Taylor stepped forward, at attention. He was wearing black sunglasses. His face appeared edged in white frost. Expressionless. "It's time to go Your Honor. You cannot stay!" he said.

"This is my home!" the judge declared. "I'm in charge, here, and I'm staying put."

"No, Your Honor," a second deputy said, coming forward through the door. "You are not in charge—of anything. By order of the court." He handed the judge a stack of court papers. The judge immediately recognized the Temporary Restraining Order on top.

"Your wife, Alice Farnsworth, has sworn out an ex-parte petition against you," Deputy Taylor said. "She accuses you of …"

"Violence," the two deputies said, in unison.

"Assault."

"Physical and verbal abuse."

"She says you've raised your hand against her."

"Insulted her."

"Mistreated her."

"Ignored her."

"She cannot live with you anymore," the second deputy said. "And the court has ruled: You must go."

"Gather your belongings," Deputy Taylor said. "You have fifteen minutes, fifteen minutes, fifteen minutes."

Judge Farnsworth flipped through the order to see whom, from the court, would have dared sign it. All his fellow judges had signed. Furious, he turned to the last page of the petition, where his wife had listed her charges.

"He's an angry, scary man," he heard her scream as he read the words. "I'm afraid of what he might do. He's changed. He drinks. He breaks things. He terrifies me!"

Suddenly, Mrs. Farnsworth appeared in the doorway, still wearing her bathrobe. She approached him, stretched out her right hand and slapped him hard across the face. "I hate you," she hissed. "And you're going to pay. My attorney says you'll pay plenty. Get out! Get out! Get out!"

Judge Farnsworth touched his throbbing cheek. He was no longer in his front hallway, but miles away, standing barefoot on a cold, dark street, still in his robe. He held a small, hastily stuffed suitcase in his right hand. He felt lost, ashamed—and alone.

As he walked, he saw what looked like his sons' college dorm on his left. Then, he was sure he saw his sons in the window, looking out at him. When he turned to enter the building, three of his fellow district court Judges, in their judicial robes, suddenly appeared before him, blocking his way. *"You cannot see your sons,"* they said, in unison. *"You cannot speak to them either—not even by phone."*

Judge Farnsworth approached them and grabbed each, in turn, by the shoulders.

"Don't you know me?" he asked. *"Don't you recognize me? I'm your colleague!"*

"Yes," they said. *"We know exactly who you are,"* and for a moment—a brief moment—Judge Farnsworth felt relieved. *"You are...the Respondent,"* they said.

"No, I'm not!" he shouted. *"I'm a judge, just like you! It's me, Judge Farnsworth!"*

"Not anymore," they said, looking back at him without expression. *"Your wife, the Honorable Alice Farnsworth, who knows you better than anyone on earth, says you're the Respondent—and we must concur!"*

"This is an outrage!" he shouted. He turned back and continued down the street, walking past courthouse employees, several of whom no longer seemed to recognize him.

"You have scared your wife," one said.

"She fears for her life," chimed another.

"She counted on you."

"She depended on you."

"To be a man."

"And, just like a man, you let her down."

"This is insane!" the judge shouted to the heavens.

"No. This is the way it's done!" the people said. "You'll get your day in court...eventually."

Next, the judge found himself standing in the lobby of a local hotel. A bellhop came to show him to his room. They boarded an elevator, went down several levels, and stepped out onto a grimy, bare hallway. The bellhop led him to a door, which opened onto a broom closet with an unmade cot inside.

"This is where you'll stay," he told him.

"I can afford better," the judge said.

"Not anymore," his wife's disembodied voice shouted, echoing through the hallway. "Not anymore!"

Suddenly, it was Monday morning a week later, and the judge found himself in the district courthouse, still dressed in his pajamas and robe. The Clerk of Court walked by.

"Regina," he said, "It's me, Judge Farnsworth."

She turned and looked at him. "You're a disgrace," she said, "showing up here, like this. The judge won't like it."

He entered the courtroom and took a seat beside his lawyer, who was dressed to the nines in pinstripes, silk tie and patent leather shoes. Before them, a credit card machine sat on the desk. He tugged repeatedly at the attorney's right arm, but the attorney didn't respond. He tugged again. Still nothing. Finally, out of the corner of his mouth, the lawyer muttered, "If you want me, pay me. Judges don't like to make attorneys work for free, you know."

Judge Farnsworth slipped his credit card into the machine and ran the ink press across it. "$2,000" the payment line read.

"Your wife has made you a fine offer," the attorney said, again out of the corner of his mouth. "She'll let you live."

"I'll let you live a little longer," he heard his wife's voice say, "so you can pay me what you owe me."

"You lied!" he shouted back. "That's perjury."

"Prove it," she said. Then her attorney joined in. "Prove it."

Then the whole courtroom joined in. "Prove it!" they shouted.

"Take the deal," Alice's attorney said. "She'll let you speak with your sons once more before you die. Take the deal," he urged. "She'll let you have your things from the house. Take the deal! She'll even drop the charges...if you give her everything she wants."

"Take the deal," his attorney whispered, "Or she'll get everything!"

"Take the deal," Alice's attorney said, growing angry. "It's her final offer."

Just then, the court clerk entered the room. "All rise," he shouted, "the district court for Montgomery County, Maryland is now in session, the Honorable Michael J. Farnsworth presiding."

He looked up and saw himself, Judge Farnsworth, enter the courtroom. He was wearing his newly pressed judge's robe and his well-known somber expression.

"Your Honor," his wife's attorney said," I move for a dismissal. After all, we covered this matter last week."

"But I wasn't here then, Your Honor," Judge Farnsworth, the respondent, said.

"Objection!" his wife's attorney said.

"Sustained," the judge replied.

"My wife lied, Your Honor," Judge Farnsworth, the respondent, said.

"Yes, of course, she did," the judge nodded, looking substantially unimpressed. "Do you have any evidence to present?"

"Did his wife, Your Honor?" his attorney asked.

"Be quiet, or I'll cite you for contempt," the judge growled from the bench.

"But I'm a good, decent man," Judge Farnsworth, the respondent, said. Then, turning to his attorney, he added "isn't that right?"

His attorney rose from his seat to address the court. "That's what he keeps telling me, Your Honor, but he isn't a judge anymore, he's the respondent. I wouldn't trust him."

"Objection," Judge Farnsworth, the respondent, said.

"Over ruled!" bellowed Judge Farnsworth, the judge.

"If you cannot prove, beyond a reasonable doubt, that the charges your wife has brought against you are false, then I'll have no alternative but to find for the plaintiff."

"This is ridiculous," Judge Farnsworth, the respondent, said.

"I find for the plaintiff," Judge Farnsworth announced from the bench. "And I hereby grant her a one-year restraining order."

Then, peering down over the front of his desk, he addressed the Respondent directly. "Judge Farnsworth," he said, "from this day forward, you may no longer speak with your wife. You may no longer visit your house. You may no longer see or speak with your sons. You may no longer discuss your 'fine points' with friends and neighbors. Each month, you will surrender to your wife half of your judicial salary, and, you will continue to pay the household mortgage. In addition, I award your wife all court costs. Case closed!" he said, at last, slowly *pounding his gavel on the bench several times.*

"No! You can't!" Judge Farnsworth shouted in his sleep, moments before he woke up in a cold sweat. The clock read 4:59 a.m.

Alice Farnsworth stirred at the sound of her husband's terrified voice. "What's the matter, Mickey?" she asked. "Did you have a bad dream?"

Judge Farnsworth was relieved to hear her voice and to see her lying in bed beside him. "Oh, thank God!" he said. "It wasn't real after all."

"What wasn't, darling?"

"Oh, you wouldn't believe me, if I told you," he said, still shaking from the experience. "Worst nightmare I ever had."

"Would it help to talk about it?"

"No, it would not!" he growled. His voice still carried some of the resentment toward her that he had experienced in his dream.

"You don't have to bite my head off," she said. "I was just trying to help."

"You've helped enough already!" he said, gruffly.

"What are you mad at me for?" she asked him.

"Nothing, nothing," he said, catching himself and softly patting her shoulder. "I'm sorry I barked at you."

"That's more like it," she said. Then, the softness returned to her voice. "All right, baby, I'm going back to sleep. What about you?"

"No. That's it for me!" the judge said, getting up. He went to the bathroom, where he turned on the light and briefly examined his cheeks for slap marks. *It seemed so real,* he said to himself. *My God, I'm still shaking!*

He brushed his teeth, washed his face, and shaved. Then, he went downstairs to the kitchen, where he made himself a strong pot of coffee, ate a light breakfast, and occasionally pinched himself for reassurance.

Chapter 30

Katie Silkwood arrived at Beverly West's townhouse office at precisely 7:30 a.m. for her pre-trial meeting. Her mother had slept over the night before so that her daughter could get herself to court on time and not be worried about the children.

Esther's cooperation had come at a price, though. Eddie had had to sleep at a nearby motel. (His wife had thrown him out several days earlier, and he had immediately moved in with Katie and the kids.)

Katie had missed his presence in her bed. It was all still so exciting. First, there had been the powerful thrill of him coming on to her at the community swimming pool, the previous summer. Initially, she hadn't taken his advances seriously, dismissing him as a flirt. After all, with his muscular build and dark good looks, he could have had anyone, so why her? Plus, he had two young children, and a darling, albeit significantly pregnant, young wife, who was at least ten years her junior.

But when he followed her into the lady's shower, there was no mistaking his intent. She had just started unfastening her bikini top, when he turned the corner, smiling. She blushed at first—she knew it—experiencing a mixture of fear, excitement, and guilt. But as he approached, she had found herself unable to stop. Slowly, she brought the straps down off her shoulders. Then, with a sheepish smile, she let the top fall away exposing her breasts. As he continued to advance, she put the soap in her hand and began rubbing it against her breasts as if she were bathing alone—and unseen.

Finally, he was up against her. As he folded her in his arms and pressed his open mouth against hers, she felt herself literally melting away. Katie could barely believe what happened next as they tore off each other's clothes and made fierce, but silent, love pressed against the ceramic wall under the warm misty shower head. The whole thing took less than five minutes, but it unleashed an erotic intensity in her that she had never known before. Afterward, they quickly dressed. She left first, while he ducked into the adjoining men's shower, not to emerge again for several minutes.

For Katie, that encounter had been her first real taste of sin, and she had found the experience entirely delicious.

After that, she was hooked. For despite its intensity, the sexual pleasure she had felt remained surprisingly fleeting. She literally couldn't get enough of it, and she wanted—desperately—to feel satiated.

From then on, she was with Eddie whenever the opportunity presented itself. She would let him into her home late on nights when Martin was out of town. On certain Saturday afternoons, while Martin thought she was off bargain hunting, they would meet at a nearby motel. She and Eddie would engage in repeated erotic acts, knowing all the while that Martin was home, dutifully watching the kids. It gave her a strong, erotic rush to know she was worshiping another man's body behind her husband's back. Just thinking about it would be enough to whip her into a frenzy again afterward, when she was lying awake in bed next to her sleeping husband.

But soon, she wouldn't have to hide her affair any longer. Beverly West had promised to help her start a new chapter in her life—a decidedly steamier one—equipped with every conceivable advantage the courts could provide. She had never imagined getting her way would be so easy—or so painless.

Katie had come to the office when and how instructed. When Beverly West heard her ring, she opened the door, took one look at her client, and broke into an enormous smile.

"You followed my instructions perfectly!" West said, noting Katie's matronly choice of an ankle-length dress, flat plain shoes, a simple, austere ponytail, her short, unmanicured nails, and her pale face that appeared to be completely devoid of makeup. "You look just like the poor wretch I will be telling Judge Farnsworth about," she said. "Come in. We'll have some tea and then briefly review the matters at hand."

They sat down on facing divans in West's office and briefly discussed Saturday morning's failed settlement talks.

"I'm sorry I couldn't spare you the expense of a trial, Katie," Beverly said. "But that husband of yours! What a fool he is, so angry and so arrogant. In short order, I'm going to teach him a lesson he'll never forget!"

Katie saw the fire in her attorney's eyes and smiled to herself. "It's all right, Beverly," she sighed. "At least you didn't have the pleasure of being married to him for eight years. And thank you for reducing your hourly fee in this case. That really helped."

"Don't mention it," West smiled.

West quickly ran down her standard checklist of pretrial items. She reviewed Katie's story of how the marriage had begun going downhill the previous summer, how they had argued increasingly and how Martin occasionally had called her some extremely unflattering things.

"When and where did he call you that?" West asked her client.

"Once, in the kitchen before a family dinner, and another time, just after we put the kids to bed."

"Who, if anyone else, ever heard his remarks?" West asked.

"Our six-year-old son, Justin, did once, I believe," Katie said.

"How do you know that?" West asked.

"Well, as I was walking by his room later that night on my way to bed. He called out my name, so I looked in on him," Katie said.

"The defense attorney may object at this point," West explained, "because your son's testimony would be considered 'hearsay' under normal circumstances. But I'm going to try and argue that it was an excited utterance, and see if the judge will buy it. Just be prepared to stop talking as soon as the objection is raised."

"Why, Beverly?" Katie asked.

"Because, my dear," West said, "judges do not like it when witnesses fail to follow the rules. And we want the judge to believe you are someone who plays by the rules, don't we?"

"Yes," Katie smiled.

"OK," West said. "Let's assume they have objected, and I've argued that what you are about to convey was an excited utterance. When the judge says 'proceed,' you continue."

"I looked in on him and found Justin was crying," Katie said. 'Why are you and Daddy yelling so much?' he asked me. 'Are you guys getting a divorce?'"

"That's great," West said. "It's important that you mention he was crying, because that adds credence to my suggestion that this was an excited utterance."

"Yes," Katie said, "but there's one thing I don't understand."

"What's that?"

"Well," Katie said, "Justin never really said it was my husband's yelling or that he had heard him call me that name. Doesn't that matter?"

"It only matters," West said, "if your husband's attorney raises the matter in his objection. Otherwise, everyone may simply assume, based on your earlier testimony that he was referring to the name-calling incident."

"What about the name's I've called him?" Katie asked.

"You only called him those things in response, right?" West asked.

"Oh, yes, of course."

"We've been over this several times now, Katie, are you clear on it?"

"Oh, yes," Katie repeated. "I'm sorry, Beverly."

"No problem," West said. "You are going to do great!"

Chapter 31

As planned, Martin met Swindell at the courthouse at eight-fifteen, forty-five minutes before the hearing's scheduled start. Martin was excited, anxious, and conflicted. He wished he could have accepted West's settlement offer, especially now that he knew the chances of settling the case during the trial were virtually nil. He hoped that the underground group had completed its covert mission and that everything had gone well. If not, he reasoned, he was screwed. Swindell, however, was completely unaware of Martin's new friends' activities, and he was looking decidedly glum.

"I've got more bad news, Mahr-tin," he said. "Remember how we figured your wife had lied about callin' the police on you, because on each occasion, you were out of town on audits?"

"Yeah," Martin said, warily.

"Well, last Tuesday, I asked the police to produce those documents, if they had them. I've got an old friend workin' there, and she agreed to expedite thin's. That was lucky for you, Mahr-tin, because they have up to ten business days to comply—even in *ex-parte* cases like yours. Anyway, one of my paralegals went over there yesterday and picked up copies of each of those police call reports."

"What?"

"Yes sir," Swindell said, "you may not have been in town, but your wife did call the police on four separate occasions regardin' domestic disturbances at your home."

"Who was she having the disturbances with then, herself?"

"Maybe," Swindell shrugged, studying his client closely. "But since she made the calls, we're now goin' to have to prove you were out of town on each occasion."

Martin sighed. "And how do we do that?"

"Leave that to me, Mahr-tin. I've got an idea or two. I didn't mention this to you before our meeting on Saturday because I thought we would settle the case, and then none of this would matter.

"We're goin' to need to be resourceful, since settlement clearly is no longer an option."

"Look, I know I screwed up. I'm sorry. Do you have to keep reminding me?"

"Well, you need to know what we're up against, Mahrtin. I ran into Beverly West in the hallway and I've never seen her so torqued. I expected flames to leap from her mouth."

"How bad could things get? You don't actually think she could get a permanent restraining order against me, do you?"

"All I'm sayin'," Swindell explained, "is that, based on my experience in district court, and in particular, dealin' with West, you never know. You just never know."

Chapter 32

At nine o'clock, the bailiff announced Judge Farnsworth to the waiting courtroom. "All rise. The District Court for the State of Maryland, Montgomery County, is now in session, the Honorable Michael J. Farnsworth presiding."

Judge Farnsworth entered the courtroom slowly and looked around as if he was experiencing this setting for the first time. Only those who knew him best would have detected anything at all unusual. For instance, they might have noticed that his typically somber expression now seemed decidedly more pained. Nothing else suggested that this hearing would be different, in any way, from any other.

The judge asked for the docket and began calling out cases. "Wilkens v. Wilkens, protective order." The clerk approached the bench and whispered something in his hear.

"I see," Judge Farnsworth said. "That matter has been settled. What other matters do we have before the court this morning?"

"Silkwood v. Silkwood, restraining order petition, Your Honor," the clerk said.

"Are the parties present?" Judge Farnsworth asked.

"Yes, Your Honor," Beverly West said. "Beverly West here, representing Mrs. Katie Silkwood, the petitioner, who is seated beside me."

"And you, Chester?" Farnsworth asked, looking at his old friend.

"Yes, Your Honor," Swindell said. "Chester T. Swindell, representin' my client, Mahr-tin Silkwood, who is seated to my right and who is the designated Respondent in this matter."

"Very well," Judge Farnsworth said. "Come forward, and let's get started."

Once the attorneys and their clients had taken their seats at their respective tables, Judge Farnsworth resumed.

"Ms. West," he asked, glancing in her direction, "what issues does the petitioner wish to bring before the court today?"

"Well, judge, we will be asking the court to make permanent the temporary restraining order and related decisions it ruled on last week. In addition, we are seeking a determination regarding Mr. Silkwood's child support obligation."

"Very well," Farnsworth said. "How many witnesses will you be calling?"

"Just my client, Your Honor."

"Mr. Swindell?" he asked. "How many witnesses do you intend to call?"

"My client is the only witness I have designated, judge."

"Very good," Farnsworth said. He made a few, brief notations. Then, without looking up, he continued, "How long do each of you think you'll need to present your cases?"

"A half day or less, judge," West said.

"The same for our side," Swindell added.

"Fine," Farnsworth said, looking up once more. "Ms. West, given the limited issues in this case I think we can dispense with opening statements, don't you agree?

West rose briefly off her seat. "Yes, Your Honor."

"Very good." Farnsworth sat up straight, folded his hands before him, and nodded at West. "Ms. West, you may proceed and call your first witness."

West stood. "I call Katie Silkwood to the stand."

Once Katie was sworn in, Beverly West asked her the perfunctory questions: her name, address, age, place of employment and marital status, and then she went right to work.

"Mrs. Silkwood," she said, "do you know why we're here this morning?"

"Yes," Katie said, "This is my husband's chance to answer the abuse charges I raised in the protective order petition one week ago."

"Correct. And would you briefly tell the court the circumstances that led you to file that protective order petition?"

"Yes. Martin and I had a good marriage for the first few years, but then about two years ago—"

Swindell stood up. "Objection! Irrelevant. Your Honor, what possible bearin' could incidents two-years old have on the petitioner's decision to seek a protective order *last week?*"

Judge Farnsworth frowned. "Sustained. Mrs. Silkwood, please try and restrict your comments to events that occurred in the immediate past."

"Perhaps, if I narrow the question, Your Honor?" Beverly West suggested.

"Proceed."

"Now, Mrs. Silkwood, could you please tell the court about the events of Thursday night a week ago?"

"We all had dinner together as we usually do," Katie said, "and everything was fine. We put the kids to bed at about eight, and then I went to the kitchen to make some herbal tea."

"What happened then?"

"Oh well, Martin came into the kitchen, and he seemed really angry."

"Objection." Swindell again rose to his feet. "The witness's opinion is irrelevant."

"Sustai—. No," Judge Farnsworth said, shaking his head and catching himself. "Overruled. The witness can express her opinion about her husband seeming to be angry. That is certainly relevant to the issue here."

"Please continue," West said to her client.

"Martin came into the kitchen, and asked if I had scheduled a meeting with a marriage counselor yet," Katie said.

"Was seeing a marriage counselor something the two of you had agreed on?"

"Objection," Swindell said. "She's leadin' the witness."

"Overruled. I think counsel is merely seeking a point of clarification," the judge said. "Let's not put her in a strait jacket. Proceed, Ms. West."

"Thank you, Your Honor." West smiled faintly at her client. "Had you and your husband made any decisions regarding seeing a marriage counselor?"

"We had talked about it, and I hadn't objected, or anything," Mrs. Silkwood said. "But I don't recall us setting up time tables or anything like that. Anyway, I said, 'No, not yet. I've been busy.' That's when he went completely ballistic on me."

Swindell stood. "Objection. The witness' answer goes beyond the scope of the question. Move to strike."

"Sustained," Judge Farnsworth said. "Strike everything after 'anything like that.'"

West continued. "Did this conversation end in a confrontation?"

"Yes."

"Would you please describe the nature of that confrontation, Mrs. Silkwood."

"He said, 'Damn it, Katie! Isn't this even a priority for you?' – or something like that. I don't remember exactly." As he said it, he knocked a plastic cup off the kitchen table, and it went sailing across the floor!"

"How did that make you feel?"

"Objection," Swindell said. "Leadin' the witness."

"Overruled."

"Well, I was scared. I jumped and I said, 'Martin, what's come over you? You're frightening me."

"What happened next?" West asked.

"Martin said, 'I wish you were scared Katie. You should be—about our marriage.' Then, he walked over to where I was standing at the counter and got real close to me, into my space and everything.

"He was about six inches away from my face. He was staring at me intently. I could feel his breath on my cheeks. 'Do you care about saving this marriage, Katie?' he asked me. I was starting to feel real uncomfortable and scared. I thought he was going to hit—."

"Objection, Your Honor. Irrelevant. The witness is givin' us a narrative."

"Overruled. Let's let her tell her story."

"Proceed, Ms. West."

West looked at Katie Silkwood. "You may continue, Mrs. Silkwood."

"Well, as I said, it looked like he was going to hit me.

'I don't get it,' he said. 'Don't you care about what happens to our family? Do you want our kids to grow up in a broken home? You used to really care about them.'"

"'That got me upset, so I said, 'How dare you question whether I care about the kids! I'm the one who's always here for them, when you go out of town every other week on business!'"

"'You know I don't have any choice in the matter, Katie. It's my job,' he said. And I said, 'Well, no one's sentenced you to work there for life. Get another job! Be a man!'

"'I am a man,' he said, 'and a damned good one, too!' Then, he announced that, as the 'man of the house,' he was going to take matters into his own hands and schedule a counseling session at the earliest opportunity with a marriage counselor we had heard good things about. 'All you'll have to do is show up, Katie,' he said, 'if that's not too much trouble.'"

"'You better make all the arrangements then, including getting a sitter for the kids,' I told him. "Then, he said he would try and schedule a session for that Saturday afternoon or the next, and I got upset."

Swindell rose to his feet. "Objection. Irrelevant, Your Honor. Now, we're not only gettin' a play-by-play narrative but dialogue, too. Mrs. Silkwood is testifyin' for both parties!"

Judge Farnsworth knitted his brow. "Sustained. Ms. West, the court is trying to give you and your client some latitude, here, but I think you need to help rein in your client."

The faintest hint of a blush was beginning to penetrate West's layer of concealer. "Certainly, your honor. Mrs. Silkwood. Katie," she said, "you indicated you got upset. Could you please tell the court why your husband's remarks upset you?"

"Because Martin knows Saturday afternoons are my personal time, when I go shopping and just chill out from being with the kids all week. He deliberately said he would schedule the appointment during my free time.

"Did you let him know you were upset?"

"Yes."

"How?"

"I spilled my tea in the sink and told him he could schedule it then, but he'd be going by himself, and I started to brush past him to leave the room."

"Did the confrontation intensify at that point?" West asked.

"Yes."

"Could you please tell us what happened?"

Swindell stood up. "Objection! Counsel's question appears to be invitin' yet more narrative."

"Sustained," Judge Farnsworth said. He sighed and gestured for West to continue.

"Did your husband do anything when you attempted to leave?" West asked.

"Yes."

"What did he do?"

"He stopped me, grabbed me by the shoulders and shook me real hard."

"Was that the extent of the confrontation?"

"No."

"What else happened?"

"He asked me what it was going to take for him to finally get through to me."

"And how did you react to that?"

"I raised my hand up like I was going to slap him."

"Then what happened?" West asked.

"He let me go."

"What did you do next?"

"I went to the bedroom and locked the door."

"Why?"

"I didn't want him to 'do anything' to get through to me."

"Did things go back to normal after that?" West asked.

"No."

"Describe what happened to disrupt the normal household routine."

"The next day, while Martin was at work, I took the kids and the dog and left the house."

"Where did you go?"

"We went to a friend's house where I knew we'd be safe. I needed time to think."

"Objection," Swindell said. "Non-responsive."

"Sustained. "Strike everything after 'friend's house.'"

"What was it about that incident that caused you to flee the house?" West asked.

"Well, that wasn't an isolated case. We had been having a lot of arguments lately, and each one seemed a little worse than the one before."

"Are you thinking of any occasions in particular?" West asked.

"Yes, the four times, in recent months, when I had called the police to the house—"

"Objection," Swindell said. "Irrelevant. Once more, Your Honor, they're attemptin' to expand the time frame!"

"Is there a reason we need to hear about these other incidents?" Farnsworth asked West.

"Well, yes, Your Honor. We contend that Mr. Silkwood had become increasingly belligerent and out-of-control in recent months. It was the escalating nature of those outbursts that made Mrs. Silkwood fear for her safety and flee."

"I'm going to allow the testimony, for now, Counselor," Judge Farnsworth said, "but you could be getting onto shaky ground. Don't make me regret it."

Both West and Swindell looked intently at the judge. Such an admonition to the petitioner's counsel was completely out of character.

Swindell leaned over toward Martin and whispered. "Somethin's up. I've known Farnsworth a long time, and I've never seen him press the petitioner's counsel like this."

"Is that good?" Martin asked.

"It looks like it could be very good for us," Swindell continued, "very good, indeed."

"OK, Mrs. Silkwood," West said. "I'd like to return to those four incidents you spoke of, when the police were called to your house. I'd like you to briefly recount what happened on each occasion and the significance of its effect on you."

"Well, the first one occurred on a Tuesday night in November, the fourth, I believe. We were arguing about a problem Justin was having in school. On this occasion, Martin got upset and threw his glass of scotch into the fireplace. I was concerned for my safety—and the safety of my kids—so I called 911."

"What happened when the police arrived?" West asked.

"Martin took off the moment he heard me on the phone. And he stayed out all night. So, he wasn't there when the police arrived."

"What did the police do?"

"They searched through the house, took down information about Martin, borrowed a picture of him, and they examined the broken glass in the fireplace. The officer was very nice. He put everything down in his report. They waited with me for nearly an hour."

"What about the second incident?" West asked.

"That happened the afternoon of Sunday, November sixteenth," Katie said. We were raking leaves and Justin ran his bicycle through them, thinking it was funny. Then, Martin took the bicycle and threw it down on the driveway with all his might. It got all scuffed up, and Justin ran to his room crying. I couldn't get him to come out."

"Did you call the police on this occasion as well?" West asked.

"Yes. They came and wrote up their report again, took a picture of the bike on the driveway and everything."

"What did they say to your husband?" West asked.

"Nothing. Martin had apologized and had gone inside to take a tranquilizer. He was sleeping upstairs when they arrived, and I asked them not to disturb him, as everything was calm once more, and I didn't want to get him riled up."

"And the police were OK with that?" West asked.

"Well, not at first. But I begged them. I explained how Martin had been under a lot of pressure lately, that he wasn't normally a violent man, and finally they said, 'OK.'"

"What was the third occasion?" West asked.

"It happened in late December, December the twenty-eighth, I believe."

"Tell us about it."

"Well," Katie said, "we had gone to my mother-in-law's home for the day—to exchange presents and have an extended Christmas for the kids. Martin and his mother don't get along well. I mean, she rides him the entire time we visit. He calls her the 'Ultra Nag.'"

"Objection," Swindell said. "Irrelevant narrative. Move to strike!"

"Sustained."

"How long did you stay there?" West asked.

"Till about four in the afternoon."

"And why did you leave at 4:00?"

"Martin and his mother don't get along," Katie said, "and he had had all he could take."

"What was the nature of the incident on this day?"

"Martin got angry and backed his car into the garage wall, messing up the fender."

"What made him so angry?" West asked.

"When we got home, he realized he had left something at his mother's house, and he would have to drive back to Virginia to get it."

"What did you do after he left?

"I called the police."

"Why?" West asked.

"I wanted them to document what had happened. I wanted them to be aware of the escalating nature of the situation."

"Did they speak with your husband on that occasion?"

"No, but they told me they were becoming concerned."

"Objection," Swindell said. "Hearsay."

"Sustained."

"When did the final incident take place?" West asked.

"That was on January eighteenth—at night."

"Describe what happened."

"Martin and Justin got into a fight and then Martin squeezed my arm."

"What was the fight about?"

"Access to the TV in the den."

"What was the issue?"

"Justin wanted to watch Disney and Martin wanted to watch the football game."

"What happened?"

"Martin locked himself in the den, and Justin banged on the door with a baseball bat for about an hour."

"What did you do while that was going on?"

"I told my son that his father had said he did not want to be disturbed. He would have to watch Disney another night."

"What did your husband do when he finally came out of the room?"

"He yelled at me for not controlling our son and grabbed me by the arm and squeezed real tight."

"What specifically led you to call 911 on that occasion?

"About a half-hour later, I looked down and saw my arm was seriously bruised."

"What happened when the police arrived?"

"The police officer tried to get me to go to a shelter—or to consider filing a petition for a protective order."

"Did you take the officer's advice?"

"No."

"Why not?"

Katie Silkwood shook her head. "I didn't want to believe things had gotten that bad."

"Thank you, Mrs. Silkwood," West said. Then looking over at Swindell, she added, "Your witness."

Chapter 33

Swindell rose slowly, took his pad in hand and approached the bench. "Very interestin' story, Mrs. Silkwood," he said. "Let me see if I understand it correctly. Your husband has been gettin' increasin'ly violent and angry lately. On four separate occasions, you called the police because of his excessive use of force or because of his out-of-control temper. And finally, last Thursday, when you saw the pattern repeatin' itself, you took matters into your own hands and fled with the children and your dog. Is that right?"

"Yes," Katie said.

"Mrs. Silkwood, rememberin' that you're under oath, I wonder if there's anythin' you may have omitted regardin' these incidents that you'd like to mention now, for the record? Or do you stand by the story as told."

"I stand by it," Katie said.

"So, if we're to believe you," Swindell said, "the police came to your house four different times in response to emergency 911 calls. On all but one of those occasions, your husband had 'fled the scene.' And on their second visit, he had been restin' after takin' a tranquilizer, and they agreed not to confront him. Is that right?"

"Yes," Katie said.

"Don't you think that's odd, Mrs. Silkwood—how the police never once saw your husband on any of those occasions?"

"Objection, Your Honor," West said. "Argumentative."

"Overruled," Judge Farnsworth said.

"I can't keep Martin at home—or anywhere else, for that matter—if he wants to leave," Katie said. "He's a grown man, and he is a lot bigger than I am."

"Isn't it true, Mrs. Silkwood, that the real reason the police never saw your husband, and the reason you—what word did you use to describe it? Ah yes," he said, referring to his notes. "The reason you 'begged' them not to disturb him on the occasion when you said he had taken the tranquilizers, was because he wasn't really home at all?"

"Of course, that's precisely what I said," Katie explained. "He wasn't home!"

"Even on the day he took the tranquilizers?" Swindell asked.

"No," she said. "He was home that time, just not the others."

"Mrs. Silkwood," Swindell continued. "Isn't it true that your husband was not only 'not at home' the four times you called 911, but that he actually was out-of-state? Wasn't he away on business?"

"Objection, Your Honor," West said. "This question has been asked and answered."

"Overruled," Judge Farnsworth said. "The question seeks further clarification. Then, turning to the witness, he said, "Please answer the question."

"What are you suggesting?" Katie Silkwood asked Swindell.

"Your honor," Swindell said, addressing the bench. "Would you please instruct the witness, to answer the question before her."

"Perhaps it would be helpful to repeat the question first," Judge Farnsworth said. He instructed the court reporter to read the question aloud from the record.

"Isn't it true," the court reporter read "that your husband was not only not at home the four times you called 911, but that he actually was out-of-state? Wasn't he away on business?"

Katie Silkwood looked at the judge, and he gestured for her to answer. She turned to Swindell. "No, that's a lie!"

"We'll see about that," Swindell said.

West stood up. "Objection, judge. Argumentative and completely inappropriate!"

"Sustained." Judge Farnsworth said. He frowned at Swindell and raised an eyebrow. "Save your arguments for the court, counselor."

"Sorry, Your Honor."

Then Swindell continued, "Mrs. Silkwood, once more rememberin' that you're under oath, is it still your contention that, on these four occasions, your husband was at home and not away on business, managin' on-site audits at his accountin' firm's clients' offices?"

"Objection!" West said, rising once more. "Counsel's question is argumentative. What's more, the question already has been asked and answered several times!"

"Sustained," Judge Farnsworth said, frowning again at Swindell.

Swindell had a sour look on his face and shook his head as he walked toward his desk and removed a set of papers from his file. He held them up in his right hand for all to see. "Your Honor, I have here four copies of police reports filed after each of the four 911 calls placed from the Silkwood home."

"Objection," Beverly West said, rising once more. "These alleged police reports have not yet been authenticated, Your Honor. Furthermore, Mr. Swindell did not apprise us, in advance of today's hearing, that he had these documents in his possession. He also failed to provide us with review copies, as is required, by law."

"That's true, judge," Swindell said, "but these documents only came into my possession over the weekend. I also have not yet moved to introduce them into evidence. I am merely asking to have them marked for identification purposes."

"Ms. West," Judge Farnsworth asked. "Do you still object?"

"No, Your Honor," West said. "However, I'd like to be permitted to review these documents first, if you don't mind."

"Certainly," Judge Farnsworth said. "Mr. Swindell, do you have copies?"

Swindell produced three sets of copies: one for the court, one for West and one for himself. He handed them around and then returned to his table, while the judge and West looked them over.

When West had completed her review, Judge Farnsworth continued. "Ms. West, do you object to these items being marked for identification?

"No, judge."

"OK," Judge Farnsworth said to Swindell, "you may proceed."

"Thank you, Your Honor," Swindell said. "If it please the court, I would like to mark these four police reports as defense exhibits A through D, for identification purposes only.

"So ordered," Judge Farnsworth said.

"Now, Mrs. Silkwood," Swindell continued, "regardin' that first 911 incident from November – I believe you said it happened on Tuesday, November fourth; is that correct?"

"Yes."

"At approximately what time that Tuesday, do you recall placin' your call to 911?"

"I don't remember," Mrs. Silkwood said. "I know it was evening, but I'm not sure."

"May I approach the witness, Your Honor?" Swindell asked.

"What for?"

"Well," Swindell said, "unless Ms. West objects, I thought I'd let Mrs. Silkwood take a look at the correspondin' report to see if it helps refresh her memory."

"No objection, Your Honor," West said.

"All right then," Judge Farnsworth said, "you may proceed."

Mrs. Silkwood took a moment to review the report before handing it back to Swindell. "Is your memory refreshed, Mrs. Silkwood?" Swindell asked.

"Yes."

"Then, could you tell the court the approximate time you placed your call?"

"Yes, I placed it at 8:43 p.m."

"Thank you," Swindell said. "And about how much time after that did the police arrive on the scene?"

"About fifteen minutes later," Mrs. Silkwood said.

"So, that would put them at your house at approximately 9:00 p.m. would it not?"

"Yes."

"Now, Mrs. Silkwood, it bein' November fourth and all, did you have a fire goin' in the fireplace that evenin'?"

"Yes, I believe we did," Mrs. Silkwood said.

"And you said the police inspected some of the glass fragments that night, didn't they?"

"Yes. They used something like a large tweezer and held each piece of broken glass up to the fire."

"Why did they do that?" Swindell asked.

"Oh, I think they said something about looking for fingerprints."

"Do you recall," Swindell asked, "if they found any?"

"No," she said. "Not on the pieces they were able to extract."

"Did they find anythin' at all of interest in the largest bottom piece that they pulled out?" Swindell asked.

"I don't know what you mean," she said.

"I mean anythin' notable about the condition of the glass fragments they were able to retrieve."

"No. I don't recall," she said.

"Mrs. Silkwood, didn't they find a few drops of Scotch still present in a bottom piece of the glass?

"Oh, yes. That's right. And officer Tilley, I think that was his name, said that showed Martin had left only a short time before I placed my call."

"Objection, hearsay," West said. "Move to strike."

"Sustained," Judge Farnsworth said. "Strike everything after "glass.""

"They found no fingerprints at all?" Swindell asked again.

"That's right."

"And they found some liquor still wet in the glass?"

"Yes."

"Now," Swindell continued, "turnin' to the second incident which happened on Sunday, November sixteenth. Do you recall precisely what time you called the police?"

"No, I don't," Mrs. Silkwood said.

"Once again, Your Honor, may I approach the witness and let her review the second incident report?"

"Yes, you may," the judge said.

Mrs. Silkwood took a few moments to review the report before handing it back to Swindell.

"Did that help refresh your memory?" he asked.

"Yes," she said.

"Could you give me the approximate time, then?"

"Yes. I called them at about three-thirty in the afternoon."

"Your Honor," Swindell said, after returning to his desk with more papers in hand, "What I have here, are copies of Mr. Silkwood's trip expense reports for four business trips that he took on the same dates as each alleged 911 call, and they are marked Defense Exhibits 'E' through 'H.' I would like to have them so marked for identification purposes."

"Objection! Inadmissible." West said, springing up from her table. "Plaintiff's counsel has not been apprised of the existence of these exhibits in advance of this hearing."

"Mr. Swindell?" Judge Farnsworth said. "Do you have anything to say in response?"

"Yes, Judge," Swindell said. "This evidence is bein' introduced for purposes of witness impeachment and, in such instances, as opposin' counsel knows, the prior disclosure rule does not apply."

"OK," Judge Farnsworth said. "Overruled."

"Your honor," West interjected, "I also object to the introduction of these documents based on the lack of a proper foundation."

Farnsworth turned to Swindell. "Do you care to respond, counsel?"

"I believe we only need proper foundation to introduce these documents into evidence, but not to have them marked for identification purposes."

"Ms. West," Judge Farnsworth asked, "do you have any further arguments you wish to make?"

"No, Your Honor."

"Thank you both," Judge Farnsworth said. "The objection is overruled. Mr. Swindell, you may mark defense exhibits E through H for identification purposes.

Swindell handed copies of the expense reports and their attached expense receipts around and then returned to the defense table.

"May I approach the witness?" he asked.

"Yes, you may."

"Mrs. Silkwood," Swindell said, handing her the expense reports, do you recognize these documents?

"I recognize the kind of document they are, but I've never seen these before."

"What kind of document are they?" Swindell asked.

"Well, they appear to be copies of travel expense report forms that Martin files with his company. But I have no way of knowing if they're real. They could be forgeries!"

"Setting aside, for a moment, the question of their authenticity. How do you know they're expense reports from your husband's firm?"

"Objection, Your Honor!" West said. "Mrs. Silkwood is not qualified to authenticate documents from her husband's firm.

"Sustained."

"That's quite all right," Swindell said. He walked over to his table and withdrew a document from a folder in his brief case. "Judge, I have here a notarized, sworn affidavit signed by one Mr. David Feldman, who is senior managin' partner at Findley, Feldman and Santori CPAs, Mr. Silkwood's employer. Mr. Feldman, in his capacity as the firm's custodian of documents, has verified the authenticity of these four expense reports."

Swindell then gave a copy of the affidavit to West and to the judge.

"I would now like to have the affidavit marked as Defense Exhibit "I" and then have it and the four expense reports introduced into evidence," Swindell said.

"Any objection, counselor?" Farnsworth asked West.

"No, Judge."

"OK, then," Farnsworth said. "Defense exhibits "E" through "I" are accepted into evidence."

Swindell was then permitted to approach the witness once more. "Mrs. Silkwood," he said, "I have in my hand what has been marked as Defense Exhibit E, which you have identified as one of your husband's travel expense reports. Would you please look at this and tell the court the period it covers?"

"Yes, it covers November four through seven."

"Now," Swindell said, "do you see two ticket stubs attached to this expense report?"

"Yes, I do," she said.

"And this one here," Swindell said, "dated November fourth, could you read the flight information contained on it?"

"Yes," she said, "It refers to a USAir flight 912 leaving from Dulles on November fourth and going to St. Louis, MO."

"And what was the flight's scheduled departure time?" Swindell asked.

Katie Silkwood froze.

"Please read it," Swindell said.

"It-it says, 8:48 p.m."

"And whose name is written on the ticket?"

"Martin Silkwood," she said.

"Now, Mrs. Silkwood, do you know approximately how long it takes to drive from your home, in Olney, to catch a flight out of Dulles airport?"

"Objection," West said. "He's calling on the witness to speculate."

"Sustained," Judge Farnsworth said.

"In the past, Mrs. Silkwood," Swindell said, "has your husband taken flights out of Dulles airport?"

"Yes."

"And on any of those occasions, did he leave from your present home address, in Olney, MD?"

"Yes."

"On average, Mrs. Silkwood," Swindell asked "how long beforehand did he leave your home in order to make those flights?"

"I'm not sure."

"Are you sayin' you don't remember?" Swindell asked.

"Objection," West said, "He's badgering the witness."

"Sustained," Judge Farnsworth said.

"OK," Swindell continued, "by your best recollection, ma'am, would your husband need to leave your home an hour before departure time—or earlier?"

"Objection, again, Your Honor," West said. "He's still asking the witness to speculate."

"Sustained."

"All right," Swindell said, taking out a handkerchief from his pocket and dabbing his perspiring face. "Mrs. Silkwood, have you ever taken a flight out of Dulles airport?"

"Yes."

"And did you leave for the airport from your present address?

"Yes."

"About how long before that flight's departure time did you leave your home?"

"I-I don't remember," she said.

Swindell frowned. "Was it less than two hours?"

"I'm not sure."

"Objection," your honor, West said. "The witness has said she doesn't know."

"Overruled," Farnsworth said. "And according to my notes, she said she didn't remember and then that she wasn't sure."

"Mrs. Silkwood, considerin' the distance between your home, in Olney, MD, and Dulles international airport and considerin' how far in advance of departure times travelers must arrive these days, just to get through security, and finally, rememberin' you're still under oath, would you be more comfortable sayin' you left two hours or three hours before your scheduled departure time?"

"Hard to say," Katie Silkwood said.

"Then, would you be more comfortable if we simply split the difference and said you left two and a half hours earlier?"

Katie Silkwood looked around for a moment as Swindell waited. "I guess I would be comfortable with that. Yes."

"OK" Swindell said, "Now, let's say your husband is a faster driver than you and that he leaves only two-and-a-quarter hours before a flight's departure time. That would still mean, would it not, that he would have had to leave your house by 6:30 p.m. on November fourth, to make his 8:48 flight. Correct?"

"Well, I guess," Mrs. Silkwood said.

"Please answer the question with either a 'yes' or a 'no' response," Swindell said.

"Yes."

"Now, Mrs. Silkwood," Swindell continued, "how reasonable is it to assume that your husband could have thrown a glass of Scotch into a roarin' fire at 6:30 p.m. and that any traces of liquid alcohol would still have been visible to police two-and-a-half hours later?"

"Objection, Your Honor," West said, rising to her feet. "My client is not a physicist or otherwise qualified to answer such a question. Mr. Swindell is once more asking her to speculate!"

"Sustained." Judge Farnsworth said.

Swindell frowned. "Mrs. Silkwood, were you surprised that the police found liquid alcohol in that glass fragment?"

West cut him off. "Objection, Your Honor. Irrelevant!"

"Sustained," Judge Farnsworth said. He stared at Swindell and gestured to him dismissively with the back of his hand. "Counselor, I suggest you move on."

Swindell looked defeated. He stood perfectly still for a moment, arms slumped at his sides. Then, he raised the hand holding his legal pad and glanced at it. Just as he appeared ready to move on to the next question, the slightest hint of a smile played on his lips. He turned away from the witness to face the bench and looked up.

"Your Honor," he said, "may I ask the court's indulgence?"

Judge Farnsworth frowned. "About what?"

"Would the court take judicial notice that it is highly unlikely that alcohol could remain in liquid form in a glass fragment that had spent more than two-and-a-half hours in an active fireplace?"

The courtroom became deathly still as all eyes turned to Judge Farnsworth. He knit his eyebrows, in deep thought, as heavy furrows briefly appeared on his forehead. He glanced at West before continuing. "Yes," he said at last. "The court takes judicial notice."

Across the room, a pencil flipped out of Beverly West's twitching hand and landed on the floor.

"Now, Mrs. Silkwood," Swindell continued, "regardin' the second incident, on Sunday, November sixteenth. You said you called 911 at about three-thirty in the afternoon, isn't that right?"

"Yes," Mrs. Silkwood said.

"And you told them your husband had thrown your son's bicycle down in anger on the driveway, damagin' it, isn't that right?"

"Yes."

"Isn't it true, Mrs. Silkwood, that you threw the bicycle down in anger?"

"Absolutely not!"

"Objection!" West said.

"Overruled."

"Weren't you the one rakin' the leaves that day?"

"No, it was Martin, who did it—"

"Mrs. Silkwood," Swindell said, "this second trip expense report which I have in my hand, marked defense exhibit F, shows that your husband was in Albany, NY the weekend of the sixteenth performin' an audit for a sheet metal manufacturin' concern. His ticket stub says he wasn't due back in at Dulles until 4:45 p.m. that Sunday."

"That's not true!"

"Well, I'd like to make this airline ticket attached to exhibit F available for the court's and the plaintiff's counsel's review," Swindell said, handing around the documents.

"You've been lyin', haven't you, Mrs. Silkwood?" Swindell asked.

"Objection!" West shouted, leaping to her feet. "Argumentative and highly improper."

"Overruled," Judge Farnsworth said.

"But Judge?"

"Overruled, Ms. West," Judge Farnsworth said, sternly. "Go ahead, Mrs. Silkwood, answer the question."

"Your Honor," West interrupted, "under the circumstances, I must advise my client not to answer the question and to invoke her Fifth Amendment privilege against self-incrimination."

"Is that what you wish to do, Mrs. Silkwood?" the judge asked.

Katie Silkwood squirmed uncomfortably in her seat. "Yes, Your Honor," she said. "On the advice of my attorney, I invoke my Fifth Amendment right."

Judge Farnsworth frowned and turned to Swindell. "All right, Mr. Swindell. You may proceed."

Swindell walked to the defense table, retrieved the two-remaining travel reports, and held them up in his right hand for all to see.

"Your Honor," he said, "the defense can take up the next hour of the court's valuable time reviewin' these final two sets of trip expense documents, if you wish. But I think we already have established clear and convincin' evidence that my client is innocent of the charges alleged in the temporary restrainin' order petition, and I therefore move for a summary dismissal of this case."

Judge Farnsworth looked at Mrs. Silkwood, and at the speechless Beverly West, as a slight hint of betrayal formed in his eyes. His cheeks reddened as he raised the gavel in his right hand.

"Based on the evidence presented today, I find the petitioner incredible, as a matter of law. Therefore, this court finds for the respondent," he said, bringing the gavel down with uncommon force. "Case dismissed!"

At that, Swindell smiled and almost skipped a step in Martin's direction. Then, a look of recognition flashed across his face. He quickly spun on his heels to address Judge Farnsworth once more.

"Your Honor," he said, "in light of the extreme degree of misrepresentation and abuse of process involved in filin' the original *ex-parte* petition and revealed through today's testimony, I move that the court agree to expunge from the public record any trace of the domestic violence and spousal abuse charges brought against my client, Mr. Martin Silkwood.

"So ordered."

Judge Farnsworth banged his gavel several times and asked everyone to be seated. "Mrs. Silkwood and Ms. West," he said. "In my thirty-odd years on the bench, I have never been as concerned about the state of our judicial system as I am at this moment.

"I now realize just how easy it apparently is for women to take advantage of this court's good intentions by bringing false charges of spousal abuse against their husbands in *ex-parte* proceedings.

"Mr. Silkwood," he said, turning toward Martin, "I want to apologize for any duplicitous role this court may have unwittingly played in advancing this case. I apologize to you, sir, for the various ways we may have aided in abusing your rights, tarnishing your reputation, and causing you and others unnecessary pain and suffering in what I can only describe as our overzealous efforts to protect the 'fairer sex.'

"For that reason, Mr. Silkwood, I am awarding you all court costs in this case. That means your wife will be responsible for paying all of Mr. Swindell's legal fees and expenses. Chester, please prepare a statement for my review at your earliest convenience."

"Yes, Your Honor," Swindell said.

"As for the petitioner and her counsel," Judge Farnsworth continued. "Neither one of you has heard the last of this matter. Court adjourned."

Chapter 34

After the hearing, Beverly West quickly and silently packed her briefcase as a stunned Katie Silkwood stood nearby, sobbing softly. The two women then repaired to a corner of the courtroom, where they spoke privately, and intently, for several minutes.

Martin met Swindell out in the hallway. Swindell was all smiles. He grabbed Martin's arm above the elbow with his left hand and gave him a firm handshake with his right. "Congratulations, Mahr-tin!" he said. "I don't think we could have hoped for a better outcome than that!"

Martin nodded. "I agree, Mr. Swindell. You did a hell of a job. Thanks so much! I'm truly grateful."

"My pleasure," Swindell said. "And please, call me Chester."

"OK."

For a moment, Swindell appeared to be looking off in the distance. Then, he sighed and raised an eyebrow. "I've got to tell you, Mahr-tin, somethin' definitely felt different in there today."

"What do you mean?"

"Well," he said, shaking his head, "it was like the ground had shifted or somethin'. I mean, Judge Farnsworth is a fair man; don't get me wrong. But I've never seen him quite so willin' to consider the respondent's point of view—or quite so determined to make the petitioner substantiate her claims. I hope it lasts!

"Considerin' all that, it turns out you were right to refuse their settlement offer."

"Where do we go from here?" Martin asked.

"Well, I suggest we file for divorce immediately—while you've still got the momentum in the case. I'd push for full custody, with liberal visitation for your wife. You just might get it. I'm guessin' some of the fight has gone out of her, and she'll be even more compliant, and gun shy, after the judge gets through with her."

"What do you think he'll do?"

Swindell raised an eyebrow as he tilted his head, contemplating the possibilities. "Well, your wife really pulled a fast one on the court, creatin' those police incidents out of nothin' – and, I suspect, West may have had a hand in that, too. That's perjury, a criminal offense with a maximum penalty of two years in jail. It's the only punishment a petitioner can face in these *ex-parte* matters.

"Do you *really* think he'd send her to jail?" Martin asked. He suddenly felt genuine concern for Katie. On the one hand, he wanted her to suffer for what she had done but not with jail time. That was too extreme. And he didn't want his kids saddled with that kind of shame, either.

Swindell saw the anxious look on Martin's face. He shook his head. "Not likely. But he's definitely not goin' to let her get away Scott-free, either. My guess: She's lookin' at some serious 'community service' time.

"What about her attorney?"

"West?" Swindell asked, a subtle smile starting to play on his lips. "I'm sure she's got a substantial fine and some additional form of penance to pay, in her immediate future.

He patted Martin on the shoulder. "Well, Mahr-tin," he said. "You've got a busy few days ahead of you. Best get started. Then, why don't you come to my office next Monday mornin', and we can start formulatin' a plan."

"Sounds good to me, Chester," Martin said. Then, the two men shook hands and went their separate ways.

Martin's next stop was his office. He arrived in the early afternoon, and when he stepped off the elevator, Monique smiled and flagged him down.

"Mr. Silkwood!" she said.

He turned and approached her, "Yes?"

"Mr. Santori and Mr. Feldman want to see you, in Mr. Santori's office."

"Now?" he asked.

She nodded eagerly.

Moments later, he rapped on Santori's door and poked his head inside. "You wanted to see me, Joe?"

He found Santori, Feldman and Rick Wainwright huddled together in the middle of the room, smiling.

Santori stepped forward, his arms spread wide. "Well, if it isn't the man of the hour! Congratulations, Marty!" Santori gave him a big bear hug.

When Santori finally let him loose, Martin stepped back and squinted at his associate. "What's going on? This isn't yet another ambush, is it? Are you going to hand me my hat?"

Santori looked crestfallen and put his hand to his chest. "Boy, that smarts. Is that really what you think of me?"

Martin raised an eyebrow. "It's been the selection *de jour* around here lately, hasn't it?"

"Yeah, I guess so," Santori shrugged. "But that's all in the past! Rick just told us about your stunning victory in court today, and we called you down here to celebrate!"

As if on cue, Wainwright produced a chilled bottle of *Pol Roger* champagne from his briefcase and quickly popped the cork. White foam overflowed the bottle and ran down its neck as Wainwright rapidly filled four flutes to the brim. Feldman then passed the tray around until everyone had a glass.

Feldman nodded his head at Martin and lifted his glass high. "To Marty Silkwood," he said, "a man with bocce-sized balls of steel. Here's to your complete, precedent-setting victory today, in Maryland District Court!"

Everyone clinked glasses, smiled, and drank to the toast.

"How did you find out?" Martin asked Wainwright.

"I placed a call to the Clerk of Court's office. Your hearing is all they're talking about up there, today. It seems Judge Farnsworth gave your wife's attorney a sizable piece of his mind—and, we understand, there's more to come!"

"That sounds about right. Swindell told me she will probably get slapped with a substantial fine...and that's just the beginning."

"Yeah," Wainwright said, nodding and smiling. "Farnsworth is on the war path now. The rumor mill says he's going to make some big changes in the way these *ex-parte* domestic violence cases get handled."

"That's all well and good," Santori said, putting his arm around Martin's shoulder. "But the important thing is that our boy is back! You've been completely exonerated, Marty. No damning paper trail will ever link you to these charges, because the case ended, officially, in dismissal!"

"Here, here!" Feldman added, refilling everyone's glasses.

"So, what's my status *vis a vis* our audit program?" Martin asked.

"You're back in the saddle, cowboy," Santori said. "You can take the lead again in the Great Plains audit, if you want, and you can roll out the training program on the scale and schedule of your choosing."

"What's the matter?" Martin asked. "Is your nephew having difficulties?"

Santori blushed crimson. "Yeah! He's turning out to be a bit of an embarrassment."

"Well, I'm going to force him to see it through," Martin said, "—with help and encouragement from me, of course."

The other men looked surprised. "Oh, maybe you didn't hear this part," Martin said. "I'm back in the house now, with the kids, and I don't know what Katie's plans are. That means, I'm going to need ample backup for our out-of-town audits. The trainee program is looking like a godsend, for me. But more importantly, it could allow us to dramatically expand our audit work...and our profits."

"Woohoo!" Feldman cheered in delight.

Santori began fumbling through his suit's vest pocket. "Uh, Marty," he said, withdrawing a white, # 10 envelope and holding it up. "Here's a little something to help you with the divorce expenses, and there's more to come."

Martin took the envelope. "Thanks," he said. Later, back in his office, he opened it and found a bonus check made out to him for $20,000.

That evening, Martin returned to his home and to his children, while his wife packed her bags and prepared to move, at least temporarily, to her mother's house. He could barely believe his good fortune at having regained so much of his former life, so quickly.

When he first arrived, he found Esther Finch standing in the foyer, waiting for Katie. She gave Martin a hug and a kiss. "I'm so glad that you're reunited with the kids," she whispered. "I hope Katie will regain her senses and return too, if you'll still have her.

"Meanwhile," she added, "should you ever need any help babysitting, please don't hesitate to call me."

Martin was touched. "Thanks, Es. You'll always be at the top of my list!"

"Thanks, honey! I'm going to wait in the living room, so you two can speak in private."

Martin heard footfalls on the stairs and turned around just in time to see his two distraught children coming in his direction. Justin bounded down in a near panic, well ahead of Monica, who had to take the steps far more slowly.

"Daddy!" Justin shouted, out of breath "Mommy's packing her clothes! She says she's going to stay at Grandma's for a few days. Make her stay! We want to be a family again!"

"Yeah, Daddy," Monica added, tears welling in her eyes. "Mommy's crying! And that makes me sad! Can't you *do* something?"

Martin sat on the bottom stair and collected his kids as they arrived and held them both close. "I'm sorry, guys! It *is* sad. It makes me feel sad, too. I wish it could be different."

Monica was suddenly a torrent of tears. "Why can't it be, Daddy? Why can't we all be together?"

Justin was crying now, and soon Martin joined them, as he rocked his kids in his arms.

"It's hard to explain guys, but this is a grown-up thing, and it can get complicated.

"What I can promise you," he added, "is that Mommy always will be an important part of your lives. You'll be able to see her whenever you want. She may be moving out, for now, but she still loves you very much, just like I do. So, please don't worry. Mommy and Daddy will work it out."

"I still wish we could all be together, like it was before," Justin said.

"I know you do." Martin rubbed Justin's mop of blond hair.

"Let's give Mommy a little time to get settled at Grandma's, and then, we'll make plans for you to see her, OK? And no matter what happens, I promise you we'll always be a family, even if we all don't live together anymore."

"Really, Daddy?" Monica asked excitedly, as she pulled away, wiped the tears from her eyes and smiled hopefully.

"Your daddy and I promise," Katie Silkwood said. She was standing at the top of the stairs with a suitcase in one hand and a smaller carrying case in the other. She put the smaller bag down momentarily, wiped a tear from the corner of her eye, and started down the steps.

"OK, guys," Martin said, standing up. He took both kids by the hand and cleared the stairs for Katie. When she reached the bottom, she put her bags down and opened her arms. Justin and Monica ran to her and she hugged them tight.

"Please don't go, Mommy!" they both said.

"It's going to be OK, you two. I promise," she said, showering them both with kisses. "I love you so much! Once grandma and I get to her house tonight, I promise, I'll call you on the phone. OK?"

She released them and Monica and Justin looked at her nodding their heads slowly and wiping away their tears.

Katie smiled. "Now, would you two go get grandma? I need to talk with Daddy for a minute, OK?"

"All right," they said. They went into the living room and ran to their grandmother, who was seated on the couch. She scooped them both up, hugged them and they said their good-byes for the night.

In the foyer, Katie Silkwood looked up at her husband. "I heard everything you said to them. Thank you. It was very generous of you."

Martin shrugged. "Don't mention it. I meant every word. The kids are the real victims in all of this, and I think we should do what we can to minimize the damage."

Katie's eyes began to well up with tears again. "Marty," she said, looking away, and sniffling, "why don't you bring them by mom's first thing in the morning on your way to work. I'll fix them breakfast, make sure they've finished their homework and take them to school. That is," she added, looking back up at him, and smiling faintly, "if that would be OK with you?

"I think that's a great idea," Martin said.

"Fine. Thank you." Katie sniffled again, stood up straight and forced a smile. "Well, I guess we should be going." She leaned forward and kissed him gently on the cheek. Then, she turned toward the living room.

"Mom," she shouted. "Are you ready to go?"

Just then, Esther and the children turned the corner from the living room. "Yes, Katie," she said. "I'm ready."

The children ran to their mother again and Katie bent down and hugged and kissed them once more. Then she stood up and collected her bags.

"OK, guys. I'll see you again real soon. And I'll call you later tonight!"

Martin got the door and Katie and Esther started out. When she was halfway through, Katie turned around smiled at Justin and Monica and blew them both a kiss. Then, they were gone.

At about 8:15 p.m., the phone rang. It was Robert Brooks. "Hi, Martin. Just checking in to see how your tour went."

"Great," Martin said. "My attorney can't stop talking about it. Thinks he's the next best thing since sliced bread. I'm sure he's already thinking about raising his fees, too, of course!"

"Glad it went so well," Brooks said. "Will you be traveling with us again, soon?"

"God, I hope not!" Martin laughed, "Although I'm beginning to realize just how helpful your tour services can be. I was probably headed 'down the river' without your expert guidance and support."

"Our pleasure," Brooks said, "The saddest part is that you needed our help in the first place! The system still has a long way to go, Marty. Well, good night."

"Good night—and thanks!" Martin said.

Martin looked at his right arm, just below the elbow, where Brooks had injected the tracking device several days earlier. He could no longer see any traces of it. Then, he watched his children playing together in front of the television set, while the dog tried to get in on the action.

"Someday, Brooks," he said softly to himself, "I expect to hear that phone ring again. And when it does, I want you to give me the chance to make this kind of difference in someone else's life."

Epilogue

Montgomery County, MD, District Courthouse, 8:35 a.m., three months later.

A line of television station vans with their satellite dishes fully deployed, hugged the curb alongside the district courthouse, on East Jefferson Street, in downtown Rockville.

Jennifer Vale, cub TV reporter for WWMD, Channel 9 News, tucked her blonde, streaked, cheerleader bangs behind her left ear, turned to face the street and smiled into the camera. Behind her, a placard-wielding crowd of women began chanting, as if on cue, "Protect defenseless women! Protect defenseless women! Protect defenseless women!" Their red and blue signs, many of which sported the

National Organization for Women (NOW) official logo, declared, "Stop this CRAP!", "Farnsworth's Folly!" and "TROs Save Lives!"

Jennifer raised the microphone to her lips. "Enraged women, including local attorneys and many former victims of domestic violence, have descended upon the Montgomery County District Courthouse today, to oppose Judge Michael Farnsworth's anticipated announcement of a new program designed to protect the rights of men accused, in civil cases, of spousal abuse and domestic violence.

"The judge's program, which he will formally unveil at a nine o'clock press conference here, twenty-five minutes from now, is nicknamed 'RAP', which stands for 'Respondent Advocate Program.' It guarantees that a court-appointed lawyer will represent the interests of the accused during secret, *ex-parte* or 'one-sided' hearings, where women can currently seek the court's protection against their allegedly abusive husbands.

"As you can see from their signs," she said, as the camera zoomed in on one of the placards that read, 'Stop this CRAP!' protesters have renamed the judge's initiative by adding the word 'Court's" in front of it.

"I am joined by Ms. Gloria Cheswick, local attorney and president of NOW's Montgomery County chapter. Gloria, what's the big deal? Why shouldn't men be represented at these hearings, where they formerly had no one looking out for their interests?"

Gloria Cheswick's shoulder-length, kinky jet-black hair framed her slightly elongated, pale face and oval, tortoiseshell glasses. She was dressed in a dark-blue pinstriped dress suit—her typical courtroom attire—and appeared ready for battle. She frowned and shook her head as a look of disgust flashed across her face. "It's all so wrong, Jennifer! These are emergency, civil proceedings designed to give vulnerable women much-needed protection. The judge's program, as I understand it, will assign the equivalent of 'public defenders' to stand in for the accused men and to cross-examine these battered women, who are courageously seeking a way to protect themselves, and their children, from violent spouses. Where's the money going to come from to pay for all of this?

"And it's so unnecessary, too," she added, "because the accused men are guaranteed a full hearing in court, within seven days, if the court issues a temporary protective order against them."

Jennifer momentarily knitted her brow in thought. "Well," she said, smiling once more, as the camera moved in for a close up, "this is obviously a complex and emotionally-charged issue that is creating a storm of controversy. We'll be covering the judge's press conference at nine and will have more on the program's pros and cons afterward.

"For now, this is Jennifer Vale, reporting for Channel 9 News, on the scene at the district courthouse, in Rockville."

Reporters from every local newspaper, television channel, radio station, and online news outlet crammed into a public hearing room on the second floor of the district courthouse, waiting for Judge Farnsworth to make his appearance. Most of the print and online reporters were still milling around the tables set up in the back, engaging in small talk as they helped themselves to free coffee, orange juice, and trays of donuts. They were dressed modestly, and informally, while the much better dressed and immaculately groomed TV reporters stood toward the front of the room. Between them, camera men and women stood at the ready behind their hand-held cameras and tripods. The dais, at the front, was top heavy with a Gordian knot of logoed microphones, representing various news outlets.

A small, frail, gray-haired woman, dressed in a drab, gray silk blouse, silver-and-turquoise necklace, and blue skirt, stepped toward the dais and slipped on a pair of black reading glasses that hung from a band around her neck. She tapped lightly on the nondescript microphone at the center of the knot and the sound reverberated through the room. She appeared to be in her early sixties and looked like a small-town librarian. When everyone quieted down, she continued.

"May I have your attention, please?" she said in a soft, grandmotherly voice. "I'm Gertie Styles, the judge's administrative aid. Thank you for coming today. If you didn't find a copy of the press release lying on your seat, please raise your hand now, and we will get you one. And now," she added, gesturing toward the door at her left, "it is my pleasure to give you, his honor, Judge Michael J. Farnsworth, chief administrative judge of The Maryland District Court."

Gertie stepped aside as Judge Farnsworth walked into the room, caught in the sudden glare of dozens of video camera lights. The judge was dressed in a charcoal-gray business suit, a blue power tie and crisp white shirt and he sported a recent tan. He looked around the room, into the glaring lights, smiled and squinted.

Behind him, Gertie turned over a white sign that was perched on an easel. Large, dark-green print announced the "Respondent Advocate Program" and then, a much smaller line of black text under it read, "A Maryland District Court Initiative." This was followed by an image of the Maryland District Court seal.

Judge Farnsworth slipped on a pair of reading glasses and took several folded sheets of paper from his vest pocket. "Ladies and gentlemen of the press," he began. "Thank you for coming. We don't hold press conferences here all that often, so I didn't know if I was going to feel like the proverbial high school nerd—I was one once—who threw a party to which no one came!" (Laughter.)

"Fortunately, Gertie knows a thing or two about filling a room, and she insisted that we invest in a generous assortment of donuts. From the look of things, it appears that did the trick!

"I'm going to read from a prepared statement and then, I'll take your questions. When I finish, I will introduce you to a few people who will be playing key roles in helping us roll out and expand this new initiative."

The judge paused, fidgeted with his papers, and then cleared his throat. "It has been said that 'the road to hell is paved with good intentions.' I have had ample proof, recently, of the accuracy of that observation.

"The 'good intentions' paving our latest 'road to ruin' are among the noblest and purest imaginable: our collective desire to protect women and children, some of the most vulnerable among us, from the dangers of domestic violence and abuse....

"Unfortunately, when emotion and 'righteous indignation' fuel reform efforts, those in charge often seem to take temporary leave of their senses and completely ignore the possibility that anyone would ever attempt to 'game' their newly reformed system. But, of course, people do try to game it. And when they do, the cure for one social ill—in this case, domestic violence—creates a whole new group of victims: innocent spouses (men, for the most part), who find themselves falsely accused of what only can be described as despicable acts: domestic violence and child abuse.

"Such charges can be personally devastating to the accused. No decent, upstanding person would ever want to be associated with them.

"Merely raising these allegations, whether true or not, can give the accuser a huge advantage in a pending divorce case. The protective orders sought in district court often come with requests for temporary awards of child custody and child support, use of the family home, the family car, and much more. And these temporary awards can quickly become permanent in divorce court.

"How does this happen and, more importantly, what's the 'big deal' that has led me to propose changes to the way we currently do business?

"My own experience on the bench has convinced me that some attorneys are now routinely using domestic violence charges as a strategy to help their clients gain the upper hand in divorce proceedings.

"Studies that I've read suggest that, nationally, men who have been falsely accused of domestic violence now number, not in the thousands or even the tens of thousands, but in the millions. That's millions of people, tried each year, in absentia, on trumped up charges and exposed to public ridicule. And it's happening, here, in America, not in some faraway country that doesn't claim to operate under the rule of law.

"As a judge, I find injustice, on such a scale, to be intolerable and personally repugnant. I cannot, in good conscience, continue to be associated with it. So, I felt compelled to find a way to make the current system and its practices work better.

"Spouses, who legitimately fear for their safety and the safety of their children, must always be able to come forward and seek protection from the court, but we also need safeguards on the courts to protect the integrity of our judicial system and the innocent.

"My solution," the judge said, pointing toward the sign behind him and to his right, "is to make sure those accused, in absentia, of domestic violence, (those we call 'respondents') have someone present in the courtroom, during those *ex-parte* hearings, to represent their interests.

"The district court will randomly select and assign family law attorneys, from local bar association lists, to serve as pro-bono respondent advocates on a rotating basis. The Advocates will serve for one day at a time and must be present for all *ex-parte* hearings held on those days. They will listen to each petitioner's testimony and then cross-examine the petitioner to make sure their allegations hold up under questioning. If the charges don't hold up, then, hopefully, the court will not grant the requested protective order, and a record of sworn testimony, including the cross examination of the petitioner, will be available for the respondent's counsel to review and for prosecutors to use in future perjury cases. Perjury, as you may know, is the only penalty that petitioners currently face if they make false accusations in these *ex-parte* proceedings."

"We will launch the RAP program here, in Montgomery County, immediately, for an initial sixty-day trial period. Then, we will expand the program to include all Maryland District Courts.

The judge folded up his papers and returned them to his vest pocket. "That concludes my prepared statement," he said. "Now, let me introduce you to two, prominent family law attorneys who have agreed to help advance this program."

He looked at the doorway located on his left. "Beverly, Chester, will you please join me?"

Beverly West, who was wearing one of her signature herring-bone dress suits, stepped forward, followed closely behind by a tall, tan Chester Swindell.

Judge Farnsworth stepped to his right to make room, behind the rostrum, for his two colleagues. "During the sixty-day trial period for this program, Beverly West has generously agreed to serve as First Advocate," Judge Farnsworth said. "She will personally be on hand for the first two weeks, representing respondents in all *ex-parte* cases brought before district court judges and commissioners. Bev will administer the launch of the program here, in Montgomery County. She will establish procedures, standards, and guidelines, which she will then teach to her successor advocates.

"Should an advocate fail to report for duty during the trial period, Bev also will fill in.

"She has donated $50,000 in seed money to cover any administrative costs required to get this program up and running. Isn't that right, counselor?" he asked, looking at West. She smiled and seemed to blanch, slightly, under her already copious, pale makeup.

"I'd also like to introduce you to Chester Swindell, who is standing to Beverly's left. Chester has, at my request, accepted the post of community liaison for the RAP program. As such, he will be receiving a small stipend to underwrite the costs for him to travel the state, speaking to men's groups about the program, answering their questions and making them aware of their rights and responsibilities under it.

"Now," Judge Farnsworth said, "I will briefly open the floor to questions. Please wait to be recognized."

Hands immediately flew up and the judge quickly pointed to a reporter standing in the front row.

"Hi, Your Honor. Tom Purdy, the Maryland Independent. It sounds like this program will hinge on your ability to get buy-in and support from family law trial lawyers. As someone who covered the courts for many years, I've seen pro bono work become rarer and rarer. In fact, most attorneys can now avoid it entirely just by making a small annual donation to Legal Aid. How do you expect to gain their support for this new initiative under the circumstances?"

"Excellent question, Tom," Judge Farnsworth said. "I think I'll let our First Advocate answer that one for me. Bev?"

West smiled. "You've raised an interesting point, Tom. In recent years, many of us have been paying the legal equivalent of 'indulgences' to sidestep the time-honored tradition of providing free assistance to the needy. But this is not a voluntary program. Judge Farnsworth, as chief administrative judge for the state's district court system, is making participation in the RAP program mandatory for all lawyers who wish to practice family law in The State of Maryland. I guess you could say that, going forward, it will be a cost of doing business."

"Explain the enforcement aspect, would you, Bev?" Judge Farnsworth said.

"Sure. Judge Farnsworth initially suggested that each attorney should pay a $2,500 fine for each instance of failing to show up for their RAP assignments. I felt that might still threaten the program's integrity. I think the court needs to set a standard that will ensure zero tolerance for noncompliance. So, at my recommendation, Judge Farnsworth changed the penalty for failing to appear to a sixty-day license suspension."

A gasp went through the crowd.

A thin, tall African American man, in the second row, quickly raised his hand. He wore a natty, olive summer-weight suit, a crisp blue button-down oxford shirt and a matching blue, black olive and gold patterned tie.

"You, sir," the judge said. He pointed at the reporter and nodded.

"Reggie Fox, of the Baltimore Sun," the reporter said. "Judge, in your prepared statement, you said, and I quote: "'My own experience on the bench has convinced me that some attorneys are now routinely using domestic violence charges as a strategy to help their clients gain the upper hand in divorce proceedings.'

"Your Honor, would you care to elaborate on that statement and, in particular, tell the public the specific incidents, in your experience, that convinced you this problem is now getting out of hand?"

Judge Farnsworth drew in his chin and stiffened his neck. "I do not care to," he said. "The people are just going to have to trust me on this one. Those involved in the specific incidents have been disciplined, and all of the state's family law attorneys have been put on notice."

The judge recognized a female reporter. "Cindy Kimball, WTTZ News," she said. "Judge Farnsworth, women's groups and, in particular, the leadership of NOW, say that your RAP program will set women's rights back fifty years. They say they will do everything in their power to unseat you in the next judicial election. Your official response, sir?"

"If keeping the courts fair, by protecting the rights of innocent men being tried in absentia, could set the women's rights movement back fifty years, Cindy, then I simply don't understand what that movement now represents. When it started, if I recall, the Women's Rights movement was all about 'equality.' Women wanted equal treatment in employment, and generally, under the law. To oppose the RAP program is to favor preferred treatment for women. The women I know want true equality not an unfair advantage. Tell NOW to 'bring it on,' and I'll take my chances that reason will prevail with the electorate."

The next question came from a slovenly looking, male reporter. "Biff Cartier, Internet Radio. Isn't this just another example of an activist judiciary overstepping its bounds, Your Honor? What makes you think the state legislature goofed, when they set up this program, and why should you be second-guessing them now?"

"Do you mean, aside from the fact that their program doesn't work?" Judge Farnsworth asked, to laughter from all sides. "At best, they thought judges would step in and cross-examine the petitioners, but that goes against our training. At heart, we are supposed to be impartial observers, not advocates. At worst, the legislature's failure to provide some form of in-court representation during *ex-parte* hearings was a huge oversight. My role, as chief administrative judge of the court, includes making sure it functions properly. I feel I'm fulfilling my mandate, nothing more."

Judge Farnsworth next selected an older, female reporter standing several rows back. "Sally Donleavy, the Washington Post," she said.

"Judge, if you were going to defend this program before the Supreme Court, what would you tell them was your legal basis for taking matters into your own hands in this way?"

"Excellent question," Judge Farnsworth said. "The current system, which allows people to press charges against others unchallenged and in 'absentia,' undermines many long-held, cherished principles of western jurisprudence. While some might argue that those principles apply 'strictly' to criminal cases, I think we're splitting hairs here, as the type of charges being brought in these civil cases are, actually, 'criminal' in nature.

"The rights I'm referring to are protected by the Bill of Rights, specifically the Fourth, Fifth, Sixth and Fourteenth Amendments. They include the guarantee of "equal protection under the law;" the right to "face our accusers," the right to "due process." and our right to be "secure in our persons, houses, papers and effects against unreasonable searches and seizures."

"All of us also have the right to expect that we will be considered innocent until proven guilty in a court of law. But for those tried, unfairly, in absentia, just the opposite is true. When these falsely accused individuals finally get their day in court, they already have been declared guilty and penalized in some way. They now must prove to the court that found them guilty, in absentia, that it made a mistake."

The judge glanced at his watch. "We have time for just one more question." Hands went up everywhere. "The young man in the middle of the back row," the judge said.

"Me?" shouted the reporter. He was a young man, who appeared to be in his early twenties.

"Yes, you," Judge Farnsworth said.

"I'd like to know in what specific ways you hope this program will make things better?"

"I'm assuming you mean in addition to the points already cited?" the judge asked.

"Yes."

"Well, I cannot think of a way in which these changes could possibly make the system work any worse than it does right now. But specifically, I think it could make many things better.

"For instance," Judge Farnsworth continued, "this one-sided, unfair treatment of people sends two very different messages to the parties in a divorce. In my opinion, it tells women they can expect preferential treatment from the courts and it invites them, to some extent, to stretch the truth, if not out-and-out lie, to get the outcomes they desire.

"At the same time, it tells men they will not get a fair shake. This realization can either encourage men to give up the fight to remain a constant, meaningful presence in their children's lives—in which case the children lose—or it can make a man want to get even with his wife, particularly if she has brought false, scurrilous charges against him. That just ratchets up the conflict in the divorce case and makes the attorneys rich.

"Once we start treating both parties fairly, I think everyone will act better and divorce cases will become less of a circus. I also think this new approach will take away the incentive attorneys presently have to try and 'game the system' on behalf of their clients. That should translate into fewer trumped-up, *ex-parte* domestic violence cases altogether.

"Finally, by making the petitioners accountable in court, I think the number of questionable cases will decline dramatically. That will benefit the true victims of domestic abuse. The courts will be able to hear their cases faster and should be able to assign them to experienced judges, rather than deputized district court commissioners. As a society, we'll also get a truer, more accurate picture of the nature, and extent, of this very real, very serious problem.

"Thank you."

Thanks for Reading*!*

Dear Reader,

I hope you enjoyed *The Reform Artists!* If you have thoughts you'd like to share with me personally, please click here (or visit http://jonreisfeld.com/contact to let me know via email.) I'm always deeply interested in what readers have to say!

And whether you loved the book or not, I would greatly appreciate it if you would please take a moment, now, while the book is still fresh in your mind, to share a brief review about it on Amazon. To save you time, here's the link the book's Amazon page: http://www.amazon.com/dp/B016RHUU4A/

Reader reviews are vitally important to book discovery, and just a few sentences will do!

Wondering what to talk about? Readers generally want to know what the reading experience was like for you and what the book means to you. They also want to know if it will reward them with an entertaining story, a believable plot, memorable characters, and useful information. Is it well-written, funny, fast-paced, plodding, exciting, or dull?

Thanks, in advance, for your help! When you're done, be sure to return to this book to download the free preview to The Last Way Station (found on the very last page)!

Best Regards,

Jon Reisfeld

About the Author

Jon Reisfeld was born in Baltimore, MD, the second of three children. He attended Northwestern University, where he graduated with a B.S. degree from the Medill School of Journalism. After college, Jon wrote for magazines and newspapers in the Washington, D.C., and Baltimore metropolitan areas before starting his own successful marketing-consulting practice. In 2012 Jon co-founded a New England writer's retreat, where he coached emerging authors. Today, he writes fiction and science fiction inspired by important social issues of our time.

Acknowledgments

No work of fiction is written in a vacuum. I would like to take this opportunity to thank the many people who read this manuscript in its various drafts, offered their encouragement and suggestions and helped make the final product stronger. While I gratefully acknowledge their input, I have taken license to add flourishes of my own in the presentation. In particular, I wish to thank Andrew J. Felser, Esq. for his thoughtful notes and corrections about certain aspects of the legislative process and for his insights on courtroom procedure; Tom McKeon, Esq. for his professional help in a time of great need; Lynn Bacharach, for her graciousness and encouragement; Lisa N. Farrell, for her help proofreading an early version of the manuscript, author Susan Setteducata for her notes, Caroline Jurney for her in-depth and extensive notes and Zachary S. Reisfeld, for his ongoing encouragement and his many helpful story edits and scene suggestions.

Read:
The Last Way Station:
Hitler's Final Journey
Also by Jon Reisfeld

What's fitting punishment for the super evil? Find out when you read this historical fantasy novelette about Adolf Hitler's final judgment, in Hell. (A quick, 75-page read. Available in Ebook and paperback formats.)

"The reader is sucked in from page one...and is only released by the surprising ending. I only wish this book had been longer. I never wanted the story to end."
Olivia, Amazon reader-reviewer

Get Your FREE sample of the First Three Chapters by clicking here

You can Find Jon Online at:
http://jonreisfeld.com (Website)
http://facebook.com/fickshuneer (Facebook page)
http://twitter.com/jonreisfeld (Twitter account)